LAURELL K. HAMILTON
selling author of the Merr
Anita Blake, Vampire Hun
Louis, Missouri with her fa

Don't miss these other Me
*Kiss of Shadows, A Caress of Twilight, Seduced by
Moonlight, A Stroke of Midnight* and *A Lick of Frost*.

And to find out more about Laurell K. Hamilton and
her books visit www.laurellkhamilton.org

www.rbooks.co.uk

MISTRAL'S KISS

Laurell K. Hamilton

BANTAM BOOKS

LONDON • TORONTO • SYDNEY • AUCKLAND • JOHANNESBURG

TRANSWORLD PUBLISHERS
61-63 Uxbridge Road, London W5 5SA
A Random House Group Company
www.randomhouse.co.uk

MISTRAL'S KISS
A BANTAM BOOK: 9780553818154

First published in Great Britain
in 2006 by Bantam Press
a division of Transworld Publishers
Bantam edition published 2007

A CIP catalogue record for this book
is available from the British Library.

Addresses for Random House Group Ltd companies outside the
UK can be found at: www.randomhouse.co.uk
The Random House Group Ltd Reg. No. 954009

Penguin Random House is committed to a sustainable future for
our business, our readers and our planet. This book is made from
Forest Stewardship Council® certified paper.

MIX
Paper from
responsible sources
FSC® C018179

Printed and bound in Great Britain by Clays Ltd, Elcograf S.p.A.

Typeset in 11/14 Palatino by
Falcon Oast Graphic Art Ltd.

To Jonathon

Worrying about the perfect words makes me miss the perfect moment. You remind me it's not perfection I'm seeking but happiness.

Acknowledgments

To Darla Cook and Sherry Ganey, who keep so much running smoothly. Mary Schuermann, best mother-in-law in the world. To my writing group, The Alternate Historians: Deborah Milletello, Mark Sumner, Rett MacPherson, Marella Sands, Tom Drennan, and Sharon Shinn. Our tenth anniversary as a group with its current members is coming in 2006. It's eighteen years from the group's inception; in 2008, we will celebrate twenty years. Can you believe it? Party, party, party. Okay, our kind of party. No drinking, certainly no drugs, just us sitting around talking, eating Debbie's amazing desserts, just us doing what we've done for a decade, being friends and helping each other succeed.

MISTRAL'S KISS

Chapter 1

I DREAMT OF WARM FLESH AND COOKIES. THE SEX I understood, but the cookies . . . Why cookies? Why not cake, or meat? But that's what my subconscious chose as I dreamt. We were eating in the tiny kitchen of my Los Angeles apartment – an apartment I didn't live in anymore, outside of dreams. The we were me, Princess Meredith – the only faerie royal ever born on American soil – and my royal guards, more than a dozen of them.

They moved around me with skin the color of darkest night, whitest snow, the pale of newborn leaves, the brown of leaves that have gone down to die on the forest floor, a rainbow of men moving nude around the kitchen.

The real apartment kitchen would have barely held three of us, but in the dream everyone walked through that narrow space between sink and stove and cabinets as if there were all the room in the world.

We were having cookies because we'd just had sex and it was hungry work, or something like that. The men moved around me graceful and perfectly nude. Several of the men were ones I'd never seen nude. They moved with skin the color of summer sunshine, the transparent white of crystals, colors I had no name for, for the colors did not exist outside of faerie. It should have been a good dream, but it wasn't. I knew something was wrong, that feeling of unease that you get in dreams when you know that the happy sights are just a disguise, an illusion to hide the ugliness to come.

The plate of cookies was so innocent, so ordinary, but it bothered me. I tried to pay attention to the men, touching their bodies, holding them, but each of them in turn would pick up a cookie and take a bite, as if I weren't there.

Galen with his pale, pale green skin and greener eyes bit into a cookie, and something squirted out the side. Something thick and dark. The dark liquid dripped down the edge of his kissable mouth and fell onto the white countertop. That single drop splattered and spread and was red, so red, so fresh. The cookies were bleeding.

I slapped it from Galen's hand. I picked up the tray to keep the men from eating any more.

The tray was full of blood. It dripped down the edges, poured over my hands. I dropped the tray, which shattered, and the men bent as if they would eat from the floor and the broken glass. I pushed them back, screaming, 'No!'

Doyle looked up at me with his black eyes and said, 'But it is all we have had to eat for so long.'

The dream changed, as dreams will. I stood in an open field with a ring of distant trees encircling it. Beyond the trees, hills rode up into the paleness of a moonlit winter's night. Snow lay like a smooth blanket across the ground. I was standing ankle-deep in snow. I was wearing a loose sweeping gown as white as the snow. My arms were bare to the cold night. I should have been freezing, but I wasn't. Dream, just a dream.

Then I noticed something in the center of the clearing. It was an animal, a small white animal, and I thought, *That's why I didn't see it*, for it was white, whiter than the snow. Whiter than my gown, than my skin, so white that it seemed to glow.

The animal raised its head, sniffing the air. It was a small pig, but its snout was longer, and its legs taller, than those of any pig I'd ever seen. Though it stood in the middle of the snowy field, there were no hoofprints in that smooth snow, no way for the piglet to have walked to the center of the field. As if the animal had simply appeared there.

I glanced at the circle of trees, for only a moment, and when I looked again at the piglet, it was bigger. A hundred pounds heavier, and taller than my knees. I didn't look away again, but the pig just got bigger. I couldn't see it happening, it was like trying to watch a flower bloom, but it was growing bigger. As tall at the shoulder as my waist, long and broad, and furry. I'd never seen a pig so fuzzy before, as if it had a thick winter coat. It looked positively pettable, that pelt. It raised that strangely long-snouted face toward me, and I saw tusks curving from its mouth, small tusks. The moment I saw them, gleaming ivory in the snow light, another whisper of unease washed through me.

I should leave this place, I thought. I turned to walk out through that ring of trees. A ring of trees that now looked entirely too even, too well planned, to be accidental.

A woman stood behind me, so close that when the wind blew through the dead trees her hooded cloak brushed against the hem of my gown. I formed my lips to say, *Who?* but never finished the word. She held out a hand that was wrinkled and colored with age, but it was a small, slender hand, still lovely, still full of a quiet strength. Not full of the remnants of youthful strength, but full of the strength that comes only with age. A strength born of knowledge accumulated, wisdom pondered over many a long winter's night. Here was someone who held the knowledge of a lifetime – no, several lifetimes.

The crone, the hag, has been vilified as ugly and weak. But that is not what the true crone aspect of the Goddess is, and it was not what I saw. She smiled at me, and that smile held all the warmth you would ever need. It was a smile that held a thousand fireside chats, a hundred dozen questions asked and answered, endless lifetimes of knowledge collected and remembered. There was nothing she would not know, if only I could think of the questions to ask.

I took her hand, and the skin was so soft, soft the way a baby's is. It was wrinkled, but smooth is not always best, and there is beauty in age that youth knows not.

I held the crone's hand and felt safe, completely and utterly safe, as if nothing could ever disturb this sense of quiet peace. She smiled at me, the rest of her face lost in the shadow of her hood. She drew her hand out of mine, and I tried to hold on, but she shook her head and said, though her lips did not move, 'You have work to do.'

'I don't understand,' I said, and my breath steamed in the cold night, though hers had not.

'Give them other food to eat.'

I frowned. 'I don't understand . . .'

'Turn around,' she said, and this time her lips did move, but still her breath did not color the night. It was as if she spoke but did not breathe, or as if her breath were as cold as the winter night. I tried to remember if her hand had been warm or cold, but could not. All I remembered was the sense of peace and rightness. 'Turn around,' she said again, and this time I did.

A white bull stood in the center of the clearing – at least that's what it looked like at first glance. Its shoulder stood as tall as the top of my head. It must have been more than nine feet long. Its shoulders were a huge broad spread of muscle humped behind its lowered head. The head raised, revealing a snout framed by long, pointed tusks. This was no bull, but a huge boar – the thing that had begun as a little pig. Tusks like ivory blades gleamed as it looked at me.

I glanced back, but knew the crone was gone. I was alone in the winter night. Well, not as alone as I wanted to be. I looked back and found the monstrous boar still standing there, still staring at me. The snow was cold under my bare feet now. My arms ran with goose bumps, and I wasn't sure if I shivered from cold, or fear.

I recognized the thick white hair on the boar now. It still looked so soft. But its tail stuck straight out from its body, and it raised that long snout skyward. Its breath smoked in the air as it sniffed. That was bad. That meant it was real – or real enough to hurt me, anyway.

I stood as still as I could. I don't think I moved at all, but suddenly it charged. Snow plumed underneath its hooves as it came for me.

It was like watching some great machine barreling down. Too big to be real, too huge to be possible. I had no weapon. I turned and ran.

I heard the boar behind me. Its hooves sliced the frozen ground. It let out a sound that was almost a scream. I glanced back; I couldn't help it. The gown tangled under my feet, and I went down. I rolled in the snow, fighting to come to my feet, but the gown tangled around my legs. I couldn't get free of it. Couldn't stand. Couldn't run.

The boar was almost on top of me. Its breath steamed in clouds. Snow spilled around its legs, bits of frozen black earth sliced up in all that white. I had one of those interminable moments where you have all the time in the world to watch death come for you. White boar, white snow, white tusks, all aglow in the moonlight, except for the rich black earth that marred the whiteness with dark scars. The boar gave that horrible screaming squeal again.

Its thick winter coat looked so soft. It was going to look soft while it gored me to death and trampled me into the snow.

I reached behind me, feeling for a tree branch, anything to pull myself up out of the snow. Something brushed my hand, and I grabbed it. Thorns cut into my hand. Thorn-covered vines filled the space between the trees. I used the vines to drag myself to my feet. The thorns were biting into my hands, my arms, but they were all I could grasp. The boar was so close, I could smell its scent, sharp and acrid on the cold air. I would not die lying in the snow.

The thorns bled me, spattered the white gown with blood, the snow covered in minute crimson drops. The vines moved under my hands like something more alive than a plant. I felt the boar's breath like heat on the back of my body, and the thorny vines opened like a door. The world seemed to spin, and when I could see again, be sure of where I was again, I was standing on the other side of the thorns. The white boar hit the vines hard and fast, as if it expected to tear its way through. For a moment I thought it would do just that; then it was in the thorns, slowing. It stopped rushing forward and started slashing at the vines with its great snout and tusks. It would tear them out, trample them underfoot, but its white coat was bedecked with tiny bloody scratches. It would break through, but the thorns bled it.

I'd never owned any magic in dream, or vision, that I didn't own in waking life. But I had magic now. I wielded the hand of blood. I put my bleeding hand out toward the boar and thought, *Bleed.* I made all those small scratches pour blood. But still the beast fought through the thorns. The vines ripped from the earth. I thought, *More.* I made a fist of my hand, and when I opened it wide, the scratches slashed wide. Hundreds of red mouths, gaping on that white hide. Blood poured down its sides, and now its squeal was not a scream of anger, or challenge. It was a squeal of pain.

The vines tightened around it of their own accord. The boar's knees buckled, and the vines roped it to the frozen ground. It was no longer a white boar, but a red one. Red with blood.

There was a knife in my hand. It was a shining white blade that glowed like a star. I knew what I needed to do. I walked across the blood-spattered snow. The boar rolled its eyes at me, but I knew that if it could, even now, it would kill me.

I plunged the knife into its throat, and when the blade came out, blood gushed into the snow, over my gown, onto my skin. The blood was hot. A crimson fountain of heat and life.

The blood melted the snow down to rich black earth. From that earth came a tiny piglet, not white this time, but tawny and striped with gold. It was colored more like a fawn. The piglet cried, but I knew there would be no answer.

I picked it up, and it curled up in my arms like a puppy. It was so warm, so alive. I wrapped the hooded cloak I now wore around us both. My gown was black now, not black with blood, but simply black. The piglet settled into the soft warm cloth. I had boots that were lined with fur, soft and warm. The white knife was still in my hand, but it was clean, as if the blood had burned away.

I smelled roses. I turned back and found that the white boar's body was gone. The thorny vines were covered in green leaves and flowers. The flowers were white and pink, from palest blush to dark salmon. Some of the roses were so deeply pink, they were almost purple.

The wonderful sweet scent of wild roses filled the air. The dead trees in the circle were dead no more, but began to bud and leaf as I watched. The thaw spread from the boar's death and that spill of warm blood.

The tiny piglet was heavier. I looked down and found that it had doubled in size. I put it onto the melting snow, and as the boar had gotten bigger, so now this piglet grew. Again, I could not see the change, but like a flower unfurling undetectably, it changed all the same.

I began to walk over the snow, and the rapidly growing pig came at my side like an obedient dog. Where we stepped the snow melted, and life returned to the land. The pig lost its baby stripes, and grew black and as tall at the shoulder as my waist, and still it grew. I touched its back, and the hair was not soft, but coarse. I stroked its side, and it nestled against me. We walked the land, and where we walked, the world became green once more.

We came to the crest of a small hill, where a

slab of stone lay grey and cold in the growing light. Dawn had come, breaking like a crimson wound across the eastern sky. The sun returns in blood, and dies in blood.

The boar had tusks now, small curling things, but I wasn't afraid. He nuzzled my hand, and his snout was softer, and more nimble, more like a great finger, than any pig's snout I'd ever touched. He made a sound that was pleasant and made me smile. Then he turned and ran down the other side of the hill, with his tail straight out behind him like a flag. Everywhere his hooves touched, the earth sprang green.

A robed figure was beside me on the hill, but it was not the grey-robed figure of the crone Goddess in winter. This was a male figure taller than I, broad of shoulder, and cloaked in a hood as black as the boar that was growing small in the distance.

He held out his hands, and in them was a horn. The curved tusk of a great boar. It was white and fresh, with blood still on it, as if he had just that moment cut it from the white boar. But as I moved over toward him, the horn became clean and polished, as if with many years of use, as if many hands had touched it. The horn was no longer white, but a rich amber color that spoke of age. Just before I touched his hands, I realized the horn was set in gold, formed into a cup.

I laid my hands on either side of his and found

that his hands were as dark as his cloak, but I knew this was not my Doyle, my Darkness. This was the God. I looked up into his hood and saw for an instant the boar's head; then I saw a human mouth that smiled at me. His face, like the face of the Goddess, was covered in shadow – for the face of deity was ever a mystery.

He wrapped my hands around the smooth horn of the cup, the carved gold almost soft under my fingers. He pressed my hands to the cup. I wondered, where had the white knife gone?

A deep voice that was no man's voice and every man's voice said, 'Where it belongs.' The knife appeared in the cup, blade-down, and it was shining again, as if a star had fallen into that cup of horn and gold. 'Drink and be merry.' He laughed then at his own pun. He raised the shining cup to my lips and vanished to the warm sound of his own laughter.

I drank from the horn and found it full of the sweetest mead I had ever drunk, thick with honey, and warm as if the heat of the summer itself slipped across my tongue, caressed my throat. I swallowed and it was more intoxicating than any mere drink.

Power is the most intoxicating drink of all.

Chapter 2

I WOKE SURROUNDED BY A CIRCLE OF FACES, IN A BED that was not mine. Faces the color of darkest night, whitest snow, the pale green of new leaves, the gold of summer sunshine, the brown of leaves trodden underfoot destined to be rich earth. But there was no pale skin that held all the colors of a brilliant crystal, like a diamond carved into flesh. I blinked up at all of them, and wondered – remembering my dream – where were the cookies?

Doyle's voice, deep and thick, as if it came from a great distance, said, 'Princess Meredith, are you well?'

I sat up, nude in the bed with black silk sheets, cold against my skin. The queen had loaned us her room for the night. Real fur, soft and nearly alive, pressed against my hip. The fur covering moved, and Kitto's face blinked up at me. His huge blue eyes dominated his pale face and held no white in all that color. The color was Seelie sidhe, but the eyes themselves were goblin. He had been a child of the last great goblin–sidhe war. His pale perfect body was barely four feet tall, a delicate man, the only one of my men who was shorter than I was. He looked child-like cuddled down in the fur, his face framed like some cherub for a Valentine's Day card. He had been more than a thousand years old before Christianity was a word. He'd been part of my treaty with the goblins. They were my allies because he shared my bed.

His hand found my arm and stroked up and down my skin, seeking comfort as we all did when we were nervous. He didn't like me staring at him without saying anything. He had been curled up close to me, and the power of the Goddess and the God in my dream must have slipped across his skin. The faces of the fifteen men standing in their circle around the bed showed clearly that they had felt something, too.

Doyle repeated his question: 'Princess Meredith, are you well?'

I looked at my captain of the guard, my lover, his face as black as the cloak I had worn in vision, or the fur of the boar that had run out into the snow and brought spring back to the land. I had to close my eyes and breathe deeply, trying to break free of the last vestiges of vision and dream. Trying to be in the here and now.

I raised my hands from the tangle of sheets. In my right hand was a cup formed of horn, the horn ancient and yellowed, held in gold that bore symbols that few outside faerie could read now. In my left hand I expected to find the white knife, but it was not there. My left hand was empty. I stared at it for a moment, then raised the cup with both hands.

'My God,' Rhys whispered, though the whisper was strangely loud.

'Yes,' Doyle said, 'that is exactly what it is.'

'What did he say when he gave you the cup of horn?' It was Abe who asked. Abe with his hair striped in shades of pale grey, dark grey, black, and white, perfect strands of color. His eyes were a few shades darker grey than most human eyes, but not otherworldly, not really. If you dressed him like a modern Goth, he'd be the hit of any club scene.

His eyes were strangely solemn. He'd been the drunk and joke of the court for more years than I could remember. But now there was a different person looking out from his face, a glimpse of what he might once have been. Someone who thought before he spoke, someone who had other preoccupations than getting drunk as quickly and as often as he could.

Abe swallowed hard and asked again, 'What did he say?'

I answered him this time. 'Drink and be merry.'

Abe smiled, wistful, sorrow-filled. 'That sounds like him.'

'Like who?' I asked.

'The cup used to be mine. My symbol.'

I crawled to the edge of the bed and knelt on it. I held the cup up with both hands toward him. 'Drink and be merry, Abeloec.'

He shook his head. 'I do not deserve the God's favor, Princess. I do not deserve anyone's favor.'

I suddenly knew – not by way of a vision – I just suddenly possessed the knowledge. 'You weren't thrown out of the Seelie Court for seducing the wrong woman, as everyone believes. You were thrown out because you lost your powers, and once you could no longer make the courtiers merry with drink and revelry, Taranis kicked you out of the golden court.'

A tear trembled on the edge of one eye. Abeloec stood there, straight and proud in a way that I had never seen him. I'd never seen him sober, as he appeared to be now. Clearly he'd drunk to forget, but he was still immortal and sidhe, which meant that no drug, no drink, could ever truly help him find oblivion. He could be clouded, but never truly know the rush of any drug.

He finally nodded, and that was enough to spill the tear onto his cheek. I caught the tear on the edge of the horn cup. That tiny drop seemed to race down the inside of the cup faster than gravity should pull it. I don't know if the others could see what was happening, but Abe and I watched the tear race for the bottom of that cup. The tear slid inside the dark curve of the bottom, and suddenly there was liquid spilling up, bubbling up like a spring from the dark inner curve of the horn.

Deep gold liquid filled the cup to its brim, and the smell of honey and berries and the pungent smell of alcohol filled the room.

Abe's hands cupped over mine in the same way I had held the cup in the vision with the God. I raised it up, and as Abeloec's lips touched the rim, I said, 'Drink and be merry. Drink and be mine.'

He hesitated before he drank, and I observed an intelligence in those grey eyes that I'd never glimpsed before. He spoke with his lips brushing the edge of the cup. He wanted to drink. I could feel it in the eager tremble in his hands as they covered mine.

'I belonged to a king once. When I was no longer his court fool, he cast me out.' The trembling in his hands slowed, as if each word steadied him. 'I belonged to a queen once. She hated me, always, and made certain by her words and her deeds that I knew just how much she hated me.' His hands were warm and firm against mine. His eyes were deep, dark grey, charcoal grey, with a hint of black somewhere in the center. 'I have never belonged to a princess, but I fear you. I fear what you will do to me. What you will make me do to others. I fear taking this drink and binding myself to your fate.'

I shook my head but never lost the concentration of his eyes. 'I do not bind you to my fate, Abeloec, nor me to yours. I merely say, drink of the power that was once yours to wield. Be what you once were. This is not my gift to give to you. This cup belongs to the God, the Consort. He gave it to me and bid me share it with you.'

'He spoke of me?'

'No, not you specifically, but he bid me to share it with others. The Goddess told me to give you all something else to eat.' I frowned, unsure how to explain everything I'd seen, or done. Vision is always more sensible inside your head than on your tongue.

I tried to put into words what I felt in my heart. 'The first drink is yours, but not the last. Drink, and we will see what happens.'

'I am afraid,' he whispered.

'Be afraid, but take your drink, Abeloec.'

'You do not think less of me for being afraid.'

'Only those who have never known fear are allowed to think less of others for being afraid. Frankly, I think anyone who has never been afraid of anything in their entire life is either a liar or lacks imagination.'

It made him smile, then laugh, and in that laughter I heard the echo of the God. Some piece of Abeloec's old godhead had kept this cup safe for centuries. Some shadow of his old power had waited and kept watch. Watched for someone who could find their way through vision to a hill on the edge of winter and spring; on the edge of darkness and dawn; a place between, where mortal and immortal could touch.

His laughter made me smile, and there were answering chuckles from around the room. It was the kind of laughter that would be infectious. He would laugh and you would have to laugh with him.

'Just by holding the cup in your hand,' Rhys said, 'your laughter makes me smile. You haven't been that amusing in centuries.' He turned his boyishly handsome face to us, with its scars where his other tricolored blue eye would have been. 'Drink, and see what is left of who you thought you were, or don't drink, and go back to being shadow and a joke.'

'A bad joke,' Abeloec said.

Rhys nodded and came to stand close to us. His white curls fell to his waist, framing a body that was the most seriously muscled of any of the guards. He was also the shortest of them, a full-blooded sidhe who was only five foot six – unheard of. 'What do you have to lose?'

'I would have to try again. I would have to care again,' said Abe. He stared at Rhys as completely as he had at me, as if what we were saying meant everything.

'If all you want is to crawl back into another bottle or another bag of powder, then do it. Step away from the cup and let someone else drink,' Rhys said.

A look of pain crossed Abeloec's face. 'It's mine. It's part of who I was.'

'The God didn't mention you by name, Abe,' Rhys said. 'He told her to share, not who with.'

'But it's mine.'

'Only if you take it,' Rhys said, and his voice was low and clear, and somehow gentle, as if he understood more than I did why Abe was afraid.

'It's mine,' Abe said again.

'Then drink,' Rhys said, 'drink and be merry.'

'Drink and be damned,' Abeloec said.

Rhys touched his arm. 'No, Abe, say it, and do your best to believe it. Drink and be merry. I've seen more of us come back into our power than you have. The attitude affects it, or can.'

Abeloec started to let go of the cup, but I moved off the bed and came to stand in front of him. 'You will bring everything you learned in this long sad time with you, but you will still be you. You will be who you were, just older and wiser. Wisdom bought at great cost is nothing to regret.'

He stared down at me with his eyes a dark and perfect grey. 'You bid me drink.'

I shook my head. 'No. It must be your choice.'

'You will not command me?'

I shook my head again.

'The princess has some very American views on freewill,' Rhys said.

'I take that as a compliment,' I said.

'But . . .' Abe said, softly.

'Yes,' Rhys said, 'it means it's all on you. Your choice. Your fate. All in your hands. Enough rope to hang yourself, as they say.'

'Or save yourself,' Doyle said, and he came to stand on the other side, like a taller darkness to Rhys's white. Abeloec and I stood with white on one side, black on the other. Rhys had once been Cromm Cruach, a god of death and life. Doyle was the queen's chief assassin, but once he had been Nodons, a god of healing. We stood between them, and when I looked up at Abeloec something moved in his eyes, some shadow of that person I had glimpsed on the hill inside the hood of a cloak.

Abeloec raised the cup, taking my hands with it. We raised the cup together and he lowered his head. His lips hesitated for a breath on the edge of that smooth horn, then he drank.

He kept tipping the cup back, until he had to

drop to his knees so that my hands stayed on the cup while he upended it. He drank it down in one long swallow.

On his knees, releasing the cup, he threw his head back, eyes closed. His body bent backward, until he lay in a pool of his own striped hair, his knees still bent underneath him. He lay for a moment so still, so very still, that I feared for him. I waited for his chest to rise and fall. I willed him to breathe, but he didn't.

He lay like one asleep, except for the odd angle of his legs – no one slept like that. His face had smoothed out, and I realized that Abe was one of the few sidhe who had permanent worry lines, tiny wrinkles at eye and mouth. They smoothed in his sleep, if it was sleep.

I dropped to my knees beside him, the cup still in my hands. I leaned over him, touched the side of his face. He never moved. I placed my hand on the side of his face and whispered his name: 'Abeloec.'

His eyes flew open wide. It startled me. Drew a soft gasp from my lips. He grabbed my wrist at his face, and his other arm wrapped around my waist. He sat up, or knelt up, in one powerful movement, with me in his arms. He laughed, and it wasn't a mere echo of what I'd heard in my vision. The laughter filled the room, and the other men laughed with him. The room rang with joyous masculine laughter.

I laughed with him, them. It was impossible not to laugh with the pure joy in his face so close to mine. He leaned in, closing the last inches between our mouths. I knew he was going to kiss me, and I wanted him to. I wanted to feel that laughter inside me.

His mouth pressed against mine. A great cry went up among the men, joyous and rough. His tongue licked light along my bottom lip, and I opened my mouth to him. He thrust himself inside my mouth, and suddenly all I could taste was honey and fruit, and mead. It wasn't just his symbol. He was the cup, or what it contained. His tongue shoved inside me until I had to open my mouth wide or choke. And it was like swallowing the thick, golden honeyed mead. He was the intoxicating cup.

I was on the floor with him on top of me, but he was too tall to kiss me deeply and press much of anything else against my naked body at the same time. Beneath us was a fur throw that lay on the stone floor. It tickled along my skin, helped every movement he made be something more, as if the fur were helping caress me.

Our skin began to glow as if we'd swallowed the moon at her ripe bursting fullness, and her light was shining out from our skin. The white streaks in his hair showed a pale luminous blue. His charcoal-grey eyes stayed strangely dark. I knew that my eyes glowed, each circle of color, green of grass, pale green jade, and that molten gold. I knew that every circle of my iris glowed. My hair cast a reddish light around my vision: It shone like spun garnets with fire inside them when I glowed.

His eyes were like some deep, dark cave where the light could not go.

Abruptly, I realized that for a long while, we hadn't been kissing. We'd simply been staring into each other's faces. I leaned up toward him, wrapped my hands around him. I'd forgotten I still held the cup in one hand, and it touched his bare back. His spine bowed, and liquid poured across his skin; though the cup had been emptied before, it was full again. Heavy, cool liquid rushed down his body and over mine, drenching us in that thick golden flow.

Pale blue lines danced across his skin. I couldn't tell if they were under his skin, inside his body, or on the surface of his glowing torso. He kissed me. He kissed me deep and long, and this time he didn't taste like mead. He tasted of flesh, of lips and mouth and tongue, and the graze of teeth along my lower lip. And still the mead ran down our bodies, spreading out, out into a golden pool. The fur underneath us flattened in the tide of it.

He spilled his mouth and hands down my body, over my breasts. He held them in his hands, gently, caressed my nipples with his lips and tongue until I cried out, and I felt my body grow wet, but not from the spreading golden pool of mead.

I watched the pale blue lines on his arm flow into shapes, flowers and vines, and move down his hand and across my skin. It felt as if someone traced a feather across my skin.

A voice cried out, and it wasn't me, and it wasn't Abeloec. Brii had fallen to his hands and knees, his long yellow hair spilling down into the growing pool of mead.

Abeloec sucked harder on my breast, forcing my attention back to him. His eyes still didn't glow, but there was that intensity in them that is a kind of magic, a kind of power. The power that all men have when they spill themselves down your body with skilled hands and mouth.

He moved his mouth over me, drinking where the mead had pooled in the hollow of my stomach. He licked the tender skin just above the hair that curled between my legs. His tongue pressed in long sure strokes over such innocent skin. It made me wonder what it would be like when he dropped lower to things that weren't so innocent.

A man's strangled cry made me look away from Abeloec's dark eyes. I knew that voice. Galen had fallen to his knees. His skin was a green so pale it was white, but now green lines traced his skin, glowing, writhing under his skin.

Forming vines and flowers, pictures. Other cries drew my attention to the rest of the room. Of the fifteen guards, most were on their knees, or worse. Some had fallen flat to the floor to writhe on their stomachs, as if they were trapped in the flowing golden liquid, as if it were liquid amber and they were insects about to be caught forever. And they fought against their fate.

Lines of blue, or green, or red, traced their bodies. I caught glimpses of animals, vines, images drawn over their skin, like tattoos that were alive and growing.

Doyle and Rhys stood in the growing tide and seemed unmoved. But Doyle stared at his hands and arms, at lines tracing those strong arms, crimson against that blackness. Rhys's body was painted with palest blue, but he didn't watch the lines; he watched me and Abeloec. Frost, also, stood in the writhing spill of liquid, but he, like Doyle, stared at the tracing of lines that glowed over his skin. Nicca stood tall and straight with his brown hair and the brilliant spill of his wings, like the sails of some faerie ship, but no lines covered his skin: He remained untouched.

It was Barinthus, tallest of all the sidhe, who had moved to the door. He stood pressed to it, avoiding the spill of mead that seemed to creep like a thing alive across the floor. He held on to the door handle as if it would not open. As if we were trapped here until the magic had its way with us.

A small sound drew me back to gaze at the bed, and Kitto still perched there, safe above the flowing mead. His eyes were wide, as if he was afraid, regardless. He was afraid of so much.

Abeloec rubbed his cheek across my thigh. It brought me back to him. Back to gazing into those dark, almost human eyes. The glow of his skin and mine had dimmed. I realized that he'd paused to let me look around the room.

Now his hands slid under my thighs, and he lowered his face, hesitating, as if he were coming in for a chaste kiss. But what he did with his mouth wasn't chaste. He plunged his tongue thick and sure across me. The sensation threw my head back, bowed my spine.

Upside down, I saw the door open, saw the surprised look on the face of Barinthus as Mistral, the queen's new captain of the guard, strode in. His hair the grey of rain clouds. Once he had been the master of storms, a sky god. Now he strode into the room and slipped on the mead, started to fall. Then it was as if the world blinked. One moment he was falling near the door; the next he was above me, falling toward me. He put his hands out to try to catch himself, and I put my arms up to keep him from falling on top of me.

His hand caught the floor, but my hand touched his chest. He shuddered above me on his knees and one hand, as if I had made his heart stutter. I touched him through the tough softness of leather armor. He was safe behind it, but the look on his face was that of a stricken man, eyes wide.

He was close enough now that I could see his eyes were the swimming green of the sky before a great storm breaks, destroying all in its path. Only great anxiety could bring his eyes to that color, or great anger. Long ago, the sky itself had changed with the color of Mistral's eyes.

My skin sang to life, glowing like a white-hot star. Abeloec glowed with me. For the first time, I saw the lines on my own skin, and the writhing lines of color marched over us, neon blue in the glow. I watched a thorny vine crawl blue and alive down my hand to unfurl across Mistral's pale skin.

Mistral's body convulsed above me, and it was as if the lines of color drew him down toward me; as if they were ropes pulling him down, down. His eyes stayed unwilling, his body fighting with muscle and might. Only when he was nearly on top of me and Abeloec, and only the force of his shoulders held his face above mine, did his eyes change. I watched that frightening storm green fade from his eyes, replaced with a blue as swimming and pure as a summer sky. I'd never known his eyes could be that blue.

The blue lines in his skin painted a lightning bolt across his cheek; then his face was too close to mine for me to see details. His mouth was upon mine, and I kissed Mistral for the second time ever.

He kissed me, as if he would breathe the air he needed to live from my mouth, as if, if his mouth did not touch mine, it would be death. His hands slid down my body, and when he touched my breasts he made a sound deep in his throat that was eager – almost a sound of pain.

Abeloec chose that moment to remind me that there was more than one mouth against my body. He fed between my legs with tongue and lips and, lightly, teeth, so that I made my own eager sounds into Mistral's mouth. It drew another of those sounds from him that was both eager and pain-filled, as if he wanted this so badly that it hurt. His hand convulsed on my breast. Hard enough that it did hurt, but in that way that pain can feed into pleasure. I writhed under both their mouths, plunging lips to Mistral, hips to Abeloec. It was at that moment that the world swam.

I THOUGHT AT FIRST IT WAS SIMPLY THE INSIDE OF MY own head, caught in pleasure. But then I realized there was no longer a fur rug, heavy with mead, under my body. I lay instead on dry twigs that poked and prodded my bare skin.

The shift of surroundings was enough to draw the attention of us all away from mouths and hands. We were in a dark place, for the only light was the glow of our bodies. But it was a brighter glow than just the three of us held. It made me look beyond the men touching me. Frost, Rhys, and Galen were like pale ghosts of themselves. Doyle was almost invisible except for the lines of power. There were others glowing in the dark, almost all the vegetative deities and Nicca, standing with his wings glowing around him. They'd gone back to being a tattoo on his back until tonight. I didn't remember Nicca touching the mead. I looked for Barinthus and Kitto, but they weren't here. It was as if the magic had picked and chosen among my men. By the glow of our bodies I saw dead plants. Withered things.

We were in the dead gardens – those once magical underground lands where legend had it that faerie had its own sun and moon, rain and weather. But I had never known any of that. The power of the sidhe had faded long before I was born. The gardens were simply dead now, and the sky overhead was only bare, empty rock.

I heard someone say, 'How?' Then those lines of color flared bright: crimson, neon blue, emerald green in the dark. It forced cries from the dark, and sent Abeloec's mouth back between my legs. Mistral's mouth pressed into mine, his hands eager on my body. It was a sweet trap, but trap it was, laid for us by something that cared little for what we wanted. The magic of faerie held us, and we would not be free until that magic was satisfied.

I tried to be afraid, but I couldn't. There was nothing but the feel of Abeloec's and Mistral's bodies on mine, and the push of the dead earth underneath me.

Chapter 3

ABELOEC'S TONGUE MADE LONG, SURE STROKES around the edge of my opening, then a caress at the top as he moved downward again. Mistral's hands played with my breasts in the same way he kissed, as if he could not fill his hands with enough of my body, as if the sensation was something that he had to have. He rolled my nipples between his fingers, and finally moved his mouth from mine to join his hands at my breasts. He took one breast into his mouth, as far as he could, as if he would truly eat my flesh. He sucked hard, and harder, until his teeth began to press into me.

Abeloec moved up to that sweet place at the top of my opening and began to roll his tongue over and around it. Mistral's teeth pressed in slowly, as if he were waiting for me to say stop, but I didn't. The combination of Abeloec's mouth, sure and gentle between my legs, and the inexorable pressure of Mistral's mouth on my breast, tight and tighter, was exquisite.

A soft breeze danced across my skin. A trickle of wind pushed strands of Mistral's hair across my body, pulling strands free from his long pony-tail. His teeth continued their relentless press. He was crushing my breast between his teeth, and it felt so good. Abeloec's tongue flicked fast and faster over that one sweet point.

The wind blew harder, sending dead leaves skittering across our bodies.

Mistral's teeth were almost met in my breast, and it hurt now. I opened my mouth to tell him to stop, but in that moment Abeloec flicked that one last time I needed. He brought me screaming, my hands flinging outward, upward, searching for something to hold on to, while Abeloec built the orgasm with tongue and mouth.

My hands found Mistral. I dug nails into his bare arms, and only when one of my hands reached for his thigh did he grab my wrist. To do it, he had to release my breast from the prison of his mouth. He pinned my hands into the dry earth, while I screamed and strained to reach him with nails and teeth. He stayed just above me, pressing my wrists into the ground. He stared down at me with eyes flickering with light. My last sight of his eyes, before Abeloec made me fling my head from side to side, fighting against the pleasure, was that they were full of lightning, flickering, dancing, so bright it made shadows on the glow of my skin.

Abeloec's hands dug into my thighs, holding me in place, while I struggled to break free. It felt so good – so good – that I thought I would lose my mind if he didn't stop. So good that I wanted him both to stop, and never to stop.

The wind blew harder. Dried, woody vines screeched in the growing wind, and trees creaked with protest, as if their dead limbs would not last the wind.

The lines of color that fed out from Abeloec, red and blue and green, grew brighter with the wind. The colors pulsed bright and brighter. Maybe because the light was so intensely colored, it didn't so much push back the darkness as make the darkness glow – as if the endless night had been brushed with neon lights.

Abeloec let go of my thighs, and the moment he did the lights dimmed, just a little. He knelt between my legs and began unlacing his breeches. His modern clothes had been ruined in last night's assassination attempt, and he, like most of the men who rarely left faerie, had few things with zippers or metal buttons.

I started to say no, because he hadn't asked, and because the magic was receding. I could think again, as if the orgasm had cleared my mind.

I was supposed to be having as much sex as I

could, for if I didn't get with child soon, not only would I never be queen, but I'd probably be dead. If my cousin Cel got someone with child before I got pregnant, he would be king, and he would kill me, and all who were loyal to me. It was an incentive to fuck that no aphrodisiac could match.

But there was something sharp under my back, and more smaller pains up and down my body. Dead branches and bits of plant poking and biting at me. I hadn't noticed it until after the orgasm, when the endorphins were receding at a rapid rate. There'd been almost no afterglow, just mind-blowing orgasm, and then this feeling of fading, of being aware of every discomfort. If Abeloec had missionary position in mind, we needed a blanket.

It wasn't like me to lose interest so quickly. If Abeloec was as talented with other things as he was with his mouth, then he was someone I wanted to bed, just for sheer pleasure. So why did I suddenly find myself with *no* upon my lips and a desire to get up off the ground?

Then a voice came out of the growing dark as the lines of color faded – a voice that froze us all where we were and sent my heart pounding into my throat. 'Well, well, well, I call for my captain of the guard, Mistral, and he is nowhere to be found. My healer tells me that you all vanished from the bedroom. I searched for you in the dark, and here you are.' Andais, Queen of Air and Darkness, stepped out from the far wall. Her pale skin was a whiteness in the growing dark, but there was light around her, light as if black could be a flame and give illumination.

'If you had stood in the light, I would have not found you, but you stand in the dark, the deep dark of the dead gardens. You cannot hide from me here, Mistral.'

'No one was hiding from you, my queen,' Doyle said – the first any of us had spoken since we'd all been brought here.

She waved him silent and walked over the dry grass. The wind that had been whipping the leaves was dying now, as the colors died.

The last of the wind fluttered the hem of her black robe. 'Wind?' She made it a question. 'There has not been wind in here for centuries.'

Mistral had left me to drop to his knees before her. His skin faded as he moved away from me and Abeloec. I wondered if his eyes still flashed with lightning, but was betting they did not.

'Why did you leave my side, Mistral?' She touched his chin with long pointed nails, raised his face so he had to look at her.

'I sought guidance,' he said in a voice that both was low and seemed to carry in the growing dark. Now that Abeloec and I had stopped having sex, all the light was fading, all the flow on everyone's skin was dying away. Soon we would stand in a darkness so absolute that you could touch your own eyeball without first blinking. A cat would be blind in here; even a cat's eyes need some light.

'Guidance for what, Mistral?' She made of his name an evil whine that held the threat of pain, as a smell on the wind can promise rain.

He tried to bow his head, but she kept her fingertips under his chin. 'You sought guidance from my Darkness?'

Abeloec helped me to my feet and held me close, not for romance, but the way all the fey do when they're nervous. We touch one another, huddling in the dark, as if the touch of another's hand will keep the great bad thing from happening.

'Yes,' Mistral said.

'Liar,' the queen said, and the last thing I saw before the darkness swallowed the world was the gleam of a blade in her other hand. It flashed from her robe, where she'd hidden it.

I spoke before I could think: '*No!*'

Her voice crawled out of the darkness and seemed to creep along my skin. 'Meredith, niece, do you actually forbid me from punishing one of my own guards? Not one of your guards, but mine, mine!'

The darkness was heavier, thicker, and it took more effort to breathe. I knew she could make the very air so heavy that it would crush the life out of me. She could make the air so thick that my mortal lungs couldn't draw it in. She'd nearly killed me just yesterday, when I interfered in one of her 'entertainments.'

'There was wind in the dead gardens.' Doyle's deep voice came so low, so deep, that it seemed to vibrate along my spine. 'You felt the wind. You remarked upon the wind.'

'Yes, I did, but now it is gone. Now the gardens are dead, dead as they will always be.'

A pale green light sprang from the darkness. Doyle holding a cup of sickly greenish flames in his hands. It was one of his hands of power. I'd seen the touch of that fire crawl over other sidhe and make them wish for death. But as so many things in faerie, it had other uses. It was a welcome light in the dark.

The light showed that it was no longer her fingertips that held Mistral's chin upward, but the edge of a blade. Her blade, Mortal Dread. One of the few things left that could bring true death to the immortal sidhe.

'What if the gardens could live again?' Doyle asked. 'As the roses outside the throne room live again.'

She smiled most unpleasantly. 'Do you propose to spill more of Meredith's precious blood? That was the price for the roses' renewal.'

'There are ways to give life that do not require blood,' he said.

'You think you can fuck the gardens back to life?' she asked. She used the edge of the blade to raise Mistral up high on his knees.

Doyle said, 'Yes.'

'This, I would like to see,' she said.

'I don't think it will work if you are here,' Rhys said. A pale white light appeared over his head. Small, round, a gentle whiteness that illumined where he walked. It was the light that most of the sidhe, and many of the lesser fey, could make at will; a small magic that most possessed. If I wanted light in the dark, I had to find a flashlight or a match.

Rhys moved, in his soft circle of light, slowly, toward the queen.

She spoke: 'A little fucking after a few centuries of celibacy makes you bold, one-eye.'

'The fucking makes me happy,' he said. 'This makes me bold.' He raised his right arm, showing her the underside of it. The light was not strong enough, and the angle not right, for me to see what was so interesting.

She frowned; then, as he moved closer, her eyes widened. 'What is that?' But her hand had lowered enough that Mistral was no longer trying to raise himself up on his knees to keep from being cut.

'It is exactly what you think it is, my queen,' Doyle said. He began to move closer to her, as well.

'Close enough, both of you.' She emphasized her words by forcing Mistral back high on his knees.

'We mean you no harm, my queen,' Doyle said.

'Perhaps I mean you harm, Darkness.'

'That is your privilege,' he said.

I opened my mouth to correct him, because he was my captain of the guard now. She wasn't allowed to simply hurt him for the hell of it, not anymore.

Abeloec tightened his hand on my arm. He whispered against my hair, 'Not yet, Princess. The Darkness does not need your help yet.'

I wanted to argue, but his reasoning was sound, as far as it went. I opened my mouth to argue, but as I looked up into his face, the argument fell away from me. His suggestion just seemed so reasonable.

Something bumped my hip, and I realized he was holding the horn cup. He was the cup, and the cup was him, in some mystical way, but when he touched it, he became more. More . . . reasonable. Or rather his suggestions did.

I wasn't sure I liked that he could do that to me, but I let it go. We had enough problems without getting sidetracked. I whispered, 'What is on Rhys's arm?'

But Abeloec and I stood in the dark, and the Queen of Air and Darkness could hear anything that was spoken into the air in the dark. She answered me, 'Show her, Rhys. Show her what has made you bold.'

Rhys didn't turn his back on her, but moved sort of sideways toward us. The soft, white sourceless light moved with him, outlining his upper body. In a battle it would have been worse than useless; it would have made him a target. But the immortal don't sweat things like that – if you can't die, I guess you can make as obvious a target of yourself as you like.

The light touched us first, like that first white breath of dawn that slides across the sky, so white, so pure, when dawn is nothing more than the fading of darkness. As Rhys got closer to us, the white light seemed to expand, sliding down his body, showing that he was still nude.

He held his arm out toward me. There was a pale blue outline of a fish that stretched from just above his wrist almost to his elbow. The fish was head-down toward his hand and seemed oddly curved, like a half circle waiting for its other half.

Abeloec touched it much as the queen had done, lightly, with just his fingertips. 'I have not seen that on your arm since I stopped being a pub keeper.'

'I know Rhys's body,' I said. 'It's never been there before.'

'Not in your lifetime,' Abeloec said.

I glanced from him to Rhys. To him, I said, 'It's a fish, why . . .'

'A salmon,' he said, 'to be exact.'

I closed my mouth so I wouldn't say something stupid. I tried to do what my father had always taught me to do, think. I thought out loud . . . 'A salmon means knowledge. One of our legends says that because the salmon is the oldest living creature, it has all the knowledge since the world began. It means longevity, because of the same legend.'

'Legend, is it?' Rhys said with a smile.

'I have a degree in biology, Rhys; nothing you say will convince me that a salmon predated the trilobites, or even the dinosaurs. Modern fish is just that, modern, on a geological scale.'

Abeloec was looking at me curiously. 'I'd forgotten Prince Essus insisted on you being educated among the humans.' He smiled. 'When you're reasoning things out, you aren't as easy to distract.' He tightened his other hand, with the cup still gripped in it.

I frowned, and finally stepped away from him. 'Stop that.'

'You drank from his cup,' Rhys said. 'He should be able to persuade you of almost anything.' He grinned as he said it. 'If you were human.'

'I guess she's not human enough,' Abeloec said.

'You're all acting as if that pale tattoo is important. I don't understand why.'

'Didn't Essus ever tell you about it?' asked Rhys.

I frowned. 'My father didn't mention anything about a tattoo on your arm.'

The queen made a derisive noise. 'Essus didn't think you were important enough to be told.'

'He didn't tell her,' Doyle said, 'for the same reason that Galen doesn't know.'

Galen was still lying in the dead garden. All the other men who had fallen to the ground were still kneeling or sitting in the dead vegetation. A soft greenish white glow began to form above Galen's head. Not a nimbus like that of Rhys, but more of a small ball of light above his head.

Galen found his voice, hoarse, and had to clear it sharply before he said, 'I don't know about any tattoos on Rhys, either.'

'None of us has told the younger ones, Queen Andais,' Doyle said. 'Everyone knows that our followers painted themselves with symbols and went into battle with only those symbols to shield them.'

'They eventually learned to wear armor,' Andais said. Her arm had lowered enough for Mistral to be comfortable on his knees again.

'Yes, and only the last few fanatical tribes kept trying to seek our favor and blessing. They died for that devotion,' Doyle said.

'What are you talking about?' I asked.

'Once we, the sidhe, their gods, were painted

53

with symbols that were our sign of blessing from the Goddess and the God. But as our power faded, so did the marks upon our bodies.' Doyle said it all in his thick-as-molasses voice.

Rhys picked up the story. 'Once, if our followers painted their bodies to mimic us, they gained some of the protection, the magic, that we had. It was a sign of devotion, yes, but once long, long ago, it literally could call us to their aid.' He looked at the faint blue fish on his arm. 'I have not held this mark for nearly four thousand years.'

'It is faint and incomplete,' the queen said from the far wall.

'Yes.' Rhys nodded and looked at her. 'But it is a beginning.'

Nicca's voice came soft, and I'd almost forgotten him, standing so still to one side. His wings began to gleam in the dark, as if their veins had begun to pulse with light instead of blood. He fanned those huge wings. They had been only a birthmark on the back of his body until a few days ago, when they had sprung from his back, real and true at last. They began to glow as if the individual colors were stained glass gleaming in sunlight that we could not see.

He held out his right hand, and showed us a mark on the outer part of the wrist, almost on the hand itself. The light was too uncertain for me to be sure of what it was, but Doyle said, 'A butterfly.'

'I have never held a mark of favor from the Goddess,' Nicca said in his soft voice.

The queen lowered her blade completely, so that it went back to being invisible in the full black skirt of her robe. 'What of the rest of you?'

'You'll be able to feel it, if you think about it,' Rhys said to the others.

Frost called a ball of light that was a dim silver-grey. It held above his head much as Galen's greenish light had. Frost began unbuttoning his shirt. He rarely went nude if he could avoid it, so I knew before he bared the perfect curve of his right shoulder that there would be something there.

He turned his arm so he could see it. The queen said, 'Show us.'

He let her see first, then turned in a slow half circle to us. It was as pale and blue as Rhys's had been, a small dead tree, leafless, naked, and the ground underneath it seemed to hint at a snow-bank. Like Rhys's salmon it was dim, and not drawn in completely, as if someone had begun the job but not finished.

'Killing Frost has never held a sign of favor,' the queen said, and her voice was strangely unhappy.

'No,' Frost said, 'I have not. I was not fully sidhe when last the sidhe held such favors.' He shrugged back into his shirt and began to button it into place. He wasn't just dressed, he was armed. Most of the others held a sword and dagger, but only Doyle and Frost had guns. Rhys had left his gun behind with his clothes in the bedroom.

I noticed a bulge here and there under Frost's shirt, which meant he held more weapons than could be easily seen. He liked being armed, but this many weapons meant something had made him nervous. The assassination attempts, maybe, or maybe something else. His handsome face was closed to me, hidden behind the arrogance that he used as a mask. Perhaps he was just hiding his thoughts and feelings from the queen, but then again . . . Frost tended to be moody.

Rhys said, 'Let Abeloec and Merry finish what they began. Let us all finish it.'

Queen Andais took in a deep breath, so that even across the dimly lit chamber I could see the rise and fall of the V of white flesh in her robe. 'Very well, finish it. Then come to me, for we have much to discuss.' She held out her hand to Mistral. 'Come, my captain, let us leave them to their pleasures.'

Mistral did not question. He stood and took her pale hand.

'We need him,' Rhys said.

'No,' Andais said, 'no, I have given Meredith my green men. She does not need the whole world.'

'Does grass grow without wind and rain?' Doyle asked.

'No,' she said, and her voice was unfriendly again, as if she would like to be angry but couldn't afford to be right now. Andais was a creature of her temper; she always indulged it. This much self-restraint from her was rare.

'To make spring, you need many things, my queen,' said Doyle. 'Without warmth and water, plants wither and die.' They stared at each other, the queen and her Darkness. It was the queen who looked away first.

'Mistral may stay.' She released his hand, then looked across the cavern at me. 'But let this be understood between us, niece. He is not yours. He is mine. He is yours only for this space of time. Is that clear to all of you?'

We all nodded.

'And you, Mistral,' the queen said. 'Do you understand?'

'My geas is lifted for this space of time with the princess alone.'

'Clearly put, as always,' she said. She turned her back as if she would walk through the wall, then turned and looked over her shoulder. 'I will finish what I was doing when I noticed your absence, Mistral.'

He dropped to his knees. 'My queen, please do not do this . . .'

She turned back with a smile that was almost pleasant – except for the look in her eyes, which even from here was frightening.

57

'You mean, do not leave you with the princess?'

'No, my queen, you know that is not what I mean.'

'Do I?' she said, danger in her voice. She glided over the dead brush and placed the point of Mortal Dread under his chin. 'You didn't come to ask the advice of my Darkness. You came to bid the princess to intercede for Nerys's clan.'

Mistral's shoulders moved as if he'd breathed deeply, or swallowed hard.

'Answer me, Mistral,' she said, a whine of rage like a razor's edge in her voice.

'Nerys gave her life on your word that you would not kill her people. You—' He stopped talking abruptly, as if she'd nudged the point close enough that he couldn't speak without cutting himself.

'Aunt Andais,' I said, 'what have you done to Nerys's people?'

'They tried to kill you and me last night, or have you forgotten?'

'I remember, but I also remember that Nerys asked you to take her life, so that you might spare her house. You gave your word that you would let them live if she died in their place.'

'I have not harmed a single one,' she said, and she looked entirely too pleased with herself.

'What does that mean?' I asked.

'I merely offered the men a chance to serve

58

their queen as a member of my royal guard. I need my Ravens at full strength.'

'Joining your guard means giving up all family loyalties and becoming celibate. Why would they agree to either of those things?' I asked.

She took the blade away from Mistral's throat. 'You were so eager to tattle on me. Tell her now.'

'May I rise, my queen?' he asked.

'Rise, cartwheel – I care not – just tell her.'

Mistral rose cautiously, and when she made no move toward him, he began to ease across the room toward us. His throat was dark in the flickering lights. She'd bled him. Any sidhe could heal such a small cut, but because Mortal Dread had done the damage, he would heal mortal slow; human slow.

Mistral's eyes were wide, frightened, but he moved easily across the dead ground, as if he weren't worried that she would do something to him as he walked away from her. I know that my shoulder blades would have been aching with the fear of the blow. Only when he was out of reach of her sword did some of the panic leave his eyes. Even then, they were that shade of tornado green. Anxiety.

'Far enough,' she said. 'Meredith can hear you from there.'

He stopped obediently, but he swallowed hard, as if he didn't like that she'd stopped him before he got back to us. I didn't blame him. The queen had magic that could destroy from this distance. She'd probably made him stop just so he would worry. She might intend him no more harm, but she wanted him to be afraid. She liked for people to be afraid of her.

'She has put metal chains of binding on all of the house of Nerys, so they can do no magic,' said Mistral.

'I can't argue with that,' I said. 'They attacked us at court, all of them. They should lose their magic for a time.'

'She has given the men the chance to become her Ravens. The women she has offered to the prince's guard, his Cranes.'

'Cel is in seclusion, locked away. He needs no guard,' I said.

'Most of the women would not agree to it, anyway,' Mistral said. 'But the queen had to be seen giving them all a choice.'

'A choice between becoming guards and what?' I asked. I was almost afraid of the answer. She'd been carrying Mortal Dread. I prayed that she hadn't executed them. She would be forsworn before the entire court. And I needed Andais on the throne until she confirmed me as her heir.

'The queen has bid Ezekiel and his helpers to wall them up alive,' said Mistral.

I blinked at him. I couldn't quite follow it all. My first thought was to protest that the queen was forsworn; then I realized she wasn't. 'They're immortal, so they won't die,' I said, softly.

'They will know terrible hunger and thirst, and they will wish to die,' Mistral said, 'but no, they are immortal, and they will not die.'

I looked past him to my aunt. 'Tricksy you,' I said. 'Very damn clever.'

She gave a little bow from the neck. 'So glad you appreciate the delicate reasoning of it.'

'Oh, I do,' and I meant it. 'You've broken no oath. In fact, technically, you're doing exactly what Nerys gave her life for. Her clan, her house, her bloodline will live.'

'That is not living,' Mistral said.

'Did you really think that the princess had enough influence with me to save them from their fate?' asked Andais.

'Once I would have gone to Essus, to ask his help with you,' Mistral said. 'So I sought the princess.'

'She is not my brother,' Andais snarled.

'No, she is not Essus,' Mistral said, 'but she is his child. She is your blood.'

'And what does that mean, Mistral? That she can bargain for Nerys's people? They have already been bargained for, by Nerys herself.'

'You are pixieing on the spirit of that bargain,' Rhys said.

'But not breaking it,' she said.

'No,' he said, and he looked so sad. 'No, the

sidhe never lie, and we always keep our word. Except our version of the truth can be more dangerous than any lie, and you'd better think through every word of any oath we give our word to, because we will find a way to make you regret you ever met us.' He sounded more angry than sad.

'Do you dare to criticize your queen?' she asked.

I touched Rhys's arm, squeezed. He looked first at my hand, then at my face. Whatever he saw there made him take a deep breath and shake his head. 'No one would dare to do that, Queen Andais.' His voice was resigned again.

'What would you give for a sign that life was returning to the gardens?' Doyle asked.

'What do you mean by *sign*?' she asked, and her voice held all the suspicion of someone who knew us all too well.

'What would you give for some hint of life here in the gardens?'

'A little wind is not a sign,' she said.

'But would the beginnings of life here in the gardens be worth nothing to you, my queen?'

'Of course it would be worth something.'

'It could mean that our power was returning,' Doyle said.

She motioned with the sword, silver gleaming dully in the light. 'I know what it would mean, Darkness.'

'And a return of our power, what would that be worth to you, Queen?'

'I know where you are going, Darkness. Do not try to play such games with me. I invented these games.'

'Then I will not play. I will state plainly. If we can bring some hint of life to these underground worlds, then you will wait to punish, in any way, Nerys's people. Or anyone else.'

A smile as cruel and cold as a winter morning curved her lips. 'Good catch, Darkness, good catch.'

My throat was tight with the realization that if he'd forgotten the last phrase, others would have paid for her anger. Someone who would have mattered to Doyle, or me, or both, if she could have found them. Rhys was right: This was a dangerous game, this game of words.

'For what shall I wait?' she asked.

'For us to bring life to the dead gardens, of course,' he said.

'And if you do not bring life to the dead gardens, then what?'

'Then when we are all convinced that the princess and her men cannot bring life back to the gardens, you are free to do with Nerys's people as you intended.'

'And if you do bring life to the gardens, what then?' she asked.

'If we bring even a hint of life back to the

gardens, you will let Princess Meredith choose the punishment of those who tried to have her assassinated.'

She shook her head. 'Clever, Darkness, but not clever enough. If you bring a hint of life back to the gardens, then I will allow Meredith to punish Nerys's people.'

It was his turn to shake his head. 'If the Princess Meredith and some of her men bring even a hint of life back to these gardens, then Meredith alone decides what punishment shall be meted out to Nerys's people.'

She seemed to think about that for a moment or two, then nodded. 'Agreed.'

'You give your word, the word of the queen of the Unseelie Court?' he asked.

She nodded. 'I do.'

'Witnessed,' Rhys said.

She waved her hand dismissively. 'Fine, fine, you have your promise. But remember, I have to agree that there is at least a hint of life. It better be some evidence impressive enough that I can't pixie out of it, Darkness, because you know I will, if I can.'

'I know,' he said.

She looked at me, then. It was not a friendly look. 'Enjoy Mistral, Meredith. Enjoy him and know that he comes back to me when this is done.'

'Thank you for loaning him to me,' I said, and kept my voice absolutely empty.

She made a face at me. 'Don't thank me, Meredith – not yet. You've only bedded him once.' She motioned at me with the sword. 'Though I see that you have found what he considers pleasure: He likes to cause pain.'

'I would have thought that he would be your ideal lover then, Aunt Andais.'

'I like to cause pain, niece Meredith, not be on the receiving end.'

I swallowed hard, so I wouldn't say what I was thinking. I finally managed, 'I did not know that you were a pure sadist, Aunt Andais.'

She frowned at me. '*Pure sadist* – that's an odd phrase.'

'I meant only that I didn't know you didn't like pain on your own body at all.'

'Oh, I like a little teeth, a little nails, but not like that.' Again she motioned at my breast. It ached where he'd bitten me, and I had a near-perfect imprint of his teeth, though he hadn't broken the skin. I would be bruised, but nothing more.

She shook her head, as if to chase away a thought, then turned, and the motion caused her black robe to swirl wide. She grabbed the edge of it, to pull it around herself. She looked back over her shoulder one last time before she stepped into the darkness and traveled back the way she'd come. Her last words were not a comfort. 'After Mistral's had his way with her, do not come crying to me that he's broken your little princess.'

And the piece of darkness where she had been was empty.

So many of us let out a sigh of relief at the same time that it was like the sound of wind in the trees. Someone gave a nervous laugh.

'She is right about one thing,' Mistral said, and his eyes held regret. 'I like causing a little pain. I am sorry if I hurt you, but it has been so long since . . .' He spread his hands wide. 'I forgot myself. I am sorry for that.'

Rhys laughed, and Doyle joined him, and finally even Galen and Frost joined in that soft masculine sound.

'Why do you laugh?' Mistral asked.

Rhys turned to me, his face still shining with laughter. 'Do you want to tell him, or do we?'

I actually blushed, which I almost never do. I kept Abe's hand in mine and drew us both across the dry, brittle grass until I stood in front of Mistral. I looked at the blood that trickled dark across his pale neck and gazed up into his eyes, so anxious. I had to smile. 'I like what you did to my breast. That's just about as hard as I like it, just this side of drawing blood with teeth.'

He frowned at me.

'You like the nail work to be harder than the teeth,' Rhys said. 'You don't mind bleeding a little from nails.'

'But only if you've done the preliminaries,' I said.

'Preliminaries?' Mistral said, and sounded puzzled.

'Foreplay,' Abeloec said.

The puzzled look faded, and something else entirely filled his eyes. Something warm and sure of itself, something that made me shiver just from him looking at me. 'I can do that,' he said.

'Then take off the armor,' I said.

'What?' he asked.

'Get naked,' Rhys called.

'I can speak for myself, thank you,' I said, glancing back at him.

He made a little motion as if to say, *Be my guest.* I turned back to Mistral. I gazed up into his face, and found that his eyes were already beginning to fade to a soft grey, like rain clouds. I smiled at him, and he smiled back, a little uncertainly, as if he wasn't used to smiling much.

'Get naked,' I said.

He grinned, a brief flash of it. 'Then what?'

'We have sex.'

'I'm first,' Abeloec said, hugging me from behind.

I nodded. 'Agreed.'

Mistral's face darkened; I could almost see clouds in his eyes. Not just the color of the irises, but the actual image of clouds floating in the pupils. 'Why is he first?' he asked.

'Because he can be part of the foreplay,' I said.

'She means, once I've fucked her, then you can do it rougher,' said Abeloec.

Mistral smiled again, but this smile was different. This was a smile that made me breathe harder. 'You really liked what I did to your breast?' he asked.

I swallowed hard, pressing myself against Abeloec's body, almost as if I were afraid of the taller man in front of me. I nodded and whispered, 'Yes.'

'Good,' he said, and he reached for the leather fastenings that held his armor in place. 'Very good,' he whispered.

Chapter 4

THE MOMENT ABELOEC LAID ME DOWN ON A BED OF castoff clothes, our skin began to glow. It was a thin layer of my guards' shirts and tunics, just enough so that I wouldn't pierce my body on the dead vegetation. It amounted to all the clothing the men were wearing, which hadn't been much – and it left them all nude. I could still feel the dry sticks, crumbling leaves, dry and withered, crushed underneath me.

It wasn't the feel of the ground in winter. No matter how cold the winter, how deep the snow, there is a feeling of waiting in the ground then – a sense that the land is merely asleep, and the sun will wake it, and spring will come. Not here. It was like the difference between a body that is deeply asleep and one that is dead. At a glance, your eyes may see no difference, but if you touch it, you know. The ground that Abeloec's body pressed me into held nothing – no warmth, breath, life. Empty, like the eyes of the dead that but a moment ago held personality, and now are like dark mirrors. The gardens weren't waiting for reawakening; they were just dead.

But we weren't dead.

Abeloec laid his naked body against mine and kissed me. The height difference meant that all he could do was kiss me, but it was enough. Enough to conjure that moonglow inside our bodies.

He raised up on his arms to stare down at my face. His skin glowed so bright that again his eyes became like dark grey caves in his face. I'd never met any sidhe whose eyes did not glow when their power came upon them. His long hair spilled out around us, and the white lines in his hair began to glow softly blue, like before. He raised higher on his arms, almost in a push-up, so that his body was suspended above mine on hands and toes.

Pale blue lines glowed through the white of his skin. Flowing images of vines and flowers, and trees, and animals. Nothing stayed, nothing lasted. There weren't that many lines, and they didn't move that fast. I should have been able to tell what kind of vine, what fruit, what animal, but beyond small, or large, it was as if my mind couldn't hold the images.

I traced the blue with my fingers, and it trailed over my hand, tickled and teased across the white glow of my own skin. And even staring at my own hand, I couldn't tell you what plant it was that grew and flowered there. It was as if I weren't meant to see it, or at least not to understand it. Not yet, maybe not ever.

I stopped trying to make sense of the flowing lines, and gazed down the length of Abeloec's body where it stretched above mine. He held himself above me like a shelter, as if he could have stayed there forever and never tired. I reached down his body, worming underneath his steady strength, until I could wrap my hand around the hard length of him.

He shuddered above me. 'I should be touching you.' His voice was strained, thick with effort, but effort for what? His arms and shoulders, and legs, were utterly still above me as if he were stone instead of flesh. It wasn't his strength that gave his voice that thick sound. At least not strength of body. Maybe strength of will.

I squeezed gently around his shaft, and he was hard, so terribly hard. His breathing changed, and I could see his stomach fluttering with the effort to stay steady above me. 'How long has it been?' I asked.

'I don't remember,' he said.

I stroked my hand up and over the head of him. His spine bowed downward, and he almost fell on top of me, but then his arms and legs went back to their firm stance. 'I thought the sidhe did not lie.'

'I do not remember *exactly*,' he said. His voice was breathy now.

I slid my other hand down to cup his balls and gently play with them.

He swallowed hard enough for me to hear it, and said, 'If you keep doing that, I'll go, and that's not how I want to go the first time.'

I continued to play with him, gently. He was so hard, quiveringly hard. Just holding him in my hands, I knew that the phrase *aching with need* wasn't merely words. He glowed and I could feel the power in him, but he did not throb with it the way the others did. It was a quieter power, this.

'What do you want the first time?' I asked, and my voice had gone deeper, thickening with the feel of him in my hands.

'I want to be inside you, between your legs – I want to make you come before I do. But I do not know if I still have that kind of discipline.'

'Then don't be disciplined. This time, the first time, don't worry about it.'

He shook his head, and the blue lines in his hair seemed to pulse brighter. 'I want to bring you such pleasure that you will want me in your bed every night. So many men, Meredith, so many men in your bed. I don't want to wait my turn. I want you to come to me again and again, because no one brings you as much pleasure as I do.'

A sound made us both turn our heads; we

found Mistral kneeling beside us. 'Hurry up and finish this, Abeloec, or I will not wait to be second.'

'Would you not worry, as I do, that you pleasure the princess?' Abeloec asked.

'Unlike you, I'll have no second chance here, Abeloec. The queen has decreed that this time is all I will ever have with the princess. So no, I am not so worried about my performance.' He ran his hand through my hair, pushing deep so that his fingers brushed my scalp. It made me cuddle my head against his hand. He closed his fingers into a fist, and was suddenly jerking my hair tight in his hand. It sped my pulse in my throat, tearing a sound from my mouth that was not pain. My skin blazed to white-hot life.

'We do not have to be gentle,' Mistral said. He leaned his face near mine. 'Do we, Princess?'

I whispered, 'No.'

He pulled my hair tighter, and I cried out. I felt rather than saw some of the other men move toward us. Mistral pulled my hair tight again, bending my neck to one side, moving my body a little out from under Abeloec. 'I am not hurting you, am I, Princess?'

'No.' All I could do was whisper.

'I don't think they heard you,' he said. He twisted his hand tight and sudden in my hair. He put his lips against my cheek and whispered, 'Scream for me.' The blue lines crawled from my skin to his, and again I saw that outline of lightning on his cheek.

I whispered, 'What will you do, if I don't scream?'

He kissed me, ever so gently against my cheek. 'Hurt you.'

My breath came out in a shudder. 'Please,' I sighed.

Mistral laughed, a wonderful deep laugh, with his face pressed against mine and his hand still tight in my hair. 'Hurry, Abeloec, hurry, or we will have to fight to see who is first.' He let go of my hair so abruptly that this motion, too, hurt a little, and forced a sound from me. Mistral turned me back over to Abeloec with my eyes unfocused, and my breath either coming too fast or nearly stopping for a moment – I couldn't quite tell. My pulse seemed uncertan if I was afraid or thrilled. But it was as if now that Mistral touched me again, he could not quite give up touching me. He kept his fingers against the side of my neck, as if he wanted to help my pulse decide.

'I do not like to cause pain,' Abeloec said. His body was not quite as happy as it had been.

'Pain is not the only way to pleasure,' I said.

His dark eyes narrowed at me from the shine of his face. 'You do not have to have pain to be pleasured?'

I shook my head, feeling the lingering ache where Mistral's hand had been. 'No.'

Doyle's deep voice came out of the dark. 'Meredith likes violence, but she also likes gentleness. It depends on her mood, and yours.'

Both Abe and Mistral looked at him. 'The queen cares nothing for our moods,' Mistral said.

'This one will,' Doyle said.

Abeloec looked down at me and began to slowly lower himself toward my body, for all the world like a push-up, except that I was in the way. His mouth found mine before his body pressed into me. He kissed me, and the blue was neon-bright and flared with lines of crimson and emerald. The lines of color flared down Mistral's hand, and it felt as if those lines were made of rope, drawing his mouth to mine, and drawing Abeloec down my body. He half knelt and half lay across my lower body. He spread my legs so that his body spilled between them. But it was his finger that found me first – testing the waters, I think.

His voice was strangled as he said, 'You're still wet.'

I would have answered but Mistral's mouth found mine, and I gave the only answer I could. I raised my hips toward Abeloec's searching hand. The next thing I felt was his hands moving to my hips. The tip of him of him rubbing against my opening.

Mistral raised his mouth from mine and half whispered, half groaned, 'Fuck her, fuck her, fuck her, please,' and the last word was drawn out into a long sigh that ended in something close to a scream.

Abeloec pushed himself inside me, and only then did he begin to throb with power. It was almost like some huge vibrator, except this vibrator was warm and alive, and had a mind and a body behind it.

That mind moved the body in rhythms that no mere mechanical aid could ever have produced. I watched Abeloec push in and out of my body like some shining shaft of light, though it was undoubtedly flesh that went in and out of me. Soft, firm, vibrating flesh.

Mistral grabbed my hair again, pulled my head back so that I could no longer watch Abeloec work his magic in my body. The look on Mistral's face would have frightened me if we'd been alone. He kissed me hard, so hard that it was bruising. I had a choice of opening my mouth to him or cutting my lips on my own teeth. I opened my mouth.

His tongue plunged inside me, as if he were trying to do to my mouth what Abeloec was doing between my legs. It was only his tongue, but he kept pushing inside, pushing until he shoved my mouth so wide that my jaw began to ache. He shoved his tongue so far down my throat that I gagged, and he drew back. I thought he did it to let me swallow and catch my breath, but he drew back so he could laugh. He let loose a roll of masculine pleasure that spilled from his mouth and danced over my skin. There was an echo to it, that laughter – an echo like distant thunder.

His pausing gave me a chance to concentrate on Abeloec. He had found a rhythm that plunged to the end of me, and out, in a rolling slide, a rhythm that would have brought me eventually. But even beyond that, his body pulsed inside mine. It was as if his magic throbbed with the rhythm of his body, so that each time he plunged deep inside me the magic throbbed harder, and vibrated faster.

I took the chance Mistral had given me to say, 'Abeloec, are you making your magic pulse in time to your lovemaking?'

His voice came tight with concentration. 'Yes.'

I started to say, *Oh, Goddess*, but Mistral's mouth found mine again, and I got only as far as, 'Oh, God—'

Mistral thrust his tongue so deep and hard into my mouth that it was like oral sex when the man is too big for comfort. If you fight it, it hurts, but if you relax, sometimes, you can do it. You can let the man have his way with your mouth without breaking your jaw. I'd never had anyone kiss me like this, and even as I fought to let him do it, I thought about him being this forceful with other things, and the thought made me open wider to him, wider to them both.

They were both so skilled, but in such opposite ways that I wondered what it would be like to have their full attention one at a time. But there was no way to ask Mistral to wait, to give us room, because I could barely breathe with his tongue down my throat, let alone speak. I wanted to speak; I wanted to stop having to fight him to breathe. My jaw was aching hard enough to distract me from Abeloec's amazing fucking. Mistral had crossed that line from *feels good* to *fucking stop*.

We hadn't arranged a sign that would let him know I wanted him to stop. When you can't speak, you usually have some prearranged way to tap out. I started pushing at his shoulders, pushing like I meant it. I wasn't as strong as a full-blooded sidhe, but I had once put my hand through a car door to scare away some would-be muggers, if that's an indication. I had bloodied my hand, but not broken it. So I pushed, and he pushed back.

He had his mouth so far inside mine that I couldn't even bite him. I was choking, and he didn't care.

I could feel the orgasm beginning to build. I did not want Abeloec's good work spoiled by the fact that I was choking.

Nails could be used for pleasure, or to make a

point. I set my nails in the firm flesh of Mistral's neck and dug them in. I carved bloody furrows in his skin. He jerked back from me, and seeing the rage on his face, again, I was glad we weren't alone.

'When I say stop, you stop,' I said. And I realized that I was angry, too.

'You didn't say stop.'

'Because you made certain I couldn't.'

'You said you liked pain.'

I was having trouble controlling my breathing, because Abeloec was still vibrating and moving inside me. I was close. 'I like pain to a point, but not a broken jaw. We'll need to lay some ground rules before . . . you . . . get . . . your turn,' and the last word was a scream as I threw my head back and my body spasmed. Mistral caught my head or I would have smashed it against the hard ground.

Abeloec's pleasure spread through me, over me, in me, in waves. Waves of pleasure, waves of power, over and over, as if here, too, he was able to control what was happening. As if he could control my release the way he'd controlled everything else. The orgasm would roll over me from my groin to every inch of my body, then it would start again, spreading from between my legs over my skin in a rush that sent my hands seeking something to hold on to, my body thrashing. My entire upper body left the ground and smashed back, over and over, while Abeloec held my hips and legs trapped against his body.

Someone was behind me, catching me, trying to hold me down, but the pleasure was too much. I could do nothing but struggle and scream, one long ragged scream after another. My fingers found flesh to tear, and strong hands held my wrist tight. My other hand found my own body, and tore at it. Another hand found that wrist, pinned it to the floor.

I heard voices over my screams: 'Go, Abeloec, just finish it!'

'Now, Abeloec!' urged Mistral.

And he did, and suddenly the world was made of white light, and it was as if I could feel his release between my legs, feel it hot and thick, and him buried as deep inside me as he could go. I floated in that white light, and found starbursts of red and green and blue. Then there was nothing, nothing but white, white light.

Chapter 5

I DIDN'T PASS OUT, NOT COMPLETELY, NOT REALLY, BUT it was as if I were boneless, helpless in the afterglow of Abeloec's power. My eyes fluttered open when the lap my head was resting in moved. I found Mistral above me, his hands still holding my wrists, still cuddling my head. 'I want you hurt, not broken,' he said, as if he saw something in my face that he had to answer.

It took me three tries to answer. 'Glad to hear it,' I finally said.

He laughed then, and began to move carefully from under me. He laid my head on the dead earth, gently. Apparently, I'd disarranged our makeshift blanket, because I could feel other patches of dry, scratchy vegetation here and there against my skin.

I turned my head and looked for the others. Abeloec was crawling a little shakily toward my head, as if he and Mistral were going to change places. It took me a moment to focus past Abe, farther into the dark beyond.

The darkness was shot with neon glow, blue, green, and red. The colors were everywhere, some individual burning lines and some entwined like string wound into rope – stronger, thicker for being joined. Doyle knelt closest to us, as if he'd tried to come to me. His sword was drawn as if there was something among us that metal could slay. His dark skin was covered in lines of blue and crimson.

Rhys was just beyond him, covered in blue and red lines, too – and there were other figures in the dark covered in green and blue lines, and images of flowering plants. I caught a shine of long pale hair. Ivi was covered in dead vines and green lines of power. Brii stood near a tree, hugging it, or tied to it with green and blue lines. But it was as if the tree had bent toward him, its thin, lifeless branches embracing his naked body like arms. Adair had climbed a tree and stood on one of the thick upper branches. He was reaching up into it, as if he saw things there that I did not. I caught glimpses of other bodies on the ground, covered in dead vegetation.

Frost and Nicca were kneeling farther away. They had lines of blue only, snaking over their bodies. They were holding someone's arms and legs. It took me a moment to realize it was Galen.

He was so covered in the bright green glow that he was nearly hidden from sight. The others seemed to be enjoying the power, or at least not to be in pain, but Galen's body seemed to be convulsing, almost as I had when Abeloec brought me, but even more violently.

Mistral's face appeared above mine, and I realized that he was holding himself above my body, much as Abeloec had earlier. But he didn't kiss me, as the other man had. He made sure that the only thing I could see was his face. 'My turn,' he said, and the look in his eyes was enough to make me frightened. Not in fear of Mistral, but fear of what was happening. Something powerful – and what would be the price? One thing I had learned early was that all power comes with a price.

'Mistral,' I said, but he was already moving down my body. The wind was back, a thin, seeking wind that touched my body like invisible fingers. The dead leaves rustled, and the vines seemed to sigh in the growing wind.

I raised up enough to look down my body at Mistral. I called his name again. He looked up at the sound of his name, but there was nothing in his face that really heard me. This was his one chance in a thousand years to have a woman. When we left the gardens, his opportunity would be gone.

If I'd known the others were safe, then I

wouldn't even have tried to argue with the look in his eyes. But I wasn't sure they were. I wasn't sure any of us were. I didn't like not knowing what was happening.

He smoothed his hands along the inside of my thighs, gentle, caressing, but that gentle movement spread my legs with him kneeling between them.

'What's happening, Mistral?'

'Are you afraid?' he asked, but he wasn't looking at my face when he said it.

'Yes,' I said, and my voice was soft in the growing wind.

'Good,' he said.

Abeloec answered me, 'I am the intoxicating cup like Medb for the kings of old. You have drunk deep.' I turned my head back to look at him where he knelt behind me.

I knew that *Medb* had been a word for 'mead,' a sovereign goddess whom nine kings of Ireland had had to mate with before she would let them rule. But most of that was only stories; no one would speak of her among the sidhe, as if she were a real goddess, a real person. I had asked, and been told only that she was the cup that intoxicates. Which had been another way of saying that she was mead. I'd been left to believe she'd never been real.

'I don't understand,' I said.

Abeloec smoothed his hand along my face. 'I

give the power of sovereignty to the queen, as Medb gave power to the kings. I was forgotten, because the world turned to chauvinism and there were no more votes for queens. I was just Accasbel. Denied my purpose. Some human literature says I am an ancient deity of wine and beer. I founded the first pub in Ireland, and was a follower of Partholon. That is all I am now to history.' He leaned in close to my face, and I lay back against the ground with his hands on either side of my face. 'Until today. I have new duties.'

Just then, Mistral's fingers found my opening, and I would have turned to look at him, but Abeloec's hands tightened on my face, kept me looking at him while Mistral began to explore me with his hand. Abeloec whispered, above my face, 'There was a time when without me, or Medb, no one ruled in Ireland, or faerie, or anywhere in the isles. The sithen brought us here for a reason. It brought everyone here for a reason, including Mistral.'

Dried leaves rushed across my body like brittle fingers tapping my stomach and breasts. 'Let us have our reason back, Meredith,' Abeloec said.

It wasn't a finger touching me down there anymore, though Mistral hadn't entered me. For someone who liked to cause pain, he was being patient, and gentle.

I whispered, 'Reason, what reason?' to Abeloec's face.

'Reason to be, Meredith. A man without a duty is only half a man.'

Mistral shoved himself inside me in one long hard movement. It spilled my upper body up off the ground, tore a scream from my mouth. Abeloec released me, and I could finally stare down my body at Mistral.

Mistral's head was flung back, eyes closed. His body was married into mine as deep as he could make it. There were no lines of color on him anymore and I realized there were none on any of the three of us. But there was something in the shining of his skin. It took me a moment to realize that something was moving *inside* his skin. It looked like a reflection of something, but it was not a reflection of anything around us.

He stayed there, frozen above me, with his lower body as snug to me as he could get it, and his upper body raised back on his hands and arms. He opened his eyes and looked down at me, and I saw clouds glide inside his eyes like windows onto some distant sky. The clouds moved as if hurried by some great wind, and I realized that that was what I was seeing inside his skin. Clouds, storm clouds roiling inside his skin.

The wind was growing, spilling my hair across my face, sending dead leaves in small whirlwinds. A storm was coming, and I was watching it grow inside Mistral's body. Mistral was the master of the winds, master of the sky, a storm god once upon a time. The first lightning flash showed in his eyes.

Once upon a time wasn't as long ago as it used to be.

Chapter 6

MISTRAL DREW OUT OF ME WITH A SIGHING SHUDDER that ran down the length of his body. Seeing him affected to that degree made my breath short and fast. At first I thought he had rain in his eyes to match the lightning; then he blinked, and I realized it was tears.

If we had been alone I would have questioned it, talked about it, but with this many other men around us, I could not. I could not point out that he was crying in front of them, nor could I ask him why and hope to get a truthful answer. But it meant a great deal to me that Mistral, master of storms, cried after he tasted my body.

Abeloec said, softly, 'It's been too long.'

Mistral looked at him, and he simply nodded with the shine of those few hard tears gliding down his cheeks. He looked down at me, and there was a gentleness on his face, a raw pain in his eyes. He kissed me, and this time it was gentle. 'I have forgotten my manners, Princess, forgive me.'

'You can kiss me with force, just don't choke me.'

He gave a small smile, and an even smaller nod. Then he laid his body carefully along the length of mine so that his testicles pressed against my groin, and the hard length of him touched me from groin to my upper stomach. He let his weight settle on top of me with a sigh, then wrapped his arms around me. He put his face to one side of mine, and it was as if he let some great tension fall away from him. It was almost as if he grew lighter at the same time that his actual weight became heavier. I laid a soft kiss against the curve of his ear, because it was the spot I could reach.

He shuddered against me again, but because he was pressed so hard against the front of my body it made me shudder, too. The wind trailed his hair and mine across my face, mingling the red and grey strands together, almost in the way the neon glow of power had wound itself together. Stronger together than apart. The clouds in his eyes spun so fast across them that it was almost dizzying to watch.

He unwound his arms from me and raised up enough to see my face. 'I don't want to kiss down the front of your body. I want to bite my way down it.'

I had to swallow hard before I could answer, in a breathy voice, 'No blood, no permanent marks, and nothing as hard as what you did to my breast. You haven't done enough prep work for that.'

'Prep work?' He made it a question.

Abeloec said, 'Foreplay.' He had been kneeling above my head, so still that I had forgotten he was there.

We both looked at him. 'Give us a little more room,' Mistral asked.

'I am the only one inside this circle with you, and I must remain.'

Circle, I thought, then I realized that he was right. The lines of blue, green, and red encircled the three of us. Everyone else was covered in them, but they formed a barrier around the three of us. It was a barrier that the wind could cross at will, but there would be other things that could not cross it. I wasn't sure what those other things would be, but I knew enough of magical circles to know that they were meant to keep some things in, and some things out. It was their nature, and tonight was all about the nature of things.

I ran my hands up Mistral's back, tracing the line of his spine, playing along the muscles that held him just above me. He closed his eyes and swallowed before he looked down at me. 'You wanted something?'

'You,' I said.

That earned me a smile. A real smile, not about sex, or pain, or sorrow, just a smile. I valued that smile the way I valued Frost's smile, and Doyle's. They had all come to me without a real smile, as if they had forgotten how to do it. By the standards that the other two men had set, Mistral was a fast learner.

I moved one hand around so I could trace his lower lip with my finger. 'Do what you wanted to do. Just remember the rules.'

His smile held an edge of something that wasn't happy now, and I wasn't sure if the parameters that I'd put on him were actually that taxing, or if I'd reminded him of something sad. 'No blood, no permanent marks, nothing as hard as what I did on your breast, because I have not done enough foreplay for that, yet.'

It was almost word for word what I'd said to him. 'Good memory.'

'Memory is all I have.' As he said it, that raw pain was back in his eyes. I thought I understood now. He was enjoying himself, and determined to enjoy himself, but when he was finished, there would be no more. The queen would put him back in the lonely cell of her rules, her jealousy, her sadism. Would it be worse to have had this moment and then be denied again? Would it cause him pain to watch me with my men, and not be a part of it? It wasn't that I was so special to him, or to them. It was simply that I was the only woman with whom the guards could break their long celibacy.

I raised myself off the ground and kissed him. 'I am yours.'

He kissed me, gently at first, then harder. His tongue thrust between my lips. I opened my mouth and let him explore my mouth. He thrust deep inside, then backed off a little, enough so that it was just a good deep kiss. The feel of his mouth drew my mouth closer to his, made my body rise up to press tighter against him, sent my arms across his back, pressed my breasts firm against his chest.

He made a small sound low in his throat, and the wind suddenly felt cool against my skin. He drew his mouth from mine, and the expression in his eyes was wild. Storm clouds rode in his eyes, but they had slowed, so that it was no longer dizzying. If I hadn't known what I was looking at, I might simply have thought his eyes were the grey of rain clouds.

He laid his face in the curve of my neck. He didn't so much kiss me as lay his lips against my skin. His breath went out in a heavy sigh that spread warmth across my skin. It made me shiver, and that was it. He set his teeth in the side of my neck, and bit me. It made me cry out and tense my fingers along his back, to trail an edge of nail across his skin.

He bit my shoulder, quick and hard. I cried out

for him, and he moved again. I don't think he trusted himself to hold my flesh in his mouth for very long. I knew he wanted to bite down harder, and I could feel the effort required to fight that urge in his lips, his hands, his entire body. He was enjoying himself, but he was struggling to keep his impulses in check.

He put his mouth into the side of the breast he had not marked and barely laid teeth. I grabbed the side of his face, not hard, but it stopped him. He lifted his gaze to mine, his mouth half opened, and I watched his expression fall. I think he expected me to tell him to stop. Even if that had been what I meant to do, I wouldn't have had the heart to say it. But regardless, it hadn't.

'Harder,' I said instead.

He gave me a wolfish grin, and again I got that glimpse of something in him that would have made me hesitate to be alone with him. But I was no longer certain if that was truly Mistral's nature, or whether centuries of denial had made him wild with need.

He set his teeth into my side and bit down hard, hard enough that I writhed under him. He moved just a little farther down my side, to my waist, and this time when I felt him begin to let go, I said, 'Harder.'

He bit me deeper this time, bit me until I felt his teeth almost meet in my skin. I cried out and said, 'Enough, enough.'

He lifted his face as if to stop completely. I smiled at him. 'I didn't say stop, I just meant that was hard enough.'

He moved to the other side of my body and bit me again without urging, hard enough that I had to tell him, almost immediately, not to go farther. He looked up at me, and whatever he saw on my face satisfied him, because he bit next to my belly button, setting his teeth so hard and fast that I had to tell him to stop.

He'd left a press of red teeth marks on my stomach. There were red marks here and there on my body, but nothing as perfect as that. A perfect set of his teeth marks in the white flesh of my body. Looking at it made me shiver.

'You like it,' he whispered.

'Yes,' I said.

The wind held an edge of dampness as it trailed across my skin. He licked low on my stomach, and the wind seemed to blow across that wet line, almost as if the wind had a mouth, too, and could blow where it wished.

Mistral pressed his mouth where he had licked, and bit me. Hard and sharp, enough to make me startle, and raise my upper body off the ground. 'Enough,' I said, and my voice was almost a yell.

The wind began to pick up, blowing more dead leaves across my body. Streaming my hair across my face, so that for a moment I couldn't see what Mistral was doing. The wind was damp, as if it rode an edge of rain. But it never rained in the dead gardens.

I felt his mouth laid on the mound between my legs, resting on the tight, curling hair. I couldn't see, but I knew what he was doing. He bit me, and I yelled, 'Enough.'

I used one hand to push my hair out of the way, so I could look down my body and see him. He gave one quick flick of his tongue between my legs. That one small touch sped my pulse and opened my mouth in a silent O.

'You know what I want to do,' he said. He spoke with his hands around my thighs, fingers digging in just a little, his face just above my groin, so close that his breath touched me there.

I nodded, because I didn't trust my voice. On the one hand, I didn't want him to hurt me; on the other, I did want him to come just to that edge of truly hurting me. I liked that edge. I liked it a lot.

I finally found my voice, and it almost didn't sound like me, so breathy, so eager. 'Go slow, and when I say enough, you stop.'

He gave that smile again that filled his cloud-dazed eyes with a fierce light, and I realized it wasn't my imagination. Lightning played through the heavy grey clouds of his eyes. It had gone away, but now it was back, and it filled them with a flashing white, white light, so that his eyes looked blind for a second. The wind slowed, and the air felt heavy, thick, and I felt an edge of electricity in the air.

He spread me wide, using his fingers, so strong, so thick. He licked the length of me, back and forth until I writhed under his mouth and hands. Only then did he press his mouth over me. Only then did he let me feel the edge of his teeth around the most intimate parts of my body.

He bit down slowly, so slowly, so carefully.

I breathed out, 'Harder.'

He obeyed.

He took as much of my flesh down there into his mouth as he could fit, and bit me. Bit me so hard that it raised my upper body completely off the ground, and I screamed for him. But I didn't scream stop, or enough. I just screamed, full-throated, spine bowing, staring down at him with wide eyes and opened mouth. I orgasmed for him, from the feel of his teeth in my most intimate flesh. I orgasmed for him, and even through the pleasure of it I changed my scream to 'Stop, stop, oh, God, stop!' Even through that most over-whelming of pleasures, I could feel his teeth going just a little too far. When something hurts in the middle of orgasm, you need to stop – things usually only hurt when the afterglow begins to fade.

Again I screamed, 'Stop,' and he stopped.

I fell back onto the ground, eyes unable to focus, fighting to breathe, unable to move. But even while my body lay helpless with the afterglow, I began to ache. I ached where his teeth had touched me there, and I knew that it was just going to hurt more later. I'd let my desire – and Mistral's – send us too far over that fine edge.

His voice came. 'I did not bleed you, and I did not bite you as hard there as I did on your breast.'

I nodded, because I couldn't speak yet. The air was so dense with the coming storm that it made it harder to breathe, almost in the way the queen could make the air too thick to breathe.

'Are you hurt?' he asked.

I found my voice. 'A little.' The ache was becoming sharper. I had only a limited time before it was simply going to hurt. I wanted him to finish before the pleasure truly did become pain.

He crawled over my body on all fours, so that he wasn't actually touching me, but he could see my face. 'Are you all right, Princess?'

I nodded. 'Help me turn over.'

'Why?'

'Because if we finish this with you on top, it's going to hurt too much.'

'I was too rough,' he said, and he sounded so sad. Lightning flashed first in one eye then the other, as if it traveled from one side of his mind to the other. The light blue lightning bolt on his cheek paled in the brightness of it.

He started to crawl off me as if he were going to stop. I grabbed his arm. 'Don't stop, bright

Goddess, don't stop. Just help me roll over. If you take me from behind, you won't be brushing up against the part of me you bruised.'

'If I have hurt you so badly, we must stop.'

My fingers tightened on his arm. 'If I wanted to stop, I would say so. Everyone else has been too afraid of hurting me, and even if you went too far, I do like it. Mistral, I like it a great deal.'

He gave an almost shy smile. 'I did notice.'

I smiled back at him. 'Then let us finish what we started.'

'If you are sure.' In the moment he said it, and meant it, I knew that I would be safe alone with him. If he was willing to pass up some of the first intercourse he'd been offered in centuries for fear of my being hurt, then he had the discipline to control himself in private. Consort preserve us, but he had more discipline than I would have had. How many men would have turned down the finish, after a start like that? Not many, not many at all.

'I am sure,' I said.

He smiled again, and something moved above us. Something grey was in motion near the high domed ceiling. Clouds – there was a tiny knot of clouds up near the ceiling. I looked into Mistral's face and said, 'Fuck me, Mistral.'

'Is that an order, my princess?' He smiled when he said it, but there was an edge of something that wasn't happy in his voice.

'Only if you want it to be.'

He looked down at me, then said, 'I would rather do the ordering.'

'Then do it,' I said.

'Turn over,' he said. His voice did not have quite the firmness it had had earlier, as if he wasn't sure I would obey.

I had recovered enough to roll over, though I was slow. He moved back until he knelt by my feet. 'I want you on your hands and knees.'

I did what he asked, or ordered. It put me looking at Abeloec, who still knelt, motionless, at the top of our makeshift blanket. I expected to see lust, or something to let me know he was enjoying the show, but that wasn't what was in his face. His smile was gentle, peaceful. It didn't match what we were doing, at least not to me.

Mistral's hands stroked my ass, and I felt him rub against my opening. The front of me was sore, but the rest of me was eager.

'You're wet,' Mistral said.

'I know,' I said.

'You really did enjoy it.'

'Yes.'

'You really do like it that rough.'

'Sometimes,' I said. The tip of him rubbed around the edge, so close, but not inside.

'Now?' He made it a question.

I lowered my upper body, so that my lower body lifted toward him, pushing against the feel of him. Only his slight movement backward kept me from taking him into my body. I made a small sound of protest. The wind held the smell of rain, the press of silent thunder. The storm was coming, and I wanted him inside me when it came.

He laughed, that wonderful masculine sound. 'I take that as a yes?'

'Yes,' I said. I pressed my cheek into the brittle leaves, my face, and hands, touching the dry ground. I had to close my eyes against the push of dead leaves and plants. I pushed my ass up at him, and asked, wordlessly, that he take me. I didn't realize I was saying anything out loud, but I must have been. For then I heard my own voice chanting, 'Please, please, please,' over and over, soft under my breath, my lips closer to the dead earth than to the man I was begging.

He pushed just the tip of himself inside me, and the wind changed instantly. It felt almost hot. I could still smell rain, but there was also a metallic smell. The scent of ozone, lightning. The air was hot and close, and I knew in that moment that it wasn't that I wanted Mistral inside me when the storm broke, but that the storm would not come until he was inside me. He *was* the storm, as Abeloec had been the cup. Mistral was the heavy press of the air, and that neck-ruffling promise of lightning.

I raised up and shoved my body onto him. He

actually stopped me with his hands on my hips. 'No,' he said, 'no, I will say when.'

I went back to pressing my upper body to the dry ground. I said, 'Mistral, please, don't you feel it? Don't you feel it?'

'Storm,' he said, and his voice seemed lower than it had been, a growling roll, as if his voice held an echo of thunder in it.

I raised up, but not to try to control him. I wanted to see him. I wanted to see if there had been other changes besides the growl of thunder in his voice. He still glowed with power, but it was as if dark grey clouds had moved in over that glow, so that I saw only the shine of his power through the veil of clouds.

He stared down at me, and his eyes flashed bright, so bright that for a moment his face was half obscured by that white, white light. The brilliance faded, leaving after-images in my vision. But without the lightning, his eyes weren't the grey of rain clouds; they were black. That blackness that rolls across the sky at midday, and sends us all running for cover, because just by looking at the sky, you know that something dangerous is coming. Something that will drown you, burn you, concuss you with the power that is about to fall from the sky.

I shivered, gazing down my body at him, shivered, because I wondered . . . was I too mortal to survive this? Was his power going to burn along my flesh, and hurt me in ways that I did not want?

It was as if Abeloec heard me thinking. He spoke, in a low, soft voice that made me look at him. He was still kneeling in front of us, but it was as if his pale skin were fading into the growing dark, as if he, himself, were dissipating into the circle of power. His hair was shot through with lines of blue, red, and green, and those lines traced the circle that held us, and on into the dark to the men beyond. His eyes held sparks of all those colors, but it was as if his power grew. He began to be that power, and not be as much Abeloec. I could tell that if he were not careful, he would become only the lines of power that traced out into the dark.

'Earth and sky is a very old dance, Meredith,' he said. 'Do not fear the power. It has waited too long for you to allow you to be harmed now.'

I found my voice in a hoarse whisper. 'Look at him.'

'Yes,' Abeloec said, 'he is the storm come to life.'

'I am mortal.'

I thought he smiled, but I couldn't be certain. I could not see his face clearly, though I knew he was only a few feet in front of me.

'In this time and place, you are the Goddess, the earth to meet the strike of the sky. Does that sound like someone who is merely mortal?'

Mistral chose that moment to remind me that he was there. He bent over my body, and bit me on the back, as his body shoved inside me. The combination of the two made me push myself tighter against him. He bit me harder, and I writhed against him, trapped between his body and his mouth.

His mouth let go, and he wrapped his arms around me. His weight lay along the back of my body, in a warm, solid line. I was supporting most of his weight, for his hands played lightly over my breasts and stomach. He was inside me, but as he had done the first time, once he was in, he had stopped moving. He spoke with his face next to mine. 'It has been too long. I will not last if you move like that.'

I turned my head, and he was close enough that when the light flashed in his eyes, I was blinded for a second. I closed my eyes and saw white and black explosions against my eyelids. I spoke with my eyes still closed. 'I can't help moving.'

He sighed, and didn't so much push himself farther inside me as writhe while he was inside me. That made me writhe, and drew a sound from him that was half pleasure, half protest.

Thunder rolled through the cavern, echoing against the bare rock walls, like some gigantic drumroll that seemed to thrum across my skin.

'Hush, Meredith, quiet. If you move, I will not last.'

'How can I not move with you inside me?'

He hugged me then, and said, 'So long since anyone reacted to my body.' He moved off my back, so that he was again on his knees, still with his body sheathed inside mine. But he pushed his hips against me and let me know that, bent over my body, he had not been completely sheathed inside me, because now the tip of him found the end of me, and I realized he might be too long for this position. If the man was too long, entering from behind could hurt. It didn't hurt yet, but it held the promise of it as he pushed gently against the inner limits of my body. The thought of what he could do to me was exciting, and a little frightening. I both wanted to feel him pound himself into me, and didn't. The thought was exciting, but it was one of those pains that worked better in fantasy than real life.

He pushed the head of himself inside me, gentle at first, then more firmly, as if he were trying to find a way deeper. He pushed slow, and firm, and tight, until I made a sound of protest.

Thunder rumbled again, and the wind gusted. I could smell rain and ozone, as if lightning had struck somewhere near, though the only lightning had been in Mistral's eyes.

'How much do you like pain?' he asked, and

his voice held thunder the way that Doyle's could hold the growl of a dog.

I thought I knew what he was asking, and I hesitated. How much do I like pain? I decided honesty was safest. I gazed back over my body until I could see him, and whatever words of caution I was about to utter died in my throat. He was something elemental. His body still held an outline, a solidness, but inside that solid line of skin were clouds, grey and black and white, boiling and writhing. The lightning flashed in his eyes again, and this time it rode down his body, a jagged line of brilliance that filled the world with the metallic smell of ozone. But it didn't affect my body like real lightning would have. Instead it was just a brilliant dance of light.

His eyes glowed in his face, lit by strike after strike of bright, white light. About every third flash, the lightning shot down his body and decorated his skin. His hair had come free of its ponytail, and that grey sheet of hair danced in the wind of his power, like some soft grey blanket trapped on a wash line as the storm thunders closer.

As many times as I'd made love to warriors of the sidhe, to creatures of faerie, the sight of him behind me still stole my words. I'd seen many wonders, but nothing quite like Mistral.

He asked again, 'How much do you like pain?' But as he spoke, the lightning flashed, the glow filling his mouth and pouring out with his words.

I said the only thing I could think of: 'Finish.'

He smiled, and his lips held an edge of that glow. 'Finish; just finish?'

I nodded. 'Yes.'

'Will you enjoy it?'

'I don't know.'

His smile widened, and his eyes flashed, and that line of light sparkled down his body. I was blind for a moment in the brilliance of it. He began to draw himself out of me. 'So be it,' he said in that deep, rolling voice. Thunder echoed him along the roof, and for a moment it seemed as if the very walls thrummed with him.

He shoved himself inside me as fast and hard as he could, and he was too long. I screamed, and it wasn't all pleasure. I tried not to, but I began to writhe, not closer, but farther away, crawling away from that hard, sharp pain.

He grabbed my hair, tight. Held me in place while he pounded himself into me.

I screamed, and this time, it held words. 'Finish, Goddess, please finish. Go, just go.'

He jerked me up on my knees, using my hair like a lever to press our bodies against each other. He was still buried in me, but the position was better. It was a little less deep and didn't hurt.

He wrapped his other arm around the front of my body, and held me tight against the front of his. He tightened the hand in my hair, drawing a sound from me that wasn't pain.

He spoke with his mouth pressed against the side of my face. 'I know that I hurt you before, but already your body forgives me. So soon, and you make pleasure noises for me.' He jerked my head back with his handful of my hair. It did hurt, but I liked it anyway. I just did.

'You like this,' he whispered against my face, and I felt wind against my face.

'Yes,' I said.

'But not the other,' he said, and the wind buffeted us, hard enough that we swayed for a moment. I rolled my eyes past him and found the ceiling crawling with clouds. Clouds that could have been the twins of the ones moving under his skin.

He jerked my hair again, brought me back to his face. 'I thought I would come too soon, and now I am taking too long.'

'You will not come until the storm does.' It was Abeloec's voice, but strangely not.

Mistral loosened his hold on my hair, so we could both look at the other man. What I saw was eyes that spun with crimson, emerald, and sapphire, as if they were full of liquid jewels. His hair was flared out around him, but not because the wind pulled it – more like the tail of a bird, or a cloak held carefully out by some invisible hands. The lines of color glowed through that hair, and went out into the dark like rope. The ropes of glowing color found dark shapes outside our circle of power. All the men out there in the dead gardens were covered in those lines. I tried to see if they were all right, but the thunder rolled through us, and it was as if the world itself shook with it.

Mistral shuddered around me, inside me, and that made me shudder. He hugged me tight with both of his strong arms. Not hurting me for a moment, not trying to. 'If taking you from behind is too much, then what else is left? I have hurt you in front, as well.'

I leaned back against his body, letting myself rest against him completely. 'If you're strong enough to keep yourself up off my body while we fuck, you won't brush the front of me.'

'Off your body?' He sounded puzzled.

'I will be facing up, you on top, but the only thing that touches me is what is inside me now.'

'If you are flat, I will not be able to get as much inside you.'

'I'll rise up to meet you.' Then I asked, 'Are you?'

'Am I what?' he asked, and the lightning in his eyes blinded me for a moment.

'Strong enough,' I said with my vision full of bright white spots.

He laughed, then, and it was like a low rumble of thunder not just in my ear, but along my body, as if the sound traveled through his very bones and into mine. 'Yes,' he said. 'Yes, I am strong enough.'

'Prove it,' I said, and my voice was a whisper that was almost lost in the sound of wind and thunder.

He let me move off him and helped me to lie down on what was left of our makeshift blanket. If we had been about to make love in standard missionary position, then I would have been more concerned about the blanket. But if we did this right, very little of me would be touching the ground.

I lay back against the hard, dry ground for a moment, my knees bent. Mistral hesitated, kneeling between them. Lightning flashed in his eyes, danced down his body, so that it looked for a moment as if the jagged bolt went from his eyes and out his leg into the ground. I heard a more distant crackle, and saw the first lightning bolt dance in the clouds at the ceiling. The smell of ozone came faint; the scent of close rain was stronger.

'Mistral,' I said, 'now – enter me now.'

'I will brush against the front of your body,' he said. 'It will hurt.'

'Enter me, and I'll show you.'

He lowered himself to me, keeping his arms locked and his body above mine. He slid himself inside me, and before he was finished, I moved up to meet him.

I raised my upper body in a sort of sit-up, more like an abdominal crunch. I couldn't hold the position forever, but I could hold it a long time, if I put my hands on either side of my thighs and held on. It held me simultaneously in position and open wide.

I watched him push himself inside me by the white moonlight glow of my own skin, and the distant flash of lightning that he'd released into the clouds above. It was almost as if now that the lighting was up there, there wasn't so very much inside him.

He began to pump his body into mine. Just the long shaft of him in and out of my body, while I held myself in a tight little ball, and he held the rest of his body above mine.

'I love watching your body move in and out of mine,' I said.

He lowered his head so that his hair trailed over me, and he could watch his own body work in and out of mine. 'Yesss,' he breathed, 'yesss.'

He started to lose his rhythm and had to look away from the sight of our bodies locked together. Soon he resumed his long sure strokes. Thunder pounded the world, lightning crackled and smashed into the ground. The storm was coming.

He began to go faster, harder, smashing himself into me. But from this position, it didn't hurt. From this position, it felt wonderful. I could feel the beginnings of my own pleasure growing inside me. 'I'm going to come soon,' I said, and it was almost a yell over the sound of wind and storm.

'Not yet,' he said, 'not yet.' I wasn't sure if he was talking to me or himself, but he suddenly seemed to give himself permission to fuck me as hard as he wanted. He drove himself in and out of me with a force that rocked my body, ground my ass into the leaves, and made me cry out with purest joy.

Lightning began to rain down from the clouds. One white-hot bolt after another, as if the clouds were screaming, and this was as fast as they could throw lightning down upon us. The ground shuddered with the beating of the lightning and the roll of the thunder. It was as if the lightning was hitting the ground as often as Mistral's body hit into mine. Over and over and over again, he rammed inside me, and over and over and over again, the lightning struck the earth. The world smelled metallic with ozone, and every hair stood to attention with the electric dance of it.

He brought me screaming, fingers digging into my own thighs, holding my place, holding my place, while the orgasm shook me, took me, and my body spasmed around his. My screams were lost in the violence of the storm, but I heard Mistral cry out above me, a second before his body thrust inside mine one last time. He came inside me, and the lightning struck the earth like a huge white hand.

I was blinded with white light. I dug my nails into my thighs to remind myself where I was, and what I was doing. I wanted his release to be everything he wished. But finally, I had to collapse to the ground, had to let my legs unbend. I lay on the dry ground, panting, trying to relearn how to breathe.

He collapsed on top of me, still inside my body. His heart was beating so fast that it felt as if it would spill out his body and touch me. Rain began to fall, gently.

His first words were breathless. 'Am I hurting you?'

I tried to raise my arm to touch him, but still couldn't move. 'Nothing hurts right now,' I said.

He let out his breath in a long sigh. 'Good.' His heart began to slow as the rain fell harder. I turned my face to the side so the drops wouldn't be hitting me full on.

I'd thought the weather inside the cavern would stop with Mistral's orgasm. But though the storm had ended, there was still a sky above us. A cloudy, rainy sky. It had not rained underground in faerie for at least four hundred years. We had a sky and rain, and we were still underground. It was impossible, but the rain on my face was warm. A spring rain, something gentle, to coax the flowers out.

He raised himself up enough to pull himself out of my body and lie by my side. I felt moisture on his face, and thought at first that it was rain. Then I realized it was tears. Had the rain come because he cried, or did one thing have nothing to do with the other? I did not know. I only knew that he cried, and I held out my arms to him.

He buried his face against my breasts, and wept.

Chapter 7

ABELOEC, MISTRAL, AND I GOT TO OUR FEET IN THE soft spring rain. It took me a moment to realize that there was light now. Not the colored shine of magic but a dim, pale light, as if there were a moon somewhere up near the stone roof of the cavern. I couldn't see the ceiling anymore. It was lost in a soft mist of clouds where the stone had been.

'Sky,' someone whispered, 'there's sky above us.'

I turned to look at the other men who had been held outside the glowing circle of Abeloec's magic. I turned to find out who had spoken, but the moment I saw the others, I didn't care. I didn't even care that it was raining, or that there was sky, or some phantom moon. All I could think was that we were missing people: a lot of people.

Frost and Rhys were white shadows in the

dimness, and Doyle a darker presence by their side. 'Doyle, where are the others?'

It was Rhys who answered. 'The garden took them.'

'What does that mean?' I asked. I took a step toward them, but Mistral held me back.

'Until we find out what is happening, we cannot risk you, Princess.'

'He is right,' Doyle said. He walked toward us, gliding graceful and nude, but there was something in the way he moved that said the fight wasn't over. He moved as if he expected the ground itself to open up and attack. Just watching him move like that scared me. Something was horribly wrong.

'Stay with Mistral and Abe. Frost with Merry. Rhys with me.'

I thought someone would argue with him, but they didn't. They followed him as they had followed him for a thousand years. My pulse was thudding in my throat, and I didn't understand what was happening, but I was almost certain in that moment that the men would never obey me as they obeyed him. I understood, as he stalked over the softening ground – with Rhys like a small, pale shadow at his side – why my aunt Andais had never made love to Doyle. Never given him a chance to fill her belly with child. She did not share power, and Doyle was a man whom other men followed. He had the stuff of kings in him. I had known that, but I hadn't been certain until this second that the other men knew it, too. Maybe not in the front of their heads, but in the very bones of their bodies, they understood what he was, what he could be.

He and Rhys moved toward a fringe of tall trees, their branches stark and dead against the soft, rainy twilight. Doyle was looking up into the trees, as if he saw something in the empty branches.

'What is that?' Mistral asked.

'I don't see . . . ,' Abe began; then I heard his breath draw in sharp.

'What, what is it?' I asked.

'Aisling, I think,' Frost whispered.

I glanced at Frost. I could remember some of the other men who had been touching the trees. Adair, for example, had climbed a tree. I remembered seeing him up in the branches in the middle of all the sex and magic. But I didn't remember seeing Aisling after the magic hit us.

'I saw Adair climbing a tree, but I don't remember Aisling,' I said.

'He vanished once we entered the garden,' Frost said.

'I thought he had been left behind in the room with Barinthus and the others,' I said.

'No, he was not left behind,' Mistral said.

'I can't see what Doyle is looking at.'

'You may not wish to,' Abe said. 'I know I don't.'

'Don't treat me like a child. What do you see? What's happened to Aisling?' I pulled away from Mistral. But he and Abe were still between me and the line of trees. 'Move aside,' I said.

They glanced at each other, but didn't move. They would not obey me as they obeyed Doyle.

'I am Princess Meredith NicEssus, wielder of the hand of flesh and blood. You are royal guards, but not royal. Don't let the sex go to your heads, gentlemen – move!'

'Do as she says,' Frost said.

They glanced at each other, but then parted so I could see. Unlike Frost, Doyle would have known not to help me, because now they weren't obeying me. They were obeying Frost. But that was a problem for another night. This night, this night, I wanted to see what everyone else had already seen.

There was a pale shape hanging from the tallest branch of the tallest tree. I thought at first that Aisling was hanging by his hands, dangling from the branch on purpose; then I realized that his hands were by his sides. He was dangling from the branch, yes, but not by his hands. The rain started to fall harder. 'The branch . . . ,' I whispered, 'it's pierced his chest.'

'Yes,' Mistral said.

I swallowed hard enough that it hurt. There

weren't many things that could bring death to the high court of faerie. There were tales of the immortal sidhe standing up after a beheading, still alive. But there were no stories about living on after your heart was gone.

Some of the other guards hadn't wanted Aisling to sleep in the bedroom with us, feeling he was too dangerous. To look upon his face had once been to fall instantly, hopelessly in love with him. Even goddesses and some gods had fallen to his power, once, or so the old stories said. So he had voluntarily kept most of his clothes on, including the gauzy veil that he wore wrapped around his face. Only his eyes were left bare.

He was a man so beautiful that all who saw him, loved him. I had ordered him to use that power on one of our enemies. She had tried to kill Galen, and almost succeeded. But I hadn't understood what I asked of him, or what I condemned her to see. She had given us information, but she had also clawed out her own eyes so she would no longer be under his power.

He had been afraid to even take off his shirt in front of me, for fear that I was too mortal to look upon his flesh, let alone his face. I hadn't been bespelled, but staring at the pale form, hanging lifeless, lost to twilight and rain, I remembered him. I remembered his skin, golden, golden as if someone had shaken gold dust across his pale, perfect body. He had sparkled in the light, not just with magic, but the way a jewel catches the light. He had glittered with the beauty of what he was. Now he hung in the rain, dead or dying. And I had no idea why.

Chapter 8

THE GROUND WAS SOFT UNDER OUR FEET AS WE walked toward Aisling's body. The sharp, dry vegetation had melted into the softening earth. Much more of this downpour and it would be mud. I had to shield my eyes with my hand to gaze up at the body in the tree.

Body, just a body. I was already distancing myself from him. Already I was making that mental switch that had allowed me to work murder cases in Los Angeles. Body, *it*, not *he*, and absolutely not Aisling. The *it* hung there, with a black branch thicker than my arm sticking out through the chest. There had to be two feet worth of branch on this side of the body. Such force it would have taken to pierce the chest of any man like that, a warrior of the Unseelie Court. A nearly immortal being, once worshipped as a god. Such beings do not die easily. He hadn't even cried out . . . or had he? Had he cried his death on the air, and I been deaf to it? Had my screams of pleasure drowned out his cries of despair?

No, no, I had to stop thinking like that, or I would run screaming.

'Is he . . . ,' Abe began.

None of the men answered him or finished his sentence. We all stared up, wordless, as if by not saying it, we'd keep it from being true. He hung so limp, like a broken puppet, but thick, and meaty, and more real than any doll. He was utterly still and limp in that heavy-limbed way that not even the deepest sleep can duplicate.

I spoke into that rain-soaked silence. 'Dead.' And that one word seemed louder than it actually was.

'How? Why?' Abe asked.

'The how is pretty apparent,' Rhys said. 'The why is a mystery.'

I looked away from what hung in the tree, out into the twilight of the gardens. I wasn't looking away from Aisling, but rather looking for the others. I tried to ignore the tightness of my throat, the speeding of my pulse. I tried not to finish the thought that had made me turn and search the dimness. Were there other men dead, or dying, in the dimness? Who else was pierced through by some magical tree?

There was nothing to see but the dead branches stretching naked toward the clouds – none of the other trees held a gruesome trophy. The tightness in my chest eased when I was sure that all the trees were empty except this one.

I barely knew Aisling. He had never been my lover, and had only been one of my guards for a day. I was sorry for the loss of him, but there were others among my guards that I cared about more, and they were still missing. I was happy they weren't decorating the trees, but that left me wondering what else might have become of them. Where were they?

Doyle spoke so close to me that I jumped. 'I do not see any of the others in the trees.'

I shook my head. 'No, no.' I looked for Frost. He stood close, but not close enough to hold me. I wanted to be comforted by one of them, but it was a child's wish. A child's wish for lies in the dark, that the monster isn't under the bed. I had grown up in a world where the monsters were very real.

'You were holding Galen, and Nicca was with you,' I said. 'What happened to them?'

Frost brushed his sodden hair from his face, the silver looking as grey as Mistral's in the dim light. 'Galen was swallowed up by the ground.' His eyes showed pain. 'I could not hold on to him. It was as if some great force wrenched him away.'

I was suddenly cold, and the warm rain wasn't enough to keep it at bay. I said, 'When Amatheon did the same thing in my vision, he went willingly. He just sank into the mud. There was no wrenching force.'

'I can only report what happened, Princess.' His voice had gone sullen. If he thought I'd criticized him, then so be it; I didn't have time to hold his hand.

'That was vision,' Mistral said. 'Sometimes on this side of the veil, it's not so gentle.'

'What's not so gentle?' I asked.

'Being consumed by your power,' he said.

I shook my head, wiping impatiently at the rain on my face. I was beginning to be irritated. The miracle of it raining in the dead gardens wasn't enough to calm the cold fear. 'I wish this rain would let up,' I said without thinking. Angry and afraid, and the rain was something I could be angry at without hurting its feelings.

The rain slackened. It went from a downpour to a light drizzle. My pulse was in my throat again, but not for the same reason. It was a miracle that there was rain here, and I hadn't meant to make it go away.

Doyle touched my mouth with a callused fingertip. 'Hush, Meredith – do not destroy the blessing of this rain.'

I nodded to let him know I understood. He took his finger away, slowly. 'I forgot that the sithen listens to everything I say.' I swallowed hard enough that it hurt. 'I don't want the rain to stop.'

We stood there, everyone tense, waiting. Yes, Aisling was dead, and many more missing, but the dead gardens had been the heart of our faerie mound once, and were more important than any one life. They had been the heart of our power. When this place had died, our power had begun to die.

I saw with relief that the warm spring drizzle kept falling. Slowly, we all let out a breath. 'Be careful what you say, Princess,' Mistral whispered.

I just nodded.

'Nicca stood up, staring at his hands,' Frost said, as if I'd asked. 'He reached out to me, but before I could touch him he vanished.'

'Vanished how?' Abe asked.

'Just vanished, as if he became air.'

'He was taken by his sphere of influence,' Mistral said.

'What does that mean?' I asked.

'Air, earth.'

I shook my hands at him, as if waving away smoke between us. 'I don't understand.'

'Hawthorne was engulfed by the trunk of that tree over there,' Rhys said. He pointed to a large greyish-barked tree. 'He didn't fight it. He went smiling. I'd bet almost anything that if we could identity it, it would be a hawthorn tree.'

'Galen and Nicca did not go smiling,' Frost said.

'They have never been worshipped as deities,' Doyle said, 'so they do not know to relax into the power. If you fight it, it will fight back. If you let it take you, then it is more gentle.'

'I know that once upon a time, some of the sidhe could travel through ground, trees, the air. But forgive me, guys, that was a thousand years before I was born. A thousand years before Galen was born. Nicca is older, but he was always too weak to be a god.'

'That may have changed,' Abe said.

'Just as Abe's power returned,' Doyle said.

Abe nodded. 'Once, so long ago that I don't want to remember, I didn't just make queens. I made goddesses.'

'What are you saying?' I asked.

He brought the horn cup in front of him. 'The Greeks believed in it, too, Princess. That the drink of the gods could make you immortal; could make you a god.'

'But they didn't drink from it.'

'The drinking is – ' He seemed to search for a word. ' – more metaphorical, at times. It was my power, and Medb's, that gave the gods and goddesses of our pantheon their marks of power. The colored lines, Princess, they paint the skin.'

Rhys looked down at his arm, where there had been that one faint fish. Now there were two, one swimming down, another swimming upward. It formed a circle, like a fish version of yin and yang. The blue lines weren't faint now – they were bright, clear blue, deeper than a summer sky. Rhys's curls had been plastered flat by the rain, so the face he turned to us seemed startled and unfinished.

'You bear both marks now,' Doyle said. With his hair in a tight braid, he looked as he always looked. He stood in the middle of all the disarray like some dark rock I might cling to.

Rhys looked up at him. 'It can't be that easy.'

'Try,' he said.

'Try what?' I asked.

The men were all exchanging some knowledge from look to look. I didn't understand.

'Rhys was a deity of death,' Frost said.

'I know that; he was Cromm Cruach.'

'Don't you remember the story he told you?' Doyle asked.

In that moment I couldn't remember. All I could think was that Galen and Nicca might be dead, or hurting, and it was somehow my fault.

'Once I brought more than just death, Merry,' Rhys said, still gazing down at his arm with its new mark.

My mind started working finally. 'Celtic death deities are also healing deities, according to legend,' I said.

'According to legend,' Rhys said. He gazed up at Aisling.

'Try,' Doyle said to Rhys, again.

I looked at Rhys. 'Are you saying you can bring him back from the dead?'

'The last time I had both symbols on my arm, I could.' He looked at me, and there was such pain on his face. I remembered what he had told me now. Once his followers had worshipped him by cutting and hurting themselves, sacrificing their blood and pain, but he had been able to heal them. Then he lost the ability to heal, and his followers thought he was displeased. They decided he wanted the deaths of others, and they began the sacrifices. He had slaughtered them all to stop the atrocities. Slain his own people to save the rest.

He had never lost the ability to kill small creatures with a touch. In Los Angeles he'd recovered the ability to kill other faerie creatures with a touch and a word. He'd killed a goblin that way, at least.

Rhys gazed up at Aisling's still form. 'I'll try.' He handed his weapons to Doyle and Frost, then touched the tree. He seemed to wait a moment, to see what the tree would do. For the first time I realized that he was wondering if the tree would kill him, too – that hadn't occurred to me.

'Is it safe for Rhys to do this?' I asked.

Rhys looked back at me. He grinned. 'If I were taller, I wouldn't have to climb.'

'I mean it, Rhys. I don't want to trade you for

Aisling. And I really don't want two of you hanging up there.'

'If I really thought you loved me, I might not chance it.'

'Rhys . . .'

'It's all right, Merry, I know where I stand.' He turned to the tree and started climbing.

Doyle touched my shoulder. 'You cannot love us all equally. There is no dishonor in that.'

I nodded, and believed him, but it still hurt my heart.

Rhys looked like some white phantom against the blackness of the tree. He was right underneath where Aisling hung. He was just about to reach out toward him when magic crawled across my skin, stopped my breath in my throat.

Doyle felt it, too, and yelled, 'Wait! Don't touch him!'

Rhys started climbing back down the tree, sliding on the rain-slicked bark.

'Rhys! Hurry!' I screamed.

The air around Aisling's body shimmered, like a heat haze, then exploded. Not in a rain of flesh and blood and bone, but in a cloud of birds. Tiny birds, smaller, more delicate than sparrows. Dozens of songbirds flew over our heads. We all fell to the ground, guarding our heads. Frost put his body over mine, protecting me from the fluttering, twittering mob. The birds looked charming, but looks can be deceiving.

When Frost raised up enough for me to see clearly again, the birds had vanished into the dimness of the trees. I stretched upward, trying to see. 'Is the cavern wall farther away than it was?' I asked.

'Yes,' Doyle said.

'The forest stretches for miles now,' Mistral said, and his voice held awe.

'They call it the dead gardens, not the dead forest,' I said.

'It was both once,' Doyle said, softly.

Rhys explained, 'This was a world at one time, Merry, a whole underground world. There were forests and streams, and lakes, and wonders to behold. But it whittled down, as our power was whittled away. Until, at the end, it was just what you saw when we entered – a bare patch where a flower garden once grew, surrounded by a fringe of dead trees.' He motioned toward the spreading trees. 'The last time I saw anything like this inside any faerie mound was centuries ago.'

Abe hugged me from behind. It startled me, and I tensed. He started to pull away from me, but I patted his arm and said, 'You startled me, that's all.'

He hesitated, then hugged me close. 'You've done this, Princess.'

I turned enough to see his face. He was smiling. 'I think you helped, too,' I said.

'And Mistral,' Doyle added. His deep voice

tried for neutral and almost made it, as much as it hurt him to say those words. He'd been convinced that the queen's ring, which now sat on my hand, had chosen Mistral for my king. Only later had I been able to convince him it wasn't so much Mistral as the fact that he was simply the first sex I'd had inside faerie while wearing the ring. Doyle had accepted that, but now he seemed to be wondering again.

'Doyle,' I said.

He shook his head at me. 'For miracles such as this, what is one person's happiness, Princess?'

I'd almost broken him of calling me princess. I had finally been Meredith, or Merry, to him, but no longer, apparently. I touched his arm. He pulled away from my touch, gently but firmly.

'You give up too easily, my friend,' Frost said.

'There is sky above us, Frost.' Doyle motioned outward with the gun in his hand. 'There is forest to walk through.' He raised his face upward, and let the warm rain fall on his closed eyes. 'It rains inside the sithen once more.' Doyle opened his eyes and looked at Frost, grabbing his arm, dark against light. 'How clear do you need your messages to be, Frost? It seems that Mistral did this.'

'I will not give up my hope, Darkness. I will not lose it, when it is so freshly won. You should not, either.'

'I've missed something,' Rhys said.

Doyle shook his head. 'You have missed nothing.'

'Now, that's too close to a lie, and we never lie,' said Rhys.

'I will not discuss this with you, here,' Doyle said. He looked past Rhys to Mistral's tall figure. It was a small look, but enough to tell me of his jealousy.

'Look to your own power, Darkness,' Abe said.

'Enough,' said Doyle. 'We must tell the queen what has happened.'

'Look at your chest, Darkness,' Abe said.

Doyle frowned at him, then looked down. My gaze followed his. It was hard to see against the black of his skin, and in the uncertain light, but . . . 'There are lines on your skin, red lines.' I moved closer, trying to decipher what Abe's power had drawn on Doyle's skin.

I started to reach out, to trace the lines on his chest. Doyle moved out of reach. 'I cannot bear much more, Princess.'

'Your body is painted with your symbol again,' Abe said. 'It is not just Mistral who is returning.'

'But it *is* he who is returning faerie to itself,' Doyle said. 'And I was ready to stand in the way of it, for my heart would not let me lose this fight. But that was before this wonder of the dead gardens come back to life, and my sign of power returning. I have served this court century after century as we lost all that we were. How could I do less than serve the court as we begin to win back what was lost? Either my oath to serve means something, or it never meant anything at all. Either I can do this for the good of our people, or I have never been the Queen's Darkness. I either do this, or I am nothing, do you not see that?'

Abe went to him, touched his arm. 'I hear you, so honorable Darkness, but I tell you that this power is a generous thing. Goddess is a generous Goddess. God is a generous God. They do not give with one hand and take with the other. They are not so cruel.'

'I have found their service most cruel.'

'Nay, you have found Andais's service cruel,' Abe said, voice soft.

A bird twittered out in the twilight woods – a sound of settling in for the night, sleepy and questioning.

A voice came out of the dimness: 'I thought you a drunken fool, Abeloec, but now I realize that it wasn't the drink making you so. It's simply your natural state.'

We all whirled toward the voice. Queen Andais stepped from the far wall, where she had emerged earlier. We had been more than careless not to realize she might come back.

Abe dropped to one knee in the mud. 'I meant no offense, my queen.'

'Yes, you did.' She walked only a little way

toward us, then stopped, grimacing. 'I am happy to see the rain and clouds, but the mud, I could have done without.'

'We are sorry that you are displeased, my queen,' Mistral said.

'The apology would sound better if you were on your knees,' she said.

Mistral dropped to his knees in the mud beside Abe. Their hair was too long, wet and heavy; it trailed into the mud. I didn't like seeing them like that. It made me afraid for them.

She waded through the now ankle-deep mud until she could have touched them, but she walked past. Instead, she reached out to trace her fingers across Doyle's chest. 'Puppy dogs,' she said, smiling.

Doyle stood impassive under the caress of her hand, though Andais had made a torture of caresses. She would tease and torment, then deny them release. She'd made a game of it for centuries.

She touched Frost's arm. 'Your tree is dark against your skin now.' She moved to Rhys, touching the dual fish. She moved to me, and I fought not to cringe away from her. She put her hand on my stomach where the exact imprint of a moth stood, like the world's most perfect tattoo. 'A few hours ago this moth fluttered, struggling to escape your skin.'

I looked down at where she touched, hoping she wouldn't go lower. She didn't like me, but she might touch my intimate parts because she knew I loathed her. Sex and hatred always mixed well for my aunt.

'My guards told me that it would become like a tattoo.'

'Did they tell you what it was?'

'A mark of power.'

She shook her head. 'The others have the outline of a creature, or an image, but your moth looks real. It is more like a photograph imprinted on your skin. That is not something that Abeloec's magic can give you. This' – she pressed hard against my stomach – 'means you can mark others. It means that those you mark are lesser powers flocking to the warmth of your fire.' She curled her arm around my waist, and pressed my body against the black robe of hers. She whispered against my ear, 'The men don't like this, no, they don't. They don't like me touching you, not one . . .' she licked the edge of my ear, 'little . . .' she licked down the curve of my neck, 'bit.' She bit me, hard and sudden, not to draw blood, but to make me jerk.

She drew her head up and said quietly, 'I thought you liked pain, Meredith.'

'Not straight out of the box, no.'

'That's not what I heard.' She let me go and walked around the group of us. 'Where are all the other men who vanished from the bedroom with you?'

'The garden has taken them,' Doyle said.

'Taken them, how?'

'Taken them into tree and flower and ground,' he said, not meeting her eyes.

'As Amatheon rose from the dirt, will they return to us, or was their death the price for this miracle?' She whispered it, but her voice seemed to echo.

'We don't know,' Doyle said.

A bird began to sing again. A high, trilling cascade of music fell from the sky, dancing over us. And as if sound could be touch, it wrapped us around in something beautiful, something just out of sight. It seemed a reminder that the dawn would come and death would not be forever. It was the sound of hope that comes each spring to let you know that winter will not last, and the land is not dead.

I could not help but smile. Mistral and Abe raised their faces upward, as if turning gratefully into a spill of warm sunshine.

Andais began to back away as the last sweet note fell upon the air. She backed toward the part of the wall that still held darkness, as if the magic's return could not touch it. 'You will make of the Unseelie Court a pale imitation of the golden court that your uncle rules, Meredith. You will fill the darkness that is our purpose with light and music, and we will die as a people.'

'Once there were many courts,' Abeloec said,

'some dark, some light, but all faerie. We did not divide ourselves into good and bad as the Christians do for their religion. We were everything at once, as we were meant to be.'

Andais did not bother to respond. Instead she simply said, 'You have brought life to the dead gardens. I will not try to pixie on my promise. Come to the Hallway of Mortality and save Nerys's people if you can. Bring that bright Seelie magic into the other heart of the Unseelie Court and see how long it survives.' With that she was gone.

We waited for a few heartbeats; then Mistral and Abe stood, mud coating their lower legs. No voice from the dark told them to get back on their knees. I let out a breath I hadn't realized I was holding.

'What did she mean when she said that our court has two hearts?' I asked.

Abe answered, 'Once every faerie mound had a garden or forest or lake at its heart. But every court also had another heart of power – one that would reflect the kind of magic the court specialized in.'

'You have brought one heart back to life,' Mistral said, 'but I am not certain it is wise to reawaken the other.'

'The hallway is a torture chamber, where most magic does not work. It's a null place,' I said.

'But once, Meredith, it was more.'

I looked at the men. 'More how?'

'Things that were older than faerie, older than us, were imprisoned there. Remnants of power from the peoples we had defeated.'

'I'm not sure I understand, Mistral.'

He looked at Doyle. 'Help me explain this.'

'Once there were creatures in the Hallway of Mortality that could bring true death to even the sidhe. They were kept there to serve as methods of execution, or torture, or simply the threat of those things. The queen did not care for them because, as you well know, she likes to do her own torturing. Watching some other being tear us limb from limb was not half so amusing to her as doing it herself.'

'And we healed better if she did it,' Rhys said.

Doyle nodded. 'Yes, she could torture us longer and more often if the things did not help.'

'What kind of things?' I asked. I didn't like how serious they'd gotten.

'Terrible things. A glimpse of them would drive a mortal mad,' he said.

'How long ago did these things vanish from the sithen?'

'A thousand years, maybe more,' he said.

'The forests haven't been gone so long as that,' I said.

'No, not quite that long.'

'Why are you all so worried?'

'Because if you, or the Goddess's power

through you, can bring this about,' Abe said, motioning at the ever-expanding forest, 'then we must prepare for the fact that the second heart of our court can come back to full life, as well.'

'Perhaps Merry is too Seelie to bring back such horrors?' Mistral said, almost hopefully.

'Her two hands of power are flesh and blood,' Doyle said. 'Those are not Seelie magicks.'

'I came to the princess for aid for Nerys's people, but I would not risk her now, not for a house full of traitors,' said Mistral.

'If we save them, they won't be traitors,' I said.

'They still believe that your mortality is contagious,' Rhys said. 'They still think that if you sit on the throne, we will all begin to age and die.'

'Do you think that Nerys's court still has enough honor to realize that I'm trying to ensure that their rulers' sacrifice wasn't for nothing? Nerys gave her life so her house would not die, and I want that to mean something.'

The men seemed to think about it for a moment. Finally Doyle said, 'They have honor, but I do not know if they have gratitude.'

Chapter 9

'DEITY MAGIC BROUGHT US HERE,' RHYS SAID, 'BUT how do we get out? There's no door anymore to the dead gardens.'

'Meredith,' Frost said.

I looked at him.

'Ask the sithen to give us a door leading out of here.'

'Do you think it will be that easy?' Rhys said.

'If the sithen wishes Merry to save Nerys's people, yes,' said Frost.

'And if it doesn't wish them saved, or if it doesn't care?'

Frost shrugged. 'If you have a better suggestion, I am listening.'

Rhys spread his hands as if to say *no*.

I looked out at the dark wall and said, 'I need a door that leads out of here.'

The darkness grew less, and a door – a large

golden door – appeared in the cave wall. I almost said, *Thank you*, but some of the older magicks don't like to be thanked – they take insult from it. I swallowed, and whispered, 'It's a lovely door.'

Carving appeared around the door frame, vines drawn through the wood as if by an invisible finger. 'That's new,' Rhys whispered.

'Let us go through, before it decides to vanish,' Frost said.

He was right. He was most certainly right. But strangely, none of us wanted to pass through the door until the invisible finger had finished drawing its vines. Only when the wood had stopped moving did Doyle touch the golden handle, and turn it. He led the way into a hallway that was almost as black as his own skin. If he stood still, he'd blend into the background.

Rhys touched the wall. 'We haven't had a black corridor like this in the sithen for years.'

'It's made of the same rock as the queen's chamber,' I whispered. I'd had so many bad experiences in the queen's shiny black-walled room that seeing the sithen turn black like that room frightened me.

Mistral was the last one through the door. When he stepped through, the door vanished, leaving a smooth black wall, untouched and unyielding.

'The hallway where Mistral and Merry had sex is turning to white marble,' Frost said. 'What caused this corridor to change to black?'

'I do not know,' Doyle said. He was looking up and down the black hallway. 'It has changed too much. I do not know where we are in the sithen.'

'Look at this,' Frost said. He was staring up at the wall across from us.

Doyle moved to stand beside him, staring at what, to me, looked like blank wall. Doyle made a harsh, hissing sound. 'Meredith, call the door back.'

'Why?'

'Just do it.' His voice was quiet, but it vibrated with urgency, as if he were forcing himself to whisper when what he wanted to do was scream.

I didn't argue with that tone in his voice. I called out, 'I would like a door back into the dead gardens.'

The door appeared again, all gold and pale wood, and carved vines. Doyle motioned Mistral to take the lead. Mistral reached for the golden handle, a naked sword in his other hand. What was happening? Why were they frightened? What had I missed?

Mistral went through with Abe behind him, me in the middle, and Rhys and Doyle following. Frost came last. But before I passed thorugh the doorway, Abe stopped, and Mistral's voice came urgent from inside the dead gardens, 'Back, go back!'

Doyle said, 'We cannot stay here in the black hallway.' Rhys was pressed against my back, Abe pressed against my front. We were frozen between the two captains of the guards, each trying to get us moving in the opposite direction.

'We cannot have two captains, Mistral,' Frost said. 'Without a single leader we are indecisive and endangered.'

'What is wrong?' I asked.

There was a sound from down the hallway – a heavy, slithering sound that froze my heart in my chest. I was afraid I recognized it. No, I had to be wrong. Then a second sound came: a high chittering sound – one that could be mistaken for birds, but wasn't.

'Oh, Goddess,' I whispered.

'Forward, Mistral, now, or we are lost,' Doyle said.

'It is not our garden beyond the door,' Mistral said.

The high-pitched bird-like sounds were coming closer, outpacing the heavy slithering weight. The sluagh, the nightmares of the Unseelie Court and a kingdom in their own right, moved fast but the nightflyers always moved faster than the rest of the sluagh. We were inside the sluagh's hollow hill; somehow we had crossed to their sithen. If they found us here . . . we might survive, or not.

'Do sluagh wait on the other side of the door?' Doyle asked Mistral urgently.

'No,' Mistral called back.

'Then go, now!' Doyle ordered.

Abe stumbled forward as if Mistral had moved suddenly out of the way. We came through the door in a rush with Doyle pushing from behind. He was like some kind of elemental force at our backs. It put us in a heap on the ground. I couldn't see anything but white flesh, and I felt the muscled weight of them all around me.

'Where are we?' Frost asked.

Rhys moved, drawing me to my feet with him. Doyle, Mistral, and Frost were all on alert, weapons out, searching for something to fight. The door had vanished, leaving us on the shore of a dark lake.

Lake may have been too strong a word. The depression was dry except for a slimy skim of water at the very bottom. Bones littered the floor of the dying lake, and the shore where we stood. The bones shone dully in the dim light that fell from the stone ceiling, as if the moon had been rubbed into the rock. All around the shore, the stone walls of the cavern rose steeply up into the gloom, surrounded only by a narrow ledge before a steep drop-off into the lake bed.

'Call the door again, Meredith,' Doyle said, his dark face still searching the dead land.

'Yes, and be more specific about our destination this time,' Mistral said.

Abe was still on the ground. I heard a sharp intake of breath, and glanced over at him. His hand was black and shiny in the dim light. 'What are these bones that they could cut sidhe flesh?'

Doyle answered him. 'They are the bones of the most magical of the sluagh. Things so fantastical that when the sluagh began to fade in power, there was not enough magic to sustain their lives.'

I clung to Rhys and whispered, 'We're in the sluagh's dead gardens.'

'Yes. Call the door, now.' Doyle glanced at me, then back to the dim landscape.

Rhys had one arm around me, the other hand full of his gun. 'Do it, Merry.'

'I need a door to the Unseelie sithen.' On the far side of the dead lake, the door appeared.

'Well, that's inconvenient,' Rhys whispered wryly, but he tucked me closer against his body.

'There is room to walk the edge, if we are careful,' Mistral said. 'We can make our way between the cavern walls and the lake bed, if we pick our way carefully around the bones.'

'Be very careful,' Abe said. He was on his feet now, but his left hand and arm were coated with blood. He still held the horn cup in his right hand, though nothing else – he'd left all his weapons behind in the bedroom. Mistral had dressed and rearmed. Frost was as armed as he had begun the night. Doyle had only what he had been able to grab – no clothes limited how much you could carry.

'Frost, bind Abeloec's wound,' said Doyle. 'Then we will start for the door.'

'It is not that bad, Darkness,' Abe said.

'This is a place of power for the sluagh, not for us,' Doyle said. 'I would not take the chance that you bleed to death for want of a bandage.'

Frost didn't argue, but went to the other man with a strip of cloth torn from his own shirt. He began to bind Abe's hand.

'Why does everything hurt more sober?' Abe asked.

'Things feel better sober, too,' Rhys said.

I looked up at him. 'You say that like you know that for certain. I've never seen you drunk.'

'I spent most of the fifteen hundreds as drunk as my constitution would let me get. You've seen Abe working hard at it – we don't stay drunk long – but I tried. Goddess knows, I tried.'

'Why then? Why that century?'

'Why not?' he asked, making a joke of it, but that was what Rhys did when he was hiding something. Frost's arrogance, Doyle's blankness, Rhys's humor: different ways to hide.

'His wound will need a healer,' Frost said, 'but I have done what I can.'

'Very well,' said Doyle, and he began to lead the way around the edge of the lake, toward the soft, gold shine of the door that had come because I called it. Why had it appeared all the way across the lake? Why not beside us, like the last two times? But then, why had it come at all? Why was the sluagh's sithen, as well as the Unseelie sithen, obeying my wishes?

The shore was so narrow that Doyle had to put his back to the wall and edge along, for his shoulders were too broad. I actually fit better on the narrow path than the men, but even I had to press my naked back to the smooth cave wall. The stones weren't cold as they would have been in an ordinary cave, but strangely warm. The lip of shore we inched across was meant for smaller things to travel, or perhaps not meant to be walked at all. The skeletons littering the shore were those of things that would have swum, or crawled, but nothing that walked upright. The bones looked like the jumbled-together remains of fish, snakes, and things that normally didn't have skeletons in the oceans of mortal earth. Things that looked like squid, except that squid did not have internal skeletons.

We were halfway around that narrow, bone-studded shore when the air wavered on its far side next to the door. For a moment the air swam, and then Sholto, King of the Sluagh, Lord of That Which Passes Between, was standing there.

Chapter 10

SHOLTO WAS TALL, MUSCLED, HANDSOME, AND looked every bit a highborn sidhe of the Seelie Court. His long hair was even a pale yellow, like winter sunshine with an edge of snow to it. His arm was in a sling, and as he turned his head to the light, a faint darkness – like a stain of bruises – touched his face. Kitto had said Sholto's own court had attacked him. They were afraid that bedding me would make Sholto completely sidhe and no longer sluagh enough to be their king.

Four robed figures stood behind him. They fanned out, some toward the golden door, some toward us. Doyle said, 'King Sholto, we are not here of our own choice. We ask forgiveness for entering your kingdom uninvited.'

I would have dropped to my knees, if there had been room, but the crumbling edge of black earth was only inches from my feet, and my back was plastered against the stone wall. There was no room for niceties on this path. There was also precious little room for the guards to fight – if they attacked us now, we were going to lose.

A blade glimmered from the edge of one of the shorter cloaked guards as he spoke. 'You are nude and nearly weaponless: only something desperate would bring you here like this, with the princess in tow.'

'It is the beginning of their invasion,' came a female voice from one of the tallest guards. I knew that voice. It was Black Agnes, Sholto's chief bodyguard, and chief among his lovers at this court. She had tried to kill me once before for jealousy's sake.

Sholto turned enough to look at her. The movement revealed that wide, pale bandages were all he was wearing on his upper body. Whatever they covered must have been a terrible wound.

'Enough, Agnes, enough!' Sholto silenced her, rumbling echoes around the cavern.

The black-robed figure of Agnes that loomed over him glanced at me. I had a moment to see the gleam of her eyes in the dark ugliness of her face. The night-hags were ugly; it was part of what they were.

One of the shorter, robed guards leaned into Sholto, as if whispering, but the echoes that hissed along the cave walls were not human speech. The high-pitched tittering of a nightflyer was coming from the human-sized figure – though it couldn't be a nightflyer, for it walked upright.

Sholto turned back to us. 'Are you saying that your queen sent you here?'

'No,' Doyle said.

'Princess Meredith,' Sholto called, 'we are within our rights to slay your guards and keep you here until your aunt ransoms you back. Darkness knows this, as does the Killing Frost. On the other hand, Mistral might have let his temper lead him astray, and Abeloec can turn up anywhere when he's lost in drink, can't he, Segna?'

The figure in the pale yellow cloak spoke in a rough voice. 'Aye, he were unhappy when he sobered up, weren't you, cup bearer?' I'd heard Abe called that before as a term of derision, but I'd never understood until tonight. It was a reminder of what he had once been; a way of rubbing his face in what he had lost.

'You taught me to be more cautious about where I passed out, ladies,' Abe said, and his voice was his usual casual, amused, bitter tone.

The two hags laughed. The other guards joined in a chorus of hissing laughter, which let me know that whatever the two shorter guards were, they were the same kind of creature.

Sholto spoke. 'Don't worry, Darkness, the hags didn't help Abe break his vow of celibacy, for that is a death sentence to all. The tearing of white sidhe flesh amuses them almost as much as sex.'

The high twittering voice came faintly again. Sholto nodded at what it had said. 'Ivar makes a good point. You are all wet and muddy, and that did not happen here in our garden.' He motioned with his good hand at the caked, drying earth and the water trapped feet below us, clearly inaccessible.

'I would ask permission to bring the princess off this ledge,' Doyle said.

'No,' Sholto said, 'she is safe enough there. Answer the question, Darkness . . . or Princess . . . or whoever. How did you get wet and muddy? I know that it is snowing aboveground; do not use that to lie.'

'The sidhe never lie,' Mistral said.

Sholto and his guards all laughed. The high tittering mixed with the rumbling bass/alto of the hags and Sholto's open, joyous laughter. '*The sidhe never lie*: Spare us that, the biggest lie of all,' said Sholto.

'We are not allowed to lie,' Doyle said.

'No, but the sidhe version of the truth is so full of holes that it is worse than a lie. We, the sluagh, would prefer a good honest lie to the half-truths that the court we are supposed to belong to feeds us. We starve on a diet of near lies. So tell us true, if you can, how came you wet and muddy, and here?'

'It rained in the dead gardens, in our sithen,' Doyle said.

'More lies,' Agnes said.

I had an idea. 'I swear by my honor – ' I began. One of the hags laughed at that, but I kept going. '– and the darkness that devours all things that it was raining in the Unseelie gardens when we left them.' I'd given not just an oath that no sidhe would willingly break – because of the curse that went with the breaking – but the oath that I'd demanded of Sholto weeks ago when he found me in California. He'd sworn the oath that he meant me no harm, and I'd believed him.

The severity of the oath silenced even the night-hags. 'Be careful what you say, Princess,' Sholto said. 'Some magicks still live.'

'I know what I swore, and I know what it means, King Sholto, Lord of That Which Passes Between. I am wet with the first rain to fall upon the dead gardens in centuries. My skin is decorated with soil reborn, dry no more.'

'How is this possible?' Sholto demanded.

'It is *not* possible,' Agnes said. She pointed one dark, muscled arm at the door. 'This is Seelie magic, not Unseelie. They conspire together to destroy us. I told you, the golden court would never have dared if they did not have the full support of the Queen of Air and Darkness.' She pointed a little dramatically at the shiny door. 'This proves it.'

'Meredith,' Doyle said softly, 'make the door go away.'

'Whispering will not make you my friend, Darkness,' Sholto said.

'I told the princess to make the door go away, so that you would understand this is not Seelie business.'

Agnes turned so suddenly that her hood fell back to reveal the dry black straw of her hair, the ruin of her complexion, covered in bumps and sores. The hags hid their ugliness, which was an exception among the sluagh. Most of them saw every oddity as a mark of beauty, or power. The hags hid themselves, though – as did the two shorter guards.

Agnes pointed the long hand with its black-taloned claws at me. 'She did not conjure this door. She is mortal, and mortal hand never made this doorway.'

'Princess, if you would,' Doyle said low but clear, so that he couldn't be accused of whispering.

I spoke loudly, so they'd hear me, and the cave caught the echo of my voice, so that it seemed to bounce along the walls. 'I need the door to go away now, please.'

There was a moment's hesitation, as if the door wanted to give me a second to reconsider; then, when I didn't, the door vanished. Sholto's guards shifted, and Agnes startled as if something had goosed her. 'Mortal flesh cannot control the sithen. Any sithen.'

'I would have agreed with you, until a few hours ago,' I said.

'How did you come here?' Sholto asked.

'I asked for a door to the dead gardens. It never occurred to me that any door I could conjure would bring me to your home, Sholto.'

'King Sholto,' Agnes corrected me.

'King Sholto,' I said dutifully.

'Why would that request bring you to our garden, Princess Meredith?' Sholto asked.

'Doyle told me to get us back to the dead gardens. I did just that: I called a door to the dead gardens. But I did not specify which garden, and you know the rest.'

Sholto stared at me. The triple gold of his irises – molten metal, autumn leaves, and pale sunshine – made his face beautiful, but it did not make the look one bit less intense. He stared at me as if he would weigh me with a look.

'This cannot be true,' Agnes said.

'If it was a lie, they'd have a better one than this,' Sholto said.

'Do you still believe everything that a piece of white sidhe flesh tells you, King Sholto? Have you learned nothing from what they did to you?' Agnes asked. I wasn't sure what she meant, but I guessed it had to do with the bandages he wore.

'Silence,' Sholto said, but there was something

in his face, the way he turned, that spoke of embarrassment. The last time I'd seen Sholto, he had hidden behind a mask of arrogance, much as Frost did. Whatever mask he had built to hide behind in court seemed to have shredded, so that he now had nothing for his emotions to hide behind.

'May we approach you, King Sholto?' I asked, and my voice was clear, but softer. The tall, elegant, arrogant man whom I'd met in Los Angeles wasn't the same man who stood before me now, shoulders slightly hunched.

'No, you may not,' Agnes said, in her strangely rich voice. Most night-hags spoke in a cackling voice, as if they'd swallowed gravel.

Sholto turned on her, and the movement cost him, for he nearly stumbled. It seemed to feed his anger. 'I am king here, Agnes, not you. Me!' He thumped himself in the upper chest. 'Me, Agnes, not you, me! I am still king here!'

He turned to us. The front of his bandages showed fresh blood, as if he'd torn stitches. Sholto was half highborn sidhe and half of the sluagh, and the sluagh were even harder to injure than the sidhe. What could have hurt him this badly?

'Bring her onto solid land, Darkness,' Sholto said.

Doyle led me forward, carefully. Rhys's hand never left my other arm. They eased me out onto the broader shoreline. The others followed, mincing their way onto secure ground.

Doyle took my hand and led me forward, very formally, toward the waiting sluagh. We had to come forward slowly, because of the bones. We'd seen what they'd done to Abe, and we were both barefoot. We'd had enough injuries for the night.

'How I hate you, Princess,' Agnes said.

Sholto spoke without turning around to look at her. 'I am very close to losing my patience with you, Agnes. You don't want that.'

'They move like shadow and light, so graceful through the bone field that is our garden,' Agnes said, 'and you watch her as if she were food and drink, and you were starving.'

The comment made me look up, away from the dangerous bones. 'Do not do this, Agnes,' he said, but his face was naked to his need. She was right about that look on his face. It was more than just lust, though it wasn't love, either. There was pain in his gaze, like a man watching something that he knew he could not have, and he wanted that thing more than anything else in the world. What had laid Sholto bare to the eyes of the world? What had stripped him to this?

Doyle stopped in a space of ground mostly clear of bones, just out of reach of the sluagh – or as far out of reach as we would get here. The other men had followed a few steps behind us, as if Doyle had given them some signal that I hadn't seen, so they wouldn't crowd Sholto and his guards. We were in the wrong. We had invaded their land, not the other way around, so we needed to be the more polite. I understood that, but looking into Sholto's face I felt like we had walked into the middle of something that had nothing to do with us.

I began to kneel and pulled Doyle down with me. I bowed my head, not just to show respect, but because I couldn't bear the look on Sholto's face anymore. I didn't deserve such a look. I was wet, splattered with mud. I must have looked like something the cat dragged in out of the storm, yet he stared at me with a desire that was painful to see. I'd already agreed to have sex with him, as he was part of the royal guard for the queen, as well as a king in his own right. He would have me, so why did he look at me the way Tantalus must have looked in Hades?

'You are princess of the Unseelie Court, in line to be queen. Why do you bow to me?' Sholto's voice tried to be neutral, and almost achieved it.

I spoke, still gazing at the ground, my hand still resting in Doyle's. 'We came to your lands accidentally, but uninvited. It is we who have trespassed. We who owe you an apology. You are King of the Sluagh, and though you are a part of the Unseelie Court, you are still a kingdom in your own right. I am only a royal princess –

perhaps heir to a throne that rules over your lands – but you, Sholto, you are already a king. A king of the dark host itself. You and your people are the last great host, the last wild hunt. They are a wondrous and fearsome thing, the people that call you king. They, and you, deserve respect in your own lands from anyone less than another high ruler.'

I heard someone shift behind me, as if one of the other guards would have protested some of what I said, but Doyle's hand was peaceful under mine. He understood that we were still in danger; besides, what I said was true. There had been a time when the sidhe understood that you respected all the kingdoms in your care, not just the ones that were blood of your blood.

'Get up, get up, and do not mock me!' Sholto's words were inexplicably rage-filled.

I looked up to find that handsome face consumed with anger, twisted with it. 'I do not understand – ' I began, but he didn't give me time to finish the sentence. He strode forward, grabbed my hand, and jerked me to my feet. Doyle came with me, tightening his grip on my other hand.

Sholto's fingers dug into my upper arm as he pulled me closer and raged inches from my face. 'I did not believe Agnes. I did not believe that Andais would allow such outrage, but now I do. Now I believe it!' He shook me hard enough to make me stumble. Only Doyle's hand kept me from falling.

I fought to keep my voice even as I said, 'I don't know what you are talking about.'

'Don't you, don't you!' He let go of me abruptly, sending me stumbling back against Doyle. Sholto dug his uninjured hand into the bandages at his chest and stomach, tearing at them.

Doyle turned his body so that I was on the other side of him, and his body would be between me and whatever was about to happen. I didn't argue with him. Sholto was moody, but I'd never seen him like this.

'Did you come so you could see what they did? Did you want to see it?' He screamed the last, filling the cave with echoes, as if the walls themselves screamed back.

I could see what was under the bandages now. Sholto's mother had been a noble lady of the Unseelie Court, but his father had been a night-flyer. The last time I'd seen Sholto's upper body bare, without him wasting magic to make it look smooth and muscled, and fully sidhe, there had been a nest of tentacles starting a few inches below the breast area to stop just above his groin. He had the full set of tentacles that the nightflyers used as arms and legs, as well as the tiny suction-tipped tentacles that were secondary sexual organs. It had been these little extras that had made me avoid taking him to my bed – Goddess help me, I'd seen them as a deformity. But that wasn't a problem now. The skin where the tentacles had been was now just raw, red, naked flesh. Whoever had done it hadn't just chopped the tentacles off, they had shaved them away, along with most of his skin.

Chapter 11

'THE LOOK ON YOUR FACE, MEREDITH — YOU DIDN'T know. You really didn't know.' His voice sounded calmer, half relieved, half reinjured, as if he hadn't expected it.

I forced myself to look away from the wound, and at his face. The eyes were too wide, his mouth open, as if he were panting. He looked like he was in shock. I found my voice, but it was a hoarse whisper. 'I did not know.' I licked my lips and tried to get hold of myself. I was Princess Meredith NicEssus, wielder of two hands of power, trying to be queen; I had to do better than this. I was huddled against Doyle, but pulled myself away. If Sholto could survive such a wound, then the least I could do was not cower in the face of it.

The high-pitched voice came from one of the shorter guards again, and Sholto spoke as if in response. 'Ivar is right. The looks on all your faces make it clear – none of you knew. On the one hand, I feel less betrayed; on the other, what it tells me about the politics at work here says it's more dangerous for our court – for both our courts.'

I stepped toward him, slowly, the way you'd approach a wounded animal. Slowly, so you don't scare him more. 'Who did this?' I asked.

'The golden court did this.'

'You mean the Seelie?'

He gave a small nod.

Doyle said, 'Only Taranis himself might be able to wrest you away from your sluagh. No other noble at his court is powerful enough to take you like that.'

Sholto looked at Doyle, a long, considering look. 'That is high praise from the Queen's Darkness.'

'It is truth. The princess said it best: The sluagh are the last of the wild hunts. The last left in all of faerie. You and your people alone still have the wild magic running through your veins. It is not a small power, King Sholto.'

'We should have heard the battle even inside our own sithen,' Frost said, and there was a question in his voice.

Sholto's eyes flicked to him, then away again, as if he suddenly found that he didn't want to meet anyone's eyes.

Segna the Gold's voice whined from out of her dirty yellow hood. 'What cannot be taken with force of arms, can easily be won with soft flesh.'

Sholto didn't tell her to be quiet. He actually hung his head, so that a sweep of his own pale hair shadowed his face. I didn't understand what Segna meant, but it had clearly hit home for him.

'I would not ask this of you,' Doyle said, 'but if Taranis's people have harmed you, then it is a direct challenge to our queen's authority. Either he believes we will not retaliate, or he believes we are not strong enough to retaliate.'

Sholto looked up then. 'Now do you understand why I thought Queen Andais had to know?'

Doyle nodded. 'Because if she had not given her permission, then this attack makes even less sense.'

'Wars have begun over less,' Mistral said.

The comment earned him a glance from Sholto. 'The last time I saw you, you sat in the consort's chair, at the feet of Princess Meredith.'

Mistral bowed. 'I was so honored.'

'I have sat in the chair, and it was an empty honor. Have you found it so?'

Mistral hesitated, then said, 'I have found it everything I would hope it to be, and more.'

I fought not to glance back at him. His voice was so careful, I knew he saw something in the king before us that I hadn't seen until now. He was desperate to know the touch of another sidhe; he wanted to have another's glow of high magic to match his own. It hadn't occurred to me that Sholto had been here in his own kingdom pining for me to keep my promise and offer him my body. Assassination attempts, murders, and more political machinations than I could keep track of had kept me from fulfilling it. But I hadn't meant to ignore Sholto.

'I did not mean it to be an empty honor, King Sholto,' I said. 'I mean to keep my promise to you.'

'Now – you will bed him now.' Segna's voice again, like a grating whine. 'It's what the Seelie bitch said, too, that once he healed up, she'd bed him.'

I stared up at him. 'You *allowed* someone to do this to you?'

He shook his head. 'Never.'

Agnes's voice, more cultured, more human than her sister hag's. 'Sholto, you have dreamt of being sidhe, completely sidhe, since you were small. Do not lie to someone who helped raise you.'

'I also wanted the wings of a nightflyer to come out of my back when I was small – do you remember that?'

She nodded, that head seeming too large for the narrow shoulders. 'You cried when you realized you would never have wings.'

'We want many things when we are children. I admit that there were times when I wished they were gone.' He made a motion as if he would touch what was no longer there, the way an amputee will try to scratch a ghost limb. His hand fell away before it made contact with the raw ruin of his stomach.

'How did they trap you, and why did they do this?' Doyle asked.

'I am a king in my own right, not just a noble of the queen's guard. If the Seelie did not see me as an unclean thing, I could have bedded one of their sidhe women long ago. But I am considered a worse crime than a mere Unseelie sidhe. Queen Andais calls me her Perverse Creature, and the Seelie truly believe that. I am a creature, a thing, an abomination to them.'

'Sholto,' I whispered.

'Don't, Princess – I have seen you flinch away from me, too.'

I moved toward him. 'At first, yes. But since then I have seen you shining in your power, with a play of colors in those extras so that they shone like jewels in the sun. I have felt your body thrumming with magic and power, your nakedness inside my body.' I touched his arm.

He didn't pull away.

'You did not fuck him,' Segna said.

'No, but I've held him in my mouth, and if you hadn't interrupted that night, we might have done more.' I had not enjoyed Sholto's extra bits, but once he had started to glow with power, his magic responding to my touch, I had seen him clearly for a shining moment. Seen him as handsome and seen that nest of tentacles not as a deformity but just as another part of him. I doubted I could have slept in the same bed with him, but sex . . . sex had seemed like a good idea in that moment. I tried to let him see that in my face now, but perhaps it showed, because he drew away and began to tell the story of the deception.

'I should have known it was a lie,' he said. 'Lady Clarisse offered to meet with me. She sent a note saying that she had glimpsed me without my shirt, and had not been able to stop fantasizing about it. I leapt at the chance, not stopping to question. I wanted so much to be with another sidhe, even if it was for only a night.'

I didn't feel guilty very often – few in faerie do – but in that moment I knew that if I had taken him to my bed, he wouldn't have been vulnerable to the Seelie's trick. Or maybe he would have been more vulnerable – we'd never know.

I tried to hug him without hurting the front of his body. Segna reached around and shoved me away.

'Do not touch her again,' Sholto snapped at Segna, and his voice was full of a choking anger.

'Now she'll cuddle you,' Segna whined, 'now she'll touch you, because the icky bits are gone.

Now she wants you, just like the other sidhe bitch.'

'She would have touched me that night in Los Angeles if you had left us alone,' he said.

Agnes reached to the other hag and drew her back. 'He is right, Segna. We bear blame in this atrocity, too.'

A tear trailed down out of the sickly yellow of Agnes's eye. She turned away so I wouldn't see. Most of faerie cried when we cried, and displayed any emotion out in the open. It was only when we got close to a throne that we learned to hide what we felt. We were meant to be a freer people than this.

'Lady Clarisse,' Sholto continued, 'took me inside the Seelie sithen. She led me cloaked through back ways to her room. Then she told me that although the tentacles fascinated her, she also feared them. She said she could not bear to have the tentacles touch her while we made love. Here I was truly a fool – I let her tie me up, so I would not accidentally brush her with the parts she feared, and said she craved.' He wouldn't meet anyone's eyes again. I watched his face redden even through the strands of his white hair. He burned with embarrassment. 'When I was helpless, other sidhe slipped into the room. They did to me what you see.'

'Was their king with them?' Doyle asked.

Sholto shook his head. 'He is not a king

who does his own dirty work. You know that, Darkness.'

'Did the king know?' Doyle said.

'They would not have done this without his knowledge,' I said. 'They fear him too much.'

'But by not being present, he has left himself room to deny it,' Sholto said. 'If I could see what he hoped to gain from this, I would believe it of him. But what does this accomplish?'

'Some of your people believed that Queen Andais did this to you, allowed it to be done. Perhaps this atrocity was committed with that as the intent. You are her strongest ally, King Sholto. If you had left her side, what then?' Doyle asked.

'The only reason for the king to want our queen shorn of her allies is that he means to make war. And if any of faerie make war on another, our treaty with America is breached. We will all be cast out of the last country that would take us in. If Taranis caused that, the rest of faerie would rise up against him, and he would be destroyed.'

We knew that Taranis had done something almost as bad earlier in the year. He had released the Nameless, a formless being. It had been made of the discarded power that all the fey had been forced to shed in order to be allowed to remain in America – one of the restrictions placed on us when President Jefferson allowed us to immigrate. The faerie had done two weirding spells in Europe, trying to control ourselves enough to live peaceably with the humans, but we had done one more here. I don't think any of the sidhe understood what we were giving up. I was born long after the spell, so that I knew our glorious past as stories, legends, rumors.

Taranis had released that trapped magic, tried to use it to kill Maeve Reed. Reed was the golden goddess of Hollywood – and once upon a time, the goddess of cinema. She had known his secret, that he was infertile, that the problem of his childlessness wasn't in the long string of wives that he kept replacing. It was him, and he had suspected it for a hundred years, when he cast Maeve Reed out of faerie for refusing his bed. She had done so on the grounds that the last wife he'd put aside had gotten pregnant by someone else. She'd told the king to his face that she thought he was infertile, and these many years later, he'd tried to take his revenge.

One of the things that prompted Queen Andais to call me back from exile had been her discovery from human doctors that she was infertile. The ruler of a faerie land *is* the land, and if they are not fertile – not healthy – the land and people die. It is a very old magic, and a true one. If Taranis had known about his infertility for a hundred years without revealing it, then he had condemned his people to death, knowingly. They killed rulers for such crimes in faerie.

'You are all entirely too quiet,' Sholto said to us.

'You know something. Something that I need to know.'

'We are not free to discuss it, not openly,' Doyle said.

'You will not be allowed to be alone with him,' Agnes said. 'We are not such fools as that.'

'I cannot argue with Agnes on this,' Sholto said. Again he made that gesture as if he would stroke the missing bits. 'I have put myself at the mercy of the sidhe once too often of late.'

'We cannot tell this tale without our queen's permission,' Doyle said. 'It would earn us, at the very least, a trip to the Hallway of Mortality.'

'I would not ask that of anyone,' Sholto said. He lowered his head, and a sound escaped him. It was almost a sob. I wanted to hug him, but I didn't want to anger his hags any further. Besides, they were partially right – I could touch him now without flinching. Still, I saw it for what it was, something cruelly done – an amputation. I had felt those muscular tentacles on my body – just a touch, but they had been real – and they'd had uses, which he now had lost.

Sholto spoke low. 'The Seelie said they were doing me a favor. That if I healed without the deformity coming back, the lady in question would keep her word and bed me for a night.'

In sympathy, I started to touch him where the bits had been, then stopped because the wound was bleeding and raw, and touching it must hurt.

'But the tentacles are part of you. It is like cutting off an arm, or worse.'

'Do you know how often I have dreamt of looking like them?' He motioned at the men at my back. 'Agnes is right. I have dreamt of looking fully sidhe for so long, and now it is as you say, I have lost pieces of myself. I have lost arms, and more.'

'The queen does not know this,' Doyle said.

'Are you certain of that, Darkness? Beyond doubt?'

Doyle started to simply say *yes*, then stopped himself. 'No, I am not certain, but she has not told us otherwise; nor have rumors to the contrary touched our court.'

'Wars have begun over less than this, Darkness. Wars between the courts of faerie.'

Doyle nodded. 'I know.'

'Agnes says that Andais had to have given Taranis her approval – even if just tacitly – or Taranis would not have risked it. Do you think my hag is right? Do you think the queen allowed this to happen?'

'The sluagh are too important to the queen, King Sholto. I cannot imagine a set of circumstances in which Andais would risk such hurt to the sluagh's vows to her court. I think it more likely that this was done, at least partially, in a bid to strip our queen of your might. Why didn't you tell the queen, the court?'

'I thought she must know. That she must have given permission. I agreed with the hags – I did not think even Taranis would dare to do this without Andais's knowledge.'

'I cannot argue your reasoning, but I do not believe she knows,' Doyle said.

'Why didn't you tell me, Sholto?' I asked. 'You once said to me that only the two of us understand what it is like to be *almost* sidhe. Almost tall enough, slender enough, almost – but not quite pure enough to be accepted.'

He almost smiled, almost. 'We may have had that in common, but as I told you in Los Angeles, no man had ever complained about your body; only envious women.'

I smiled at him. 'About my breasts, you were right.' That earned me a smile in return, which, given that awful wound, made me breathe more easily. 'But I am too short, too human looking for most of the sidhe, male or female, to let me forget it.'

'I told you then: They were fools,' Sholto said. He took my hand in his and raised it up for a kiss, but when he tried to bend over me, the pain stopped him in midmotion.

I pressed his hand to my cheek. 'Sholto, oh, Sholto.'

'I had hoped to hear tenderness in your voice, but not for this reason. Don't pity me, Meredith, I could not bear it.'

I didn't know how to respond. I just held his hand against my face, and tried to think of anything I could say that wouldn't make him feel worse. How could I not feel pity?

'When did this happen, King Sholto?' Doyle asked.

Sholto looked past me to the other man. 'Two days ago, just before your second press conference.'

'The one during which two murders were committed,' Rhys said.

Sholto looked at him. 'You caught your murderer, though the human police don't know it yet. I hear you're trying to let him heal from the torture before showing him to the human police.'

'Our queen made a mess of him,' Rhys said.

'He is guilty?' Sholto made it a question.

'We believe so,' Doyle said.

'But you are not certain?'

'What was done to your stomach, Queen Andais did to every inch of Lord Gwennin.'

Sholto winced, and nodded. 'One would do much to stop such pain.'

'Even confess to something you did not do,' Doyle said.

I looked at Doyle then. 'Do you think Gwennin is innocent?'

'No. Nor do I believe he acted completely alone. Andais was using his own intestines as a

172

leash on him, Meredith. He would have been a fool not to confess.'

Sholto pressed my hand to his face. Segna tried to interfere but Agnes stopped her, and the other two guards moved between Sholto and the hags. I caught a glimpse of one of the guard's faces. Oblong eyes full of nothing but color, thin lipless mouth, and a face that was a strange mix of humanoid and nightflyer. They were like Sholto, but no one would have ever have mistaken them for sidhe. The eyes, though – the eyes were goblin eyes. The guard stared at me with his face that looked only half formed, the nostrils mere slits. I did not look away. I stared, memorized his face, for I had never seen another quite like it.

'You do not find me ugly.' The guard's voice held that edge of twittering – almost bird-like, but deeper.

'No,' I said.

'Do you know what I am?'

'The eyes are goblin blood, but the face is night-flyer. I'm not sure about the rest,' I said.

'I am half-goblin and half-nightflyer.'

'Ivar and Fyfe are my uncles on my father's side,' Sholto said.

The second guard spoke for the first time. His voice was deeper, more 'human.' He gave me the full gaze of his face. His eyes were the same oblongs of color, a deep rich blue, but he had more nose, more lower jaw. If he'd been taller, he might have passed for a goblin. But the skin wasn't quite the right texture. 'I am Fyfe, brother to Ivar.' He gave the hags an unfriendly look. 'Our king felt the need of some male guards, who were not conflicted about what to do with his body. We guard it, and that is all.'

'This insult was not for lack of our ability to guard,' Agnes said. 'You, too, will be helpless when he chases his next bit of sidhe flesh. He won't want an audience, and he will go with her alone.'

'Enough, Agnes. Enough, all of you.' Sholto pressed my hand tighter against his face. 'Why didn't I tell you, Princess? How could I admit that Seelie did this to me? That I was not warrior enough to save myself? That I fell into their trap, because they offered me what you had promised? Agnes is right in one thing: I am near blinded by my desire to be with another sidhe, so blinded that I let a Seelie woman bind me. So blinded I believed her lie that she was fascinated with my bits, but afraid of them, too.' He shook his head. 'I am King of the Sluagh, and even bound I should have had enough magic to save myself from this.' He let go of me, stepped back.

'The Seelie have magic that we do not,' Frost said.

'The sluagh have magic that the Seelie have never possessed,' I said. I touched Sholto's arm. He flinched, but didn't pull away. I squeezed his arm, and wanted so badly to hold him, to try to chase this pain away. I rested my head against his bare arm. My throat closed up, and I was suddenly choking on tears. I began to weep, clutching at his arm. I couldn't stop.

He pulled me away from him enough to see my face. 'You waste tears on me – why?'

I had to struggle to speak. 'You are beautiful, Sholto, you are – don't let them make you think otherwise.'

'Beautiful now that he's butchered,' Segna said, looming over us, pushing her way past the uncles.

I shook my head. 'You broke in on us in Los Angeles. You saw what I was doing with him. Why would I have been doing those things if he was less than beautiful to me?'

'All I remember from that night, white flesh, is that you killed my sister.'

I had, but by accident. That night, in fear for my life, I had lashed out with magic I hadn't known I had. It had been the first night that my hand of flesh had manifested. It was a terrible power – the ability to turn living beings inside out, but they did not die. They lived on, impossibly on, with their mouths lost inside a ball of flesh, and still they screamed. I'd had to cut her to bits with a magical weapon to finally end her agony.

I don't know what shadows showed on my

face, but Sholto reached for me. Reached for me, to hold me, to give comfort, and it was too much for Segna. She shoved the other two guards away as if they were straw before a storm wind. She struck at me, shrieking her rage.

Suddenly there was movement behind me, and in front of me. All the guards moved at once, but Sholto was closest. He used his own body to shield me, so Segna's razor claws sliced his own white skin. He took the brunt of the blow meant for me, and even what was left of that strike staggered me backward, numbing my arm from shoulder to elbow. It didn't hurt, because I couldn't feel it.

Sholto pushed me into Doyle's arms, and pivoted in the same movement. The movement was so fast that it surprised Segna, made her stumble nearer the edge of the lake. Sholto's good arm was a pale blur as he smashed into her. The blow sent her over the edge. She seemed to hang there in midair, her nearly naked body revealed by the wings of her cape. Then she fell.

Chapter 12

SHE LAY JUST ABOVE THE LOW WATER, IMPALED ON A series of spiked bones jutting out of her from throat to stomach. She hung there, caught, bleeding, like a fish caught on some terrible hook.

I think Sholto's guards expected her to simply draw herself off the spined ridge of the boned creature. Agnes, especially, seemed to be waiting, patient, unworried. 'Come on, Segna, get up.' Her voice was impatient.

Segna lay there and bled, her legs flailing, exposing her most intimate parts as she struggled. The hags wore a leather belt from which hung a sword and a pouch, but that, and their cloaks, were all. Her body was both larger than a human's and more wizened, as if she were a shrunken giant.

I saw the wide eyes, the fright on her face. She wasn't going to just get up. Sometimes, being mortal, I recognized real damage faster, because on a visceral level, I knew it was a possibility. Creatures who are immortal, or nearly so, don't understand the disasters that could befall them.

'Ivar, Fyfe, go to her.'

'With due respect, King Sholto,' Fyfe said, 'I would stay here, and send Agnes down.'

Sholto started to argue, but Ivar joined the argument. 'We do not dare leave Agnes up here with you alone. The princess will have guards, but you will be unprotected.'

'Agnes would not hurt me,' Sholto said, but he was staring at Segna as if he were finally realizing just how bad it might be.

'We are your guards, and your uncles. We would be poor at both duties if we left you alone with Agnes now,' Ivar said in his bird-like voice. People always expected the nightflyers to have hissing, ugly voices, but Ivar sounded like a song-bird – or how a songbird might sound if it could speak as humans do. Most of the nightflyers sounded like that.

'Segna is a night-hag,' Agnes said. 'A mere bone will not bring her down.'

'I tripped on such a bone coming into your garden,' Abe said, and raised his cloth-wrapped arm at her. Blood had soaked through much of the cloth.

'The bones hold old magic,' Doyle said. 'Some of them are things that hunted the sidhe and the other sluagh before they were tamed by your early kings.'

'Do not lecture me about my own people,' Agnes said.

'I remember a time when Black Agnes was not a part of the sluagh,' Rhys said, softly.

She glared at him. 'And I remember a time when you had other names, white knight.' She spat in his direction. 'We have both fallen far from what we once were.'

'Go with Ivar, Agnes. Go see to your sister,' Sholto said.

She glared at him. 'Do you not trust me?'

'I once trusted the three of you more than any other, but you bloodied me before the Seelie got hold of me. You cut me up first.'

'Because you sought to betray us with some white-fleshed slut.'

'I am king here, or I am not, Agnes. You either obey me, or you do not. You will go down with Ivar to help Segna, or I will see it as a direct challenge to my authority.'

'You are gravely wounded, Sholto,' said the hag. 'You cannot win against me in this weakened state.'

'It is not about winning, Agnes. It is about being king. Either I am your king, or I am not. If I am your king, then you will do as I say.'

'Do not do this, Sholto,' she whispered.

'You raised me to be king, Agnes. You told me

that if the sluagh do not respect my threat, then I will not be king for long.'

'I did not mean—'

'Go with Ivar, now, or it ends between us.'

She reached out to him, as if to touch his hair.

He jerked back and yelled, 'Now, Agnes, go now, or it will end badly between us.'

Fyfe threw back his cloak, revealing his weapons, and each of his hands touched a sword hilt, ready for a cross-draw.

Agnes gave Sholto one last look that was more despair than anger. Then she followed Ivar down the steep slope of the lake, using her claws to dig into the soil, so she wouldn't slide into the bones that spiked the earth.

Ivar was already wading through the still water. It came above his waist, which meant the water was deeper than it had looked. He had to strain to lay a hand over Segna's heart between the hanging weight of her breasts. He turned that lipless, unfinished face to look at Sholto, and the look did not communicate good news.

Agnes was taller than Ivar, and had an easier time in the water – it came only to her thighs. She waded to the other hag, and when she reached her let out a wail of despair.

Sholto collapsed to his knees on the side of the lake. 'Segna,' he said, and there was real grief in his voice.

I knelt beside him, touched his arm. He jerked

away. 'Every time I am with you, someone I care about dies, Meredith.'

Ivar called up, 'I am not certain she is dying. Gravely injured. She may yet live.'

Agnes was petting her sister's face. But I could see the gaping mouth, the labored breathing. Blood bubbled from the chest wound when she breathed, poured down her mouth. It would have been death to most.

'Can she survive it?' I asked, softly.

'I do not know,' Sholto said. 'Once it would not have been a killing blow, but we have lost much of what we were.'

'Abeloec's wound from the bones is still bleeding,' Doyle said.

Sholto's head drooped, hiding his face in a curtain of that white hair. I was close enough to hear him crying, though so softly that I doubted anyone else would hear it. I pretended not to notice, as was only respectful for a king.

Segna reached out to him. She spoke in a voice thick and bubbling with her own blood, 'My lord, mercy.'

He raised his face, but kept his hair like a shield on either side, so only I, kneeling beside him, could see the tracks of tears on his face. His voice came clear and unemotional; you would never have known the pain in his eyes from that voice. 'Do you ask for healing, or for death, Segna?'

'Healing,' she managed to say.

He shook his head. 'Get her off the bones.' He looked at Fyfe. 'Go help them.'

Fyfe hesitated for a moment then slid, carefully, down the slope to join his brother in the still, thick water. The three of them managed to slide Segna free of most of the bones. One of them seemed caught on Segna's own ribs, and Agnes snapped that spine so that they could lower her into their arms. She was writhing in pain, and coughing blood.

Agnes raised a tearstained face. 'We are not the people we once were, King Sholto. She dies.'

Segna reached a shaking hand out to him. 'Mercy.'

'We cannot save you, Segna. I am sorry,' said Sholto, for it now seemed clear that this was the case.

'Mercy,' she said again.

Agnes said, 'There is more than one kind of mercy, Sholto. Would you leave her to a slow death?' Her voice managed to be both tear-choked and hot with hatred. Such words should burn coming out.

Sholto shook his head.

Ivar's high-pitched voice came. 'It is your kill, Sholto.'

'*Their* kill – the king's and the princess's,' Agnes said, giving me a look of such venom that I fought not to flinch. If a look could still kill among us, I would have died from that look in her eyes. She spat into the water.

'She did not strike the blow, I did,' Sholto said as he came to his feet. He actually stumbled, and I caught him, helped him stand. He didn't jerk away, which let me know he was badly hurt. I could see the bleeding wound that Segna had made, but I didn't think it was that wound that made me him stumble. Nor was it the amputation that weakened him now. There are wounds that never show on the body that are deeper and more hurtful than anything that bleeds.

'My apologies, Sholto, but the hag is right,' Ivar's high voice said reluctantly, 'Segna bled you both. If the princess was not a warrior, then she would be free of this, but she is a sidhe of the Unseelie Court, and all who claim that are warriors.'

'The princess has killed more than once in challenge,' Fyfe said.

'If she will not help finish Segna, then she will never be acknowledged as queen of the sluagh,' Agnes said. She stroked Segna's face, a surprisingly gentle gesture given her dagger-like talons.

I heard Doyle sigh. He moved close enough to whisper to me, 'If you do not help make this kill, Agnes will spread the rumor that you are not a warrior.'

'And that would mean what?' I whispered back.

'It could mean that when you sit on the throne

of the Unseelie Court, the sluagh will not come to your call, for they are a warrior people. They will not be led by someone who is unbloodied in battle.'

'I've been bloodied,' I said. The numbness was sliding away, and now the pain was sharp and tearing. The wound was bleeding freely. What I needed was to get medical attention, not to wade around in slimy water. 'I'll need a dose of antibiotics after this.'

'What?' Doyle and Sholto both asked.

'I'm mortal. Unlike the rest of you, I can get an infection, blood poisoning. So after we crawl around in that water, I'll need antibiotics.'

'You can truly catch all that?' Sholto asked.

'I've had the flu, and my father made sure I had all my childhood immunizations – he wasn't sure how much I could withstand or heal.'

Sholto gazed at me, studying my face. 'You are fragile.'

I nodded. 'Yes, I am, by the standards of faerie.' I looked up at Doyle. 'You know, there are times when I'm not sure I want to be in charge here.'

'Do you mean that?'

'If there was a better alternative than my cousin, yes, I mean it. I'm tired, Doyle, tired. As much as I wanted to come back home to faerie, I'm beginning to miss L.A. almost as much. To put some distance between me and all this killing.'

'I told you once, Meredith, that if I could bear to give the court to Cel, I would leave with you.'

'Darkness,' Mistral said, 'you cannot mean that.'

'You have not been outside faerie except for small trips. You have not seen that there are wonders outside our hills.' He touched my face. 'There are some wonders that will not fade when we leave here.'

He had told me that he would give up everything and follow me into exile. Frost and he, both. When they first thought that the queen's ring, a relic of power, had chosen Mistral as my king Doyle had broken down and said he could not bear it, to watch me with another. He had pulled himself together and remembered his duty, as I'd remembered mine. Would-be queens and kings did not run away and hide, and give their countries over to insane tyrants like my cousin Cel. He was crazier than his mother, Andais.

I stared up into Doyle's face and I wanted him. Wanted to run away with him. Frost came up beside us. I gazed at my two men. I wanted to wrap them around me like a blanket. I did not want to climb down into that stinking hole and wade through razor-sharp bones and dirty water to kill someone I hadn't meant to even hurt.

'I don't want this kill.'

'It must be your choice,' Doyle said softly.

Rhys joined us. 'If we're talking about running away to L.A. permanently, can I come, too?'

I smiled at him, touched his face. 'Yes, you come, too.'

'Good, because once Cel's on the throne, the Unseelie Court won't be safe for anyone.'

I closed my eyes, rested my forehead against Doyle's bare chest for a minute. I pressed my cheek against him, held him tight, so I could listen to the slow, steady beat of his heart.

Abeloec, who had been quiet, spoke next to my face: 'You have drunk deep of the cup, of both cups, Meredith. Wherever you go, faerie will follow you.'

I looked at him, trying to hear all the double meanings in what he'd said. 'I don't want this kill.'

'You must choose,' Abeloec said.

I clung to Doyle for a moment more, then tore myself away. I forced myself to stand straight, shoulders back, though the shoulder Segna had torn ached and stung. If my body didn't heal itself, I'd need stitches. If we could ever get back to the Unseelie Court, there were healers who could fix me up. But it was as if something, or someone, didn't want me getting back there. I didn't think it was political enemies, either – I was beginning to feel the hand of deity pushing firmly in my back.

I'd wanted the Goddess and the God to move

among us again – all of us had wanted that. But I was beginning to realize that when the gods move, you either get out of the way or get swept along for the ride. I wasn't sure getting out of the way was an option for me.

I caught the faintest scent of apple blossoms, a small ... what? Warning, reassurance? The fact that I wasn't sure if it was a warning of danger or a spiritual embrace pretty much summed up my feelings about being the Goddess's instrument: Be careful what you wish for.

I looked at Sholto, with his wound seeping blood onto his bandages. He and I had both wanted to belong, truly belong, to the sidhe. To be honored and accepted among them. Look where it had gotten us.

I held my hand out to him, and he took it. He took it, and squeezed it tight. Even in all this horror and death, I felt in that one touch how much it meant to him to touch me at all. Somehow, the fact that he still wanted me so much made it all the worse.

'I tried to share life with you, Meredith, but I am King of the Sluagh, and death is all I have to offer.'

I squeezed his hand. 'We are both sidhe, Sholto, and that is a thing of life. We are Unseelie sidhe, and that is a thing of death, but Rhys reminded me what I'd forgotten.'

'What had you forgotten?'

'That the deities among us who brought death also once brought life. We are not meant to be split apart like this. We are not light and dark, evil and good; we are both and neither. We have all forgotten what we are.'

'What I am in this moment,' said Sholto, 'is a man who is about to slay a woman who was my lover, and my friend. I can think of nothing beyond this moment – as if when she dies at my hand, I will die with her.'

I shook my head. 'You won't die, but you may wish you could, for a moment.'

'Only for a moment?' he asked.

'Life is a selfish thing,' I said. 'If you pass through the sorrow, outrun the horror, you will begin to want to live again. You will be glad you didn't die.'

He swallowed hard enough for me to hear it. 'I don't want to pass through this.'

'I'll help you.'

He almost smiled, and it was like a ghost flitting across his face. 'I think you've helped enough.' With that he let go of my hand and eased himself over the edge, using his good hand to keep himself from sliding through the bones.

I didn't look back at anyone. I just eased myself over the edge and followed. Looking back wouldn't make me feel better. Looking back would simply make me want to ask for help. Some things you have to do yourself. Sometimes what it means to lead is simply that you can't ask for help.

I found that the bones weren't sharp on every point – it was mostly the spines on the tops that were vicious. I grasped softer, rounder-looking bones, using them as handholds. It took all my concentration to get down to the water without losing my grip or cutting my hand.

The water was surprisingly warm, like bathwater. The soil underneath it was soft, and mushy, silt rather than mud. The footing was uncertain, and again I let myself sink into concentration on the task at hand. I focused on finding footing, avoiding anything that felt like a bone. I did not want to think about what I was about to do.

Segna had tried to kill me twice now, but I couldn't hate her. It would have been so much easier if I could have hated her.

Chapter 13

IF I HADN'T BEEN AFRAID OF GETTING STABBED ON THE bones, I would have swum out to where Sholto and Agnes stood holding Segna. The other two guards, Ivar and Fyfe, were still in the water, still close, but not holding the fallen woman. The water reached to my shoulders, stinging in the claw marks that Segna had made on me, and plenty deep enough to swim in, if it hadn't hidden those bones beneath its surface. My blood trailed into the black water, lost.

Sholto was cradling Segna's head and upper body as well as he could with only one good arm. Agnes was still beside him, helping hold her sister hag above the water. I stumbled on the soft bottom and went under. I came up sputtering.

Agnes's voice came clear to me as she said to Sholto, 'How can you want that weak thing? How can that be what you want?'

I heard earth sliding, water moving. I turned to find Doyle and Frost in the water, wading toward me.

Agnes yelled, 'It is her kill or she will never be queen.'

'We do not come to kill for her,' Doyle said.

Frost said, 'We come to guard her, as your king's guard protects him.' His face was an arrogant mask. His pale, expensive suit soaked up the dirty water. His long silver hair trailed in the water. Somehow, he seemed more dirtied by the water than anyone else, as if it spoiled his white-and-silver beauty more grievously.

Doyle's blackness just seemed to melt into the water. The fact that his long braid trailed in the water didn't bother him. The only thing he worried about keeping clean was his gun. Modern guns shoot just fine wet, but he'd begun using firearms when dry powder meant life or death, and old habits die hard.

I waited for them to reach me, because I wanted the comfort of their presence while I did this. What I really wanted to do was fall into their arms and start screaming. I didn't want to kill anymore – I wanted life for my people. I wanted to bring life back to faerie, not death. Not death.

I waited, and let their hands give me solace. Let them lift me above the soft, treacherous bottom and guide me through the water. I didn't collapse against them, but I let myself take courage from the strength of their hands.

A bone brushed my leg. 'Bone,' I said.

'A ridge of bone, by the feel of it,' Doyle said.

'Are you hoping Segna dies before you get here?' Agnes asked, voice derisive. The tears shining on her face made me discount the tone. She was losing someone she had lived with, fought beside, loved, for centuries. She'd hated me before this; now she'd hate me even more. I did not want her as my enemy, but it seemed as if no matter what I did, I couldn't avoid it.

'I'm trying not to share her fate,' I said.

'I hope you do,' Agnes said.

Sholto, tears plain on his face, looked at her. 'If you ever raise a hand to Meredith again, I will be done with you.'

Agnes stared at him, searched his face, as she held Segna's body. She stared into the face of the man she loved. Whatever she saw there made her bow her head. 'I will do as my king bids.' The words were bitter; it seemed to tighten my own throat just to hear them. They must have burned in Agnes's throat.

'Swear it,' Sholto said.

'What oath would you have of me?' she asked, head still bowed.

'The oath that Meredith gave, that will do.'

She shivered, and it wasn't from cold. 'I swear

by the darkness that eats all things that I will not harm the princess here and now.'

'No,' Sholto said, 'swear that you will never harm her.'

She bowed lower, dry black hair trailing into the water. 'I cannot make that oath, my king.'

'Why can you not?'

'Because I mean her harm.'

'You will not swear to never hurt her?' He sounded surprised.

'I will not; cannot.'

Ivar of the bird voice said, 'May I suggest, Your Highness, that she swear the oath to not harm the princess now, so we can all move about freely. We can deal with her treachery later, once we've dealt with the urgencies of the present moment.'

Sholto clutched Segna to him, and her yellowed hands with their broken claws grasped at him. 'You are right,' he said. He looked at Agnes, who was still bent over the water and Segna's body. 'Make what oath you will, Agnes.'

She straightened up, the water streaming from her hair. 'I swear by the darkness that eats all things that I will not harm the princess in this moment.'

'May I suggest something, King Sholto?' Doyle asked.

'Yes,' Sholto answered, though his eyes were on the dying woman in his arms.

'Black Agnes should add to her oath that she will

not harm the princess while we are here in your garden.'

Sholto just nodded and whispered, 'Do as he says, Agnes.'

'Do the sidhe guards give orders to our king now?' she said.

'Do it, Agnes!' he screamed at her, and the scream ended in a sob. He folded his body over Segna and wept openly.

She glared at me, not Doyle, while she spoke, and each word seemed dragged out of her. 'I swear by the darkness that eats all things that I will not harm the princess while we stand in the dead gardens.'

'I think that is as good as we get from her,' Frost said, voice low.

Doyle nodded. 'Aye.'

They both looked at me, as if they knew this was a bad idea. I addressed their look aloud. 'There's no way around this, only through it. We have to live through this moment to get to the next.'

Sholto raised his face enough to say, 'Segna will not live through this moment.'

He hadn't been this upset in Los Angeles when I'd done something much more horrible to Nerys the Grey, his other hag. I didn't point this out, but I couldn't help noting it. They had both been his lovers – but then again, I knew better than most that you don't feel for your lovers all the same.

Segna meant something to him, and Nerys had not. Simple, painful, true.

I looked past the dying hag to Black Agnes, who watched Sholto intently. I realized in that moment that she didn't just weep for Segna's death, but like me remembered that he hadn't wept for Nerys. Was she wondering if he would weep for her? Or did she already know that he had loved Segna more? I wasn't sure, but I could tell it was a raw and painful thought that cut across her features. She stared at the weeping king, and her thoughts carved loss across her face. She would not come out of this night's work simply mourning Segna.

She seemed to feel the weight of my gaze, because she turned. She looked at me, the grief in her face changing into a fine, burning hatred. I saw my death in her eyes. Agnes would kill me, if she could.

Doyle's hand tightened on my arm. Frost stepped over the bones in front of us, hidden by the water, and put his broad shoulders in the way of Agnes's look, as if her look alone could somehow hurt me. That time was past. But there would be more nights, and more ways of making one mortal princess dead.

'She has given her oath,' Sholto said in a choked voice. 'It is all we can do tonight.' That last was some acknowledgment that he saw what we saw in Agnes's face. I'd liked to have believed that he could keep a tight enough rein on the hag, but her look said there would not be a leash of honor, or love, stronger than her hate.

I didn't want to kill Segna, didn't want to end her life while Sholto wept for her. And now I knew that I must also kill Agnes or she'd see me dead. I might not do the deed myself, and it might not happen today, but I would have to call for her death. She was too dangerous, too well placed among the sluagh to be allowed to live.

As I let the thought come all the way up to the front of my mind, I didn't know whether to laugh, or weep. I didn't want to kill one hag, and had hated killing the first, yet I was already planning the death of the third.

Frost and Doyle lifted me over the hidden ridge of bones. They half floated me to Sholto, where he cried over the hag. They tried to let me go, but I sank to my chin when they released me. They grabbed me in the same moment, both fishing me higher above the black water.

'She must stand on her own two feet for this kill,' Agnes said, her voice holding some of the deadly heat of her look.

'I don't know if I'm tall enough,' I said.

'I have to agree with the hag,' Fyfe said. 'The princess must stand on her own for the kill to be hers.'

Frost and Doyle exchanged glances, still holding me between them. 'Let me down slowly,' I said. 'I think I can touch bottom.'

They did what I asked. If I kept my chin pointed up, I could just barely keep the dirty water out of my mouth.

'We have no weapons with us that will kill the immortal,' Doyle said.

'Nor we,' Ivar said.

Sholto looked at me, his face raw with grief, and I fought to meet that look. He moved, and a tiny wave slapped my face. I began treading water, so I could keep my head above the surface. As I did so, my leg brushed something – I thought it was a bone, but it moved. It was Segna's arm, limp in the water. My leg brushed it again, and the arm convulsed.

'The bones are a killing thing,' I said.

Then Segna said in a rattling voice, thick with things that should never be in the throat of the living, 'Kiss me one . . . last . . . time.'

Sholto leaned over her with a sob.

Ivar moved everyone back to give us room. He made certain that Agnes moved back, too, which meant that Segna's body began to sink below the water. I moved forward, tried to help catch her, as I treaded water. I got a hand on her body, felt the weight of her cloak wrap around my legs. I felt her tense a heartbeat before her arm, which was behind me now, swept forward. I had time to turn and put both hands on her arm, to keep the claws from my side.

'Merry!' Doyle yelled.

I had time to see her other arm sweeping up behind me. I let go of the arm I was already fending off, and tried to sweep the second arm away from me. Segna's body rolled under the water, and took me with her.

Chapter 14

I HAD TIME TO TAKE A BREATH, THEN WE WERE UNDER-water. Segna's face loomed under the dirty water. Her mouth opened, screaming at me, blood blossoming from her mouth. My hands dug desperately into her arms, too small to encircle them, as I forced them away from me and she dragged me deeper into the water.

Too late I realized that there were other ways to kill me than claws – she was trying to impale me on submerged bone. I kicked my feet to stay above the bone, to not let her spit me upon it. The point of bone held me on its tip, and I kicked and pushed to keep it from piercing my skin. Segna pushed and fought against me. The strength in her arms and body was almost too much for me. She was wounded, dying, and it was all I could do to keep her from killing me.

My chest was tight; I needed to breathe. Claws, bones, and even the water itself could kill. If I couldn't push her off me, all she had to do was simply hold me underwater.

I prayed, 'Goddess help me!'

A pale hand shone in the water, and Segna was pulled backward, my grip on her arms pulling me with her. We broke the surface together, both of us gasping for breath. Her breath ended in a spattering cough that covered my face in her blood. For a moment I couldn't see who had pulled her back. I had to blink her blood out of my eyes to see Sholto with his arm across her upper body. He held her one-armed and yelled, 'Get out, Meredith, get out!'

I did what he said: I let her go and pushed backward, trusting that there were no bones just behind me.

Segna didn't try to catch me. She used her newly freed hands to claw down Sholto's arm, making a crimson ruin of his white flesh.

I treaded water, looking around for Doyle and Frost, and the others. There were no others. I was paddling in a lake – a deep, cold lake – no longer the shallow, stagnant pool we'd been wading in before. There was a small island close at hand, but the shore was far away, and it was not a shore I knew. I screamed, 'Doyle!' But there was no answer. In truth, I hadn't expected one, for I could already see that we were either in a vision, or somewhere else in faerie. I didn't know which, and I didn't know where.

Sholto cried out behind me. I turned in time to see him go under in a wash of red. Segna struck at the water where he'd vanished with the dagger from her belt. Did she realize it was him she attacked now, or did she still think she was killing me?

I screamed, 'Segna!'

The sound seemed to reach her, because she hesitated. She turned in the water and blinked at me.

I pushed myself high enough out of the water so she could see me. Sholto had not yet resurfaced.

Segna screamed at me, the sound ending in a wet cough. Blood poured down her chin, but she started moving toward me.

I screamed, 'Sholto!' hoping Segna would realize what she'd done and turn back to rescue him. But she kept swimming, weakly, toward me.

'He is only white flesh now,' she growled, in that too thick, too wet voice. 'He is only sidhe, not sluagh.'

So much for her helping Sholto – obviously it was up to me. I took a good breath and dived. The water was clearer here, and I saw Sholto like a pale shadow sinking toward the bottom, blood trailing upward in a cloud.

I screamed his name, and the sound echoed

through the water. His body jerked, and just then something grabbed my hair and yanked me upward.

Segna pulled me through the water. I could see that she was making for the bare island. My naked back hit the rocks, scraped along them, as she struggled from the lake. She pulled me with her, until both of us were free of the water. She lay panting on the rock, her hand still tangled in my hair. I tried to ease away from that hand, but it convulsed tighter, wrenching my hair as if she meant to take it out by the roots. She started dragging me closer to where she lay.

I fought to get up on all fours so she wouldn't scrape more of my skin off on the bare rock. In order to do so, I had to take my gaze off her for an instant.

It was a mistake. She jerked me down with that strength that could have torn a horse apart. Jerked me down, onto my stomach. I wedged an arm under my body to keep me off the rocks.

Then I saw that she still held the dagger. She pressed it to my cheek. I gazed at her along the line of the blade. She was lying down, almost flat against the rocks.

'I'll scar you,' she said. 'Ruin that pretty face.'

'Sholto is drowning.'

'The sluagh cannot die by water. If he is sidhe enough to drown, then let him.'

'He loves you,' I said.

202

She made a harsh sound that spattered her chin with more blood. 'Not as much as he loves the thought of sidhe flesh in his bed.'

I couldn't argue with that.

The tip of her blade wavered above my cheek. 'How much sidhe are you? How well do you heal?'

I thought it was a rhetorical question, so I didn't answer it. Would she die of her wounds before she hurt me, or would she heal?

She coughed blood onto the stones, and it was as if she wondered the same thing. She used her grip on my hair to force me onto my back, dragging me closer as she did it. I couldn't stop her – I could not fight against such strength. She crawled on top of me and put her blade tip over my throat. I grabbed her hand, wrapped both my hands around it, and still trembled with the effort to hold her off me.

'So weak,' she gasped above me. 'Why do we follow the sidhe? If I were not dying, you could not hold me off.'

My voice came out tight with strain as I said, 'I'm only part sidhe.'

'But you're sidhe enough for him to want you,' she growled. 'Glow for me, sidhe! Show me that precious Seelie magic. Show me the magic that makes us follow the sidhe.'

Her words were fatal. She was right. I had magic. Magic that no one else had. I called my hand of blood. As I summoned it, I tried not to think about the fact that I could have done it sooner – before she hurt Sholto.

I wielded the hand of blood. I could have made her bleed out from just a tiny cut, and these were not tiny cuts. I started to glow under the press of her body. My body shone through the blood she was dripping on me. I whispered, 'Not Seelie magic, Segna, *Unseelie* magic. Bleed for me.'

She didn't understand at first. She kept trying to shove the blade into my throat, and I kept holding her just off me. She dug her hand into my hair so that her claws raked my scalp, bloodied me. I called blood, and her wounds gushed.

The blood poured over me, hot – hotter than my own skin. I turned my head away to keep my eyes clear of it. My hands grew slippery with her blood, and I was afraid that her knife would slip past my defenses before I could bleed her out. So much blood; it poured and poured and poured. Could a night-hag bleed to death? Could they even be killed this way? I didn't know, I just didn't know.

The tip of her knife pierced my skin like a sharp bite. My arms were shaking with the effort to keep her off me. I screamed, 'Bleed for me!' I spat her blood out of my mouth, and still her knife wormed another fraction into my throat. Barely, barely below the skin – I wasn't hurt yet, but I would be soon.

Then her hand hesitated, pulled backward. I blinked up at her through a mask of her own blood. Her eyes were wide and startled. There was a white spear sticking out through her throat.

Sholto stood above her, bandages gone, his wound bare to the air, both hands gripping the spear. He pulled the spear out with a wrenching motion. A fountain of blood spilled out of her neck. I whispered, 'Bleed.' She collapsed in a pool of crimson, the knife still clasped in her hand.

Sholto stood over her and drove the white spear into her back. She spasmed underneath him, her mouth opening and closing, hands and feet scrabbling at the bare rock.

Only when she stopped moving completely did he take the spear out. He stood swaying, but used the tip to send her dagger spinning into the lake. Then he collapsed to his knees beside her, leaning on the spear like a crutch.

By the time I staggered to him, I wasn't glowing. I was tired, and hurt, and covered in my enemy's blood. I fell to my knees beside him on the bloody rock, and I touched his shoulder, as if I wasn't sure he was real. 'I saw you drown,' I said.

He seemed to have trouble focusing on me, but said, 'I am sidhe and sluagh. We cannot die by drowning.' He coughed hard enough that he doubled over, throwing up water onto the rock, as he clung to the white shaft of the spear. 'But it hurts as if it were death.'

I embraced him, and he winced, covered in wounds new and old. I held him more carefully, clinging to him, covering his upper body in Segna's blood.

His voice came rough with coughing. 'I'm holding the spear of bone. It was one of the signs of kingship once for my people.'

'Where did it come from?' I asked.

'It was in the bottom of the lake, waiting for me.'

'Where are we?' I asked.

'It's the Island of Bones. It used to be in the middle of our garden, but it has become the stuff of legend.'

I touched what I'd thought was rock, and found he was right. It was rock, but the rock had once been bone. The island was made up of fossils. 'It feels awfully solid for a legend,' I said.

He managed a smile. 'What in the name of Danu is going on, Meredith? What is happening?'

I smelled roses, thick and sweet.

He raised his head, looked around him. 'I smell herbs.'

'I smell roses,' I said, softly.

He looked at me. 'What is happening, Meredith? How did we get here?'

'I prayed.'

He frowned at me. 'I don't understand.'

The smell of roses grew thicker, as if I were standing in a summer meadow. A chalice appeared in my hand, where it lay against Sholto's naked back.

He startled away from the touch of it as if it had burned him. He tried to turn too quickly, and it must have pained the open wound on his stomach, for he winced, sucking in his breath sharply. He fell back onto his side, the spear still gripped in one hand.

I held up the gold-and-silver cup so that it caught the light. It was really only then that it sank in that there was light here. It was sunlight, glinting on the cup, and warm on my skin.

For my life, I couldn't remember if there had been sun a moment ago. I might have asked Sholto, but he was focused on what was in my hand, and whispered, 'It can't be what I think it is.'

'It is the chalice.'

He gave a small shake of his head. 'How?'

'I dreamt of it, as I dreamt of Abeloec's horn cup, and when I woke it was beside me.'

He leaned heavily on the spear, and reached toward the shining cup. I held it out toward him, but his fingers stopped just short of it, as if he feared to touch it.

His reluctance reminded me that things could happen if I touched one of the men with the chalice. But weren't we in vision? And if so, would that hold true? I looked at Segna's body, felt her blood drying on my skin. Was this vision, or was it real?

'And is not vision real?' came a woman's voice.

'Who said that?' Sholto asked.

A figure appeared. She was hidden completely behind the grey of a hooded cloak. She stood in the clear sunlight, but it was like looking at a shadow – a shadow with nothing to give it form.

'Do not fear the touch of the Goddess,' the figure said.

'Who are you?' Sholto whispered.

'Who do you think I am?' came the voice. In the past, she had always either appeared more solid or been only a voice, a scent on the wind.

Sholto licked his lips and whispered, 'Goddess.'

My hand rose of its own accord. I held the chalice out to him, but it was as if someone else were moving my hand. 'Touch the chalice,' I whispered.

He kept his grip on the spear, leaning on it, as he stretched out his other hand. 'What will happen when I touch it?'

'I don't know,' I said.

'Then why do you want me to do it?'

'She wants you to,' I said.

He hesitated again with his fingers just above the shining surface. The Goddess's voice breathed around us with the scent of summer roses: 'Choose.'

Sholto took in a sharp breath and blew it out, like a sprinter, then touched the gold of the cup. I smelled herbs, as if I had brushed against a border of thyme and lavender around my roses. A black-cloaked figure appeared beside the grey. Taller, broader of shoulders, and somehow – even shrouded by the cloak – male. As the cloak could not hide the Goddess's femininity, so the cloak could not hide the God's masculinity.

Sholto's hand wrapped around the chalice, covering my hand with his, so that we both held the cup.

The voice came deep, and rich, and ever changing. I knew the voice of the God, always male, but never the same. 'You have spilled your blood, risked your lives, killed on this ground,' he intoned. That dark hood turned toward Sholto, and for a moment I thought I saw a chin, lips, but they changed even as I saw them. It was dizzying. 'What would you give to bring life back to your people, Sholto?'

'Anything,' he whispered.

'Be careful what you offer,' the Goddess said, and her voice, too, was every woman's, and none.

'I would give my life to save my people,' Sholto said.

'I do not wish to take it,' I responded, because the Goddess had offered me a similar choice once. Amatheon had bared his neck for a blade, so that life could return to the land of faerie. I had refused, because there were other ways to give life to the land. I was descended from fertility deities, and I knew well that blood was not the only thing that made the grass grow.

'This is not your choice,' she said to me. Was there a note of sorrow in her voice?

A dagger appeared in the air in front of Sholto. Its hilt and blade were all white, and gleamed oddly in the light. Sholto's hand left the chalice and grabbed for the knife, almost by reflex. 'The hilt is bone. It is the match to the spear,' Sholto said, and there was soft wonder in his voice as he gazed at the dagger.

'Do you remember what the dagger was used for?' said the God.

'It was used to slay the old king. To spill his blood on this island,' Sholto replied obediently.

'Why?' the God asked.

'This dagger is the heart of the sluagh, or was once.'

'What does a heart need?'

'Blood, and lives,' Sholto answered, as if he were taking a test.

'You spilled blood and life on the island, but it is not alive.'

Sholto shook his head. 'Segna was not a suitable sacrifice for this place. It needs a king's blood.' He held the knife out toward the God's shadowy figure. 'Spill my blood, take my life, bring the heart of the sluagh back to life.'

'You are the king, Sholto. If you die, who will

take back the spear, and bring the power back to your people?'

I knelt there, the blood growing tacky on my skin. I cradled the chalice in my hands, and had a bad feeling that I knew where this talk was going.

Sholto lowered the knife and asked, 'What do you want of me, Lord?'

The figure pointed at me. 'There is royal blood to spill. Do it, and the heart of the sluagh will live once more.'

Sholto stared at me, the look on his face full of shock. I wondered if my face had looked that way when the choice had been mine. 'You mean for me to kill Meredith?'

'She is royal blood, a fit sacrifice for this place.'

'No,' Sholto said.

'You said you would do anything,' the Goddess said.

'I can offer my life, but I cannot offer hers,' Sholto said. 'It isn't mine to give.' His hand was mottled with the force of his grip on the hilt of the knife.

'You are king,' the God said.

'A king tends his people, he doesn't butcher them.'

'You would condemn your people to a slow death for the life of one woman?'

Emotions chased over Sholto's face, but finally he dropped the knife on the rock. It rang as if it were the hardest metal rather than bone. 'I cannot, will not harm Meredith.'

'Why will you not?'

'She is not sluagh. She should not have to die to bring us back to life. It is not her place.'

'If she wishes to be queen over all of faerie, then she will be sluagh.'

'Then let her be queen. If she dies here, she will not be queen, and that will leave us with only Cel. I would bring life back to the sluagh and destroy all of faerie in one blow. She holds the chalice. The chalice, my lord. The chalice after all these years is returned. I do not understand how you can ask me to destroy the only hope we have.'

'Is she your hope, Sholto?' the God asked.

'Yes,' he whispered. There was so much emotion in that one word.

The dark figure looked at the grey. The Goddess spoke. 'There is no fear in you, Meredith. Why not?'

I tried to put it into words. 'Sholto is right, my lady. The chalice has returned to us, and magic is returning to the sidhe. You use my body as your vessel. I do not think you would waste all that on one bloody sacrifice.' I glanced at Sholto. 'And I have felt his hand in mine. I have felt his desire for me. I think it would destroy something in him to kill me. I do not believe my God and Goddess so heartless as that.'

'Does he love you then, Meredith?'

'I do not know, but he loves the idea of holding me in his arms. That I know.'

'Do you love this woman, Sholto?' the God asked.

Sholto opened his mouth, closed it, then said, 'It is not a gentleman's place to answer such questions in front of a lady.'

'This is a place for truth, Sholto.'

'It's all right, Sholto,' I said. 'Answer true. I won't hold it against you.'

'That's what I'm afraid of,' he said softly.

The look on his face made me laugh. The laughter echoed on the air like the song of birds.

'Joy will suffice to bring this place back to life,' the Goddess said.

'If you bring life to this place with joy, then you will change the very heart of the sluagh. Do you understand that, Sholto?' the God said.

'Not exactly.'

'The heart of the sluagh is based on death, blood, combat, and terror. Laughter, joy, and life will make a different heart for the sluagh.'

'I am sorry, my lord, but I do not understand.'

'Meredith,' the Goddess said, 'explain it to him.' The Goddess was beginning to fade, like a dream as dawn's light steals through the window.

'I do not understand,' Sholto said.

'You are sluagh and Unseelie sidhe,' the God said; 'you are a creature of terror and darkness. It is what you are, but it is not all you are.' With that, the dark shape began to fade, too.

Sholto reached out to him. 'Wait, I don't understand.'

The God and Goddess vanished, as if they'd never been, and the sunlight dimmed with them. We were left in gloom. It was the twilight of the underground of faerie these days – not the aberration of the momentous sunlight that had bathed us moments ago.

Sholto yelled, 'My God, wait!'

'Sholto,' I said. I had to say it twice more before he looked at me.

His face was stricken. 'I don't know what they want from me. What am I to do? How do I bring the heart of my people back with joy?'

I smiled at him, the mask of blood cracking with it. I had to clean off this mess. 'Oh, Sholto, you get your wish.'

'My wish? What wish?'

'Let me clean off some of this blood beforehand.'

'Before what?'

I touched his arm. 'Sex, Sholto, they meant sex.'

'What?' The look on his face, so astonished, made me laugh again. The sound echoed across the lake, and again I thought I heard birdsong.

'Did you hear that?'

'I heard your laughter, like music.'

'This place is ready to come back to life, Sholto, but if we use laughter and joy and sex to make it happen, then it will be a different place than it was before. Do you understand that?'

'I'm not sure. We are going to have sex here, now?'

'Yes. Let me wash off some of the blood, and then yes.' I wasn't sure he'd heard anything else I'd said. 'Have you seen the new garden outside the throne room doors in the Unseelie sithen?'

He seemed to have to fight to concentrate, but finally he nodded. 'It's a meadow with a stream now, not the torture area the queen had made of it.'

'Exactly,' I said. 'It was a place of pain and now it's a meadow with butterflies and bunnies. I'm part Seelie Court, Sholto, do you understand what I'm saying? That part of me will impact the magic we do here and now.'

'What magic will we perform here and now?' he asked, smiling. He was still leaning heavily on the spear, the raw wound of what the Seelie had done to him bare to the air. I'd had enough of my own injuries to know that just the touch of air hurt when the skin was abraded. The bone knife lay next to Sholto's knees. Truthfully, I'd thought it might vanish when the God and Goddess went – for he had refused to use it for its true purpose. Nevertheless, Sholto was still surrounded by major relics of the sluagh. He'd been visited by deity. We knelt in a place of legend, with the possibility of bringing his people to a rebirth of their powers. And all he seemed to be able to think of was the fact that we might be having sex.

I looked in his face. I tried to see past the almost shy anticipation there. He seemed afraid to be too eager. He was a good king, yet the promise of sex with another sidhe had chased all the cautions from his mind. I could not allow him to leap in, though, until I was sure he understood what might happen to his people. He had to understand or . . . or what?

'Sholto,' I said.

He reached out to me. I took his hand to keep him from touching my face. 'I need you to hear me, Sholto, to truly hear me.'

'I will listen to anything you say.'

He was willing to follow my lead. I'd noticed that about him in L.A. – that the dominant, frightening king of the sluagh became submissive in intimate situations. Had Black Agnes taught him that, or Segna? Or was he just wired that way?

I patted his hand, more friendly than sexual. 'What I bring to sex magic is meadows and butterflies. Some of the corridors in the Unseelie mound are turning to white marble with veins of gold.'

His face became a little more serious, less amused. 'Yes, the queen was most upset,' he said. 'She accused you of remaking her sithen in the image of the Seelie Court.'

'Exactly,' I said.

His eyes widened.

'I didn't do it on purpose,' I said. 'I don't control what the energy does with the sithen. Sex magic isn't like other magicks – it's wilder, and has more a mind of its own.'

'The sluagh are wild magic, Meredith.'

'Yes, but wild sluagh and wild Seelie magic aren't the same.'

He turned my hand palm-up. 'You bear the hand of flesh and the hand of blood. Those are not Seelie powers.'

'No. In combat I seem to be all Unseelie, but in sex magic it is the Seelie in my blood that comes out. Do you understand what that might mean for your sluagh?'

All the light seemed to drain from his face, so somber now. 'If we have sex, and the sluagh are reborn, you might remake the sluagh in your image.'

'Yes,' I said.

He stared at my hand as if he'd never seen it before. 'If I had taken your life, then the sluagh would have remained what they are: a terrible darkness to sweep all before us. If we use sex to bring life back to my people, then they may become more like the sidhe, or even the *Seelie* sidhe.'

'Yes,' I said, 'yes.' I was relieved that he finally understood.

'Would it be so terrible if we were more sidhe?'

He almost whispered it, as if he spoke to himself.

'You are their king, Sholto. Only you can make this choice for your people.'

'They would hate me for making this choice.' He stared at me. 'But what other choice is there? I will not spill your life away, not even to bring life back to all of my kingdom.' He closed his eyes and let go of my hand. He began to glow, soft, and white like the moon rising through his skin. He opened his eyes, and the triple gold of his irises gleamed. He traced a glowing fingertip across the palm of my hand, and it drew a line of cold white fire across my skin. I shuddered from that small touch.

He smiled. 'I am sidhe, Meredith. I understand that now. I am sluagh, too, but I am also sidhe. I want to be sidhe, Meredith. I want to be fully sidhe. I want to know what it feels like to be what I am.'

I drew my hand back from him, so I could think without the press of his power against my skin. 'You are king here. You must make this choice.' My voice was a little hoarse.

'It is no choice,' he said. 'You dead, and lost to all of faerie – or you in my arms? It is no choice.' He laughed then, and his laughter, too, echoed across the lake. I heard chimes, or birds, or both. 'Besides, Darkness and Frost would kill me if I took you as a sacrifice.'

'They would not slay the king of the sluagh and bring war to faerie,' I said.

'If you truly believe that their loyalties are still to faerie rather than to you alone, then you do not see their eyes when they look at you. Their vengeance would be terrible, Meredith. The fact that there are still assassination attempts against you only shows that some of the sidhe do not yet understand how short-leashed the queen has kept Darkness and Frost. Especially Darkness,' he said, his voice going low. His face looked haunted. He shook the thought away and looked back at me. 'I have seen the Darkness hunt. If Hell Hounds, Yeth Hounds, still existed among us, they would belong to the sluagh, to the wild hunt, and the blood of that wild hunt still runs through Doyle's veins, Meredith.'

'So you do not kill me for fear of Doyle and Frost?'

He looked at me, and for a moment let the veil drop from those glowing eyes. He let me see his need, such need, as if it should have been carved in letters across the air. 'It is not fear that impels me to spare your life,' he whispered.

I gave him a smile, and the chalice still gripped in my hand pulsed once against my skin. The chalice would be part of what we did. 'Let me wash some of this blood away. Then I will put my glow against yours.'

His own glow began to fade a little, his burning eyes cooling to as normal as they ever got. It was hard to call his triple-gold irises normal, even by sidhe standards, though. 'I am hurt, Meredith. I would have had our first time together be perfect. I'm not certain how much good I'm going to be to you tonight.'

'I'm hurt, too,' I said, 'but we'll both do our best.' I stood up and found my body stiff with injuries I hadn't even realized I'd suffered – small wounds that I must have received in the fight.

'I will not be able to make love the way you wish it,' he said.

'How do you know what I wish?' I asked as I made my way slowly across the rough and smooth of the rock.

'You had quite an audience for Mistral's turn with you. The rumors have grown, but if even part of it is true, I will not be able to dominate you as he did.'

I slid into the water. It found every small cut and scrape. The water was cool and soothing, but at the same time it made the wounds burn. 'I don't want to be dominated right now, Sholto. Make love to me – let it be gentle between us, if that is what we want.'

He laughed again, and I heard bells. 'I think gentle is all I'm capable of tonight.'

'I do not always want rough, Sholto. My tastes are more varied than that.' I was shoulder-deep in the water now, trying to get the blood off me. The blood began to dissolve in the water, washing away almost more easily than it should have.

'How varied are your tastes?' he asked.

I smiled at him. 'Very.' I dunked under the water in a bid to get the blood off my face, out of my hair. I came up gasping, wiping the runnels of pinkish water from my face. I went under two more times until the water ran clear.

Sholto was at the edge of the island when I came up the last time. He was standing, using the spear like a crutch. The white knife was tucked carefully through the cloth of his pants, the way you'd stick a pin through: in, then out, so the point was exposed to the air. He offered me his hand. I took it, though I could have gotten out by myself, and I knew that bending over must hurt him.

He lifted me out of the water, but his eyes never got to my face. His gaze stayed on my body, my breasts, as the water ran down them. There are women who would have taken offense, but I wasn't one of them. In that moment he wasn't a king, he was a man – and that was just fine with me.

Chapter 15

SHOLTO LAY NAKED BEFORE ME. I'D NEVER SEEN HIM like that, lying naked, and waiting, knowing that we didn't have to stop.

The first and only time I'd seen him completely nude he'd still had extras. But he had used his own personal magic then to make his stomach look like the perfect six-pack abs. Even to the touch, I hadn't been able to feel what I'd known was there. He was very good at personal glamour, but then he'd spent years hiding that bit of deformity.

Now he lay back, using his own pants as some small cushion against the stone. The Seelie had skinned him from just below his ribs to just above his groin. I'd seen the wound, but now it loomed larger. The pain must have been a fearsome thing.

He had laid the white spear and the bone knife to one side of him. I had set the chalice on the other side of him. We would make love between the chalice, symbol of the Goddess, and two symbols that were oh, so masculine.

The air above his body wavered, like heat off a road, and the next moment there was no wound. He was back to creating the illusion of that perfect six-pack. Of all my lovers, only Rhys had it for real. 'You don't need to hide, Sholto,' I said.

'The look on your face is not the look I want to see the first time we make love, Meredith.'

'Take the glamour away, Sholto, let me truly see you.'

'It is no more beautiful than what used to be there.' His voice was sad.

I touched the smooth skin of his shoulder. 'You were beautiful. You are beautiful.'

He gave me a smile as sad as his tone. 'Meredith, no lies, please.'

I studied his face. He was as fair of face as Frost, who was one of the most perfect men I'd ever seen. I said out loud, 'The queen once called you the most perfect sidhe body she had ever seen. You are wounded, you will heal; it has not changed the perfection of you.'

'The queen said that it was a pity that one of the most perfect sidhe bodies she'd ever seen was ruined by such deformity.'

Okay, maybe mentioning the queen's words hadn't been a good idea. I tried again. I crawled to his face and leaned over to touch his lips with mine. But it was a cold kiss, and he barely responded. I drew back. 'What is wrong?'

'In Los Angeles, even the sight of you clothed hardened my body. Tonight I am weak.'

I gazed down the long length of his body to find that he was still soft, and as small as he got. He was one of those men that wasn't truly small even when soft; a shower, not a grower.

I had magic in me that could bring a man to life, as it were, but it was Seelie magic. I wanted to use less Seelie magic in this union, not more. Although Sholto had made the decision to accept the risk, I feared for the sluagh. I feared them losing their identity as a people.

Of course, there were other ways to bring a man to life besides magic.

I crawled, carefully, on the bare rocks, until I knelt by his hip. 'You aren't weak, Sholto, you're hurt. There is no shame in that.'

'To see you nude and not to react is shameful.'

I gave him the smile he needed and said, 'I think we can fix that.'

'Magic?' he said, staring down his body at me.

I shook my head. 'No magic, Sholto, just this.' I traced my hand over his thighs, reveling in the smooth skin. The fey didn't have much body hair, but I think the fact that he was part nightflyer – a creature that had no hair – made him utterly smooth. Smooth as a woman and so soft, yet terribly male from the bottoms of his feet to the top of his head. I traced along the inside of his thighs and he spread them for me, so that I could sweep upward and touch the silken skin between his legs. He was still soft and loose as I rolled those delicate balls in my hand.

The touch bowed his spine, sending his head back, eyes closed. But with the pleasure came a sound of pain. The movement had hurt the butchered skin across the middle of his body. What progress I'd made wilted in the face of such pain.

He threw his arm across his eyes and made a sound between a sob and a yell. 'I will be useless to you tonight, Meredith. I will be useless to my people. I will not bring us back to life with death, and I cannot bring us back with life.'

'I would wait until you were healed, Sholto, if I could. But this night is about bringing life back to faerie. Console yourself – we will have other nights, or days. Other times, after you are healed, to do what we want to do. Tonight, we do what we must.'

He uncovered his eyes and gazed down at me. His face held such despair.

'I can't think of any intercourse position that isn't going to hurt you, and you don't like pain,' I said.

'I did not say I did not like pain, but not this much.'

I stored that away for future reference. 'I know.

There are limits for most of us beyond which pain is just pain.'

'I am sorry, Meredith, but I fear I have reached that point with these wounds.'

'We'll see,' I said. I leaned back over his body until I could kiss the front of him. I drew him, gently, into my mouth. The only other time I'd had him in my mouth he had been long and hard, and eager. Tonight his body was quiet, loose, and still.

At first, I was almost impatient, but I let that go. This was not a moment for impatience, or hurrying – this was Sholto's first time with another sidhe. This was one of his most treasured dreams, and he was coming to it hurt, and not at his best. He'd probably fantasized this moment, and now none of his fantasies was coming true. Reality was a harsher mistress than imagination.

I let go of the impatience. I stopped wondering what Doyle and Frost and the others must be thinking. I let go the thought that my powers were growing and I had no idea what they would do next. I let all the worries go, and gave myself over to this moment. I gave myself over to the sensation of him in my mouth.

I had been denied the chance to give oral sex to most of my lovers. They didn't want to risk spilling their seed anywhere but between my legs, wasting a chance to father the next heir to the throne – a chance to make themselves king to my queen. I didn't blame them, but I loved oral sex, and I'd missed performing it. The few times I'd been able to persuade anyone, he had already been excited – big, hard, which was a pleasure all its own – but I liked the feel of a man when he was small. So much easier to take all of him in my mouth. No straining, no fighting all that length or width.

I rolled him in my mouth, sucking gently, at first. But I wanted to enjoy all the sensation I could while he remained small, so I increased in intensity. I could feel him moving in my mouth, the skin sliding, the meat of him so easy to work with. I sucked him fast and faster, until he cried out, 'Enough, enough.'

I moved to the loose roll of his balls, licking along the skin, sliding all that silkiness between my lips and tongue. I watched him grow larger as I played with his balls. I rolled one testicle, carefully, into my mouth so I could play with all of it. He was too big for me to try to take both in at the same time; it would be too easy to injure such tender parts. The last thing I wanted to do was cause him any new pain.

His eyes were wild as they looked down his body at me. The gold of his eyes started to glow – molten gold in the center, amber shot through with sun, then a pale yellow-gold like elm leaves in fall. One moment his eyes were all that glowed, and the next that light exploded down his body, as if white light were liquid running just under his skin. His skin glowed even underneath the red ruin, as if he were carved of rubies set in ivory, with the sun glowing through the white and red of his body.

I moved over his body, not with him inside, but with a knee on either side of his hips. I gazed down at him, wanting to remember the beauty of him the first time. The glow had spread to the tips of his hair, as if every strand were dipped in moonlight. He was a thing of light and magic, but as I used my hand to help slide him inside me, he was all silken skin, and muscle.

I slipped the head of him inside me, and found I was almost too tight. I'd performed all the fore-play on him, and received none for myself. I was wet from the pleasure, but tight, so very tight.

He managed to gasp out, 'You're not open enough.'

'Is it hurting you?' My own voice sounded whispery.

'No,' he whispered.

'Then I want to feel you force your way into me. I want to feel each inch push inside while I'm this tight.' I wriggled my hips a little lower, fight-ing for each delicious inch. I was so tight that he touched every bit of me, sliding heavy and slow over that spot inside me.

I meant to have him inside me as deep as he'd go before my release, but my body had other ideas. It was as if my body being so tight around his made his body press just right, just exactly right against that one spot. One moment I was trying to be so careful, easing him inside me, and the next I was screaming my orgasm, my body bucking around his, the movement forcing more of me down the shaft of him faster than I would have managed without it. And as long as I could keep pushing him inside me the orgasm kept going. It kept on as I shoved him inside me, and somewhere before the last inch of him went inside, he started helping to push.

I sat on top of him with our bodies wedded as close as man and woman could be, the orgasm dancing me above him. I was aware, vaguely, that my skin was glowing – a moon shine to match his own. The wind of my own power blew my hair around my face, garnets sparkling in fire. My eyes glowed so brightly that I could see the colored shadows of the green and gold of my own eyes at the edges of my vision. I screamed and writhed above him on wave after wave of pleasure. This had not been planned, or achieved with skill, but more by luck; a key sliding into a lock at the perfect moment. Our bodies took that moment and rode it.

I heard him scream my name, felt his body buck under mine, felt him drive himself home as hard and as fast as he could. He hit the end of me, and that orgasmed me again. I threw my head back and screamed his name to the heavens.

He went still underneath me, but I couldn't focus my eyes enough to see him, not really. My vision ran in streamers of colors. I collapsed forward, and forgot. Forgot that he was still hurt. Forgot that I was wearing the queen's ring on my right hand; the ring that had once belonged to a real fertility goddess.

I had a second to realize that the skin of his stomach under my hands was no longer raw, but felt smooth and perfect. I blinked down, fighting through pleasure's afterglow to see him. His stomach was as flat and perfect as his illusion once had been, but this was no illusion. He had his tentacles back, but as a tattoo so bright and lifelike that a glance made them seem real. They were a picture, drawn upon his skin.

I saw all that in three blinks of an eye, but there was no next blink, for the ring suddenly came to life. It was like being plunged into water with an electric current in it. It was not enough to kill, but enough to hurt.

Sholto yelled under me, and not from pleasure.

I tried to take the ring away from his body, but my hand seemed glued to his newly decorated skin. The power blew out from us, as if the magic spilled away over the bare rock. I could breathe again.

Sholto gasped, 'What was that?'

'The ring.'

He gazed down his body at me, and my hand pressed to his abdomen. His fingers touched the tattoo, a look on his face of wonder, and of loss. It was as if he'd been given his dearest wish, and in the same moment experienced a loss that would haunt him forever.

I heard metal rolling along rock. The sound made me turn. The chalice was rolling toward us, though the ground was utterly flat. I looked to the other side and found the spear of bone rolling from the other side. They were going to touch us at the same time.

'Hold on,' I said.

'To what?'

'To me.'

He grabbed my arms, and my hand was freed from his stomach. I grabbed his arms without thinking, putting the ring against his bare skin, again. Sometimes Goddess pulls us by the hand down our path, and sometimes she gets behind us and pushes off the cliff edge.

We were about to be pushed.

Chapter 16

WOOD, METAL, FLESH; ALL OF IT HIT US AT ONCE. WE were left clinging to each other in the center of a blast of power that splashed the lake up over the island. We drowned for a moment, then the world literally moved. It felt as if the island bucked up and dropped down again.

The water cleared, the earth stopped moving, and the chalice and spear were gone. We were left wet and gasping, huddled naked together. I was afraid to let go, as if our arms around each other – our bodies still wedded together – were all that kept us from falling off the face of the earth.

Voices came, yells, shouts. I picked out Doyle's voice, Frost, and Agnes's harsh call. The voices made us both turn, blinking water out of our eyes. On the shore, which was a lot farther away than it had been before, were all our guards. We were back in the dead gardens of the sluagh, but the lake was full of water now, and the Island of Bones was in the middle of it.

Doyle dived into the water, his dark body cutting the surface. Frost followed him. The other guards did the same. Sholto's uncles discarded their cloaks and hit the water after my guards. Only Black Agnes stayed on the shore.

I looked down at Sholto; I was still on top of him. 'We're about to be rescued.'

He smiled up at me. 'Do we need rescuing?'

'I'm not sure,' I said.

He laughed then, and the sound echoed against the bare stone of the cavern. He hugged me tight, and laid a gentle kiss on my cheek. He breathed his words against my skin: 'Thank you, Meredith.'

I pressed my cheek against his and whispered back, 'You are most welcome, Sholto.'

He buried his hand in my wet hair and said, softly, 'I have long desired you to whisper my name like that.'

'Like what?' I asked, face still pressed against his.

'Like a lover.'

I heard movement behind us, and Sholto released his hold on my hair. I kissed him on the lips, before I lifted my body to see who had made the island first.

Doyle – of course it was Doyle – walked toward us. He gleamed black and shining, water dripping down his nakedness. The light caught blue and purple gleams from his skin as he moved toward us. The light seemed to dazzle on his skin and on the water – reflected brilliance. My skin was warm in the light. Sunlight, it was sunlight again. Like noonday come to this shadowy place.

There was a green haze to the bare rock where Sholto and I lay. That haze took the shape of tiny stems, reaching out over the rock, anchoring themselves as Doyle came to stand beside us.

His face struggled for an expression, and finally settled on that stern face, the one that had frightened me as a child when he stood at my aunt's side. Somehow the expression wasn't nearly as frightening with him naked, and given my now so intimate knowledge of him. The Queen's Darkness was my lover, and I could never again see him as that threatening figure, simply the queen's assassin, her black dog to fetch and kill.

I stared up at him, still pressed tight in Sholto's arms. I sat up, and his arms fell away from me, reluctantly. Since I was still riding his body, it wasn't as if he stopped touching me. His hands slid down my arms, staying in contact. I glanced at Sholto's face and found him looking not at me, but at Doyle.

Sholto's face was defiant, almost triumphant. I didn't understand the look. I glanced at Doyle, and saw behind that stern face a flash of anger.

234

For the first time in weeks I remembered how they had both found me in Los Angeles. They had fought, both convinced that the queen had sent each of them to kill me.

But there had been something personal about that fight. I couldn't remember what they had said to each other that made me think they had some kind of bad history, but I had felt it. The looks they gave each other now confirmed that I was missing something. Some disagreement, or challenge, or even grudge between these two men. Not good.

Rhys came up the slope of the rock, dripping like wet ivory. He stopped short of us all, as if he also sensed, or saw, the tension.

What do you do when you're naked with one lover, and another lover is standing there? Sholto was not my king, or husband. I took my hand from him and offered it to Doyle. Doyle hesitated a moment, his gaze on his rival and not on me. Then those black eyes moved to me. His expression never truly changed, but some breath of harshness left him. Or perhaps some touch of gentleness returned to him.

There was movement behind him, and Frost and Mistral struggled up the slope. They were dressed, and weapons bulged everywhere. Frost actually caught Mistral's arm as the other man slipped. The clothes and weapons had slowed them down.

Now they stood there, Frost's hand on Mistral's arm. Mistral was almost on his knees, from his slip, but they had frozen, staring at us. They hadn't just caught a whiff of tension. Their reaction said clearly that there was bad blood between Sholto and Doyle.

Doyle took my hand in his. The moment he touched me the tightness in my chest, which I hadn't even known was there, loosened.

He lifted me upward, off the other man. Sholto's hands, all of his body, let me go with such reluctance. The sensation of him drawing out of deep within my body shivered through me. Only Doyle's grip kept my knees from buckling.

Sholto raised his arms to help catch me, his hands on my thighs. Doyle pulled me in against his body, half lifting me over Sholto's body. Sholto let me go; otherwise it would have been like a tug-of-war, not seemly behavior for a king.

I stood there wrapped in Doyle's arms, staring up at his face, trying to decipher what he was thinking. Around me the tiny plants unfurled tiny leaves, and the world suddenly smelled of thyme, that sweet, green herb scent that Sholto had said he sensed when I was smelling roses.

The delicate herbs tickled along my foot, as if reminding me that there were some things more important than love. Staring up into Doyle's face, I wasn't sure that was right. In that moment I wanted him happy. I wanted him to know that

236

I wanted him happy. I wanted to explain that Sholto had been lovely, and the power had been immense, but that in the end, he meant nothing to me, not when I had Doyle's arms around me.

But you can't say that out loud, not with the other man lying behind you. So many hearts to juggle, including my own.

The herbs touched me again, wound around my ankle. I glanced down at the greenery, and thought of my favorite thymes. My gran had grown them in the herb garden behind the house where my father raised me – so many varieties. Lemon thyme, silver thyme, golden thyme. At that thought, the plants around my ankle were suddenly tinged with yellow. Some of the leaves on some of the plants turned silver, others became pale yellow, and some that bright sunny yellow. There was a scent of faint lemon on the air, as if I had crushed one of the pale yellow leaves between my fingertips.

'What did you do?' Doyle whispered, his deep voice thrumming along my spine so that I shivered against him.

My voice was soft, as if I didn't want to say it too loudly: 'I just thought that there is more than one kind of thyme.'

'And the plants changed,' he said.

I nodded, staring at them. 'I didn't say it out loud, Doyle. I only thought it.'

He hugged me. 'I know.'

Mistral and Frost were with Rhys now. They did not approach us, and again I wasn't sure why. They waited, as if they needed permission to come closer – the way they would have waited to approach Queen Andais.

I thought it was me they waited on, but I should have known better. Sholto said behind me, 'The sidhe do not usually stand on ceremony, but if you need permission, then I give it. Come closer.'

Mistral said, 'If you could see yourself, King Sholto, you would not ask why we stand on ceremony.'

The comment made me look back at Sholto. He was sitting up, but where he had been lying was an outline of herbs. Peppermint, basil – as I recognized them, I smelled their perfumes. But the herbs spreading out from where he had lain, where we had lain, wasn't what made the men stop. Sholto was wearing a crown; a crown of herbs. Even as we watched, the delicate plants wove like living fingers through his hair, creating a wreath of thyme and mint. Only the most delicate of the plants, entwining themselves as we watched.

He raised a hand, and the moving plants touched his fingers as they had touched my ankle. I was wearing an anklet of living thyme, gold-flecked leaves, smelling of green life and lemons. The tendril wrapped around his fingers like a happy pet. He lowered his hand and stared at it. The plant wove itself into a ring as we watched – a ring that bloomed on his hand, the delicate spray of white blossoms more precious than any jewel. Then his crown burst into bloom, shades of white, blue, lavender. Finally, the blooms spread across the island, so that the ground was nearly solid with tiny, airy flowers, moving not in a breeze – for there was none – but nodding as if the flowers were speaking to one another.

'A crown of flowers is not a crown for the king of the sluagh!' Agnes shouted, harsh, from the shore. She was on hands and knees, hidden completely under her black cloak. I saw the flash of her eyes, as if there was a glow to them; then she lowered her head, hiding from the light. She was a night-hag. They didn't travel at noon.

Ivar spoke, but I couldn't see him. 'Sholto, King, we cannot approach you in this burning light.'

His uncles were half-goblin – which, depending on the type of goblin, might make sunlight a problem. But they were also half-nightflyer, and that definitely made sunlight a problem.

'I would that you could come to me, Uncles,' Sholto said.

Doyle's arms tightened around me, a warning. 'Be careful what you say, Sholto; you do not understand the power of the words of someone whom faerie itself has crowned.'

'I do not need advice from you, Darkness,' Sholto said, and again there was bitterness in his voice.

The sunlight faded, and a soft twilight began to fall. There was the sound of splashing, then Ivar and Fyfe came up upon the island. They were nude except for enough clothing to hold their weapons. They fell to one knee before him, heads bowed. 'King Sholto,' Ivar said, 'we thank you for sending the light away.'

Sholto said, 'I didn't . . .'

'You are crowned by faerie,' Doyle said again. 'Your words, perhaps even your thoughts, will shape what will happen this night.'

I said, 'I thought – only thought – that there is more than one variety of thyme, and it changed the herbs. What I thought about became real, Sholto.'

Agnes called from the shore, 'You have freed us from the light, King Sholto. You have given us back the Lost Lake and the Island of Bones. Will you stop there, or will you give us back our power? Will you remake the sluagh while the magic of creation still burns through you, or will you hesitate and lose this chance to bring us back into ourselves?'

'The hag is right, Your Highness,' Fyfe said. 'You have brought us back the magic of making, wild magic, creation magic. Will you use it for us?'

In the dying light I watched Sholto lick his lips. 'What would you have of me?' he asked carefully. I heard in his voice what was beginning to be in my mind, a touch of fear. You could police your words, but policing your own thoughts – that was harder, so much harder.

'Call the wild magic,' Ivar said.

'It is here already,' Doyle said, 'can you not feel it?' His heart sped under my cheek. I wasn't sure I understood exactly what was happening, but Doyle seemed both frightened and excited. Even his body was beginning to react, pressed against the front of mine.

The two kneeling figures looked at Doyle. 'Do not look to Darkness,' Sholto said. 'I am king here.'

They looked back at him, and bowed again. 'You are our king,' said Ivar. 'But there are places we cannot follow you. If the wild magic is real again, then you have two choices, king of ours: You can remake us into a thing of flowered crowns and noonday suns, or you can call the old magic, and remake us into what we once were.'

'Darkness is right,' Fyfe said. 'I can feel it like a growing weight inside me. You can change us into what she wants us to be' – he pointed at me – 'or you can give us back what we have lost.'

Sholto then asked something that made me

241

think even better of him than I already did. 'What would you have of me, Uncles, what would you have me do?'

They glanced first at him, then at each other, then carefully down at the ground again. 'We want to be what we once were. We want to hunt as we once did. Give us back what has been lost, Sholto.' Ivar held out his hand toward his king.

'Do not remake us in the sidhe bitch's image,' Agnes yelled from the shore. It was a mistake.

Sholto yelled back at her, 'I am king here. I rule here. I thought you loved me once. But I know now that you only raised me to take the throne because you wished to sit upon it. You cannot rule, but you thought you could rule through me. You and your sisters thought to make me your puppet.' He stood and screamed at her. 'I am no one's puppet. I am King Sholto of the Sluagh, I am the Lord of That Which Passes Between, Lord of Shadows. Long have I been lonely among my own people. Long have I wanted some to look as I do.' He slammed a hand into his chest. It made a thick, meaty sound. 'Now you tell me I have the power to do just that. You have envied the sidhe their smooth skin, their beauty that turns my head. So have what you envy.'

A wail came from Agnes, but it was too dark to see what was happening on the shore. She screamed, a horrible sound – a sound of loss, and pain, as if whatever was happening to her hurt.

I heard Sholto say, softly, 'Agnes.' The sound in that one word let me know that he wasn't so terribly certain of what he wanted, or what he had done.

What had he done?

His uncles abased themselves, faces pressed to the herbs. 'Please, King Sholto, we beg you, do not remake us into sidhe. Do not make us only lesser versions of the Unseelie. We are sluagh, and that is a proud thing. Would you strip us of all that we have kept over the years?'

'No,' Sholto said, and there was no anger in his voice now. The screams from the shore had taken away his anger. He understood now how dangerous he was in this moment. 'I want the sluagh to be powerful again. I want us to be a force to be reckoned with, negotiated with. I want us to be a fearsome thing.'

I spoke before I could think: 'Not just fearsome, surely.'

'I want us to have a terrible beauty then,' he said, and it was as if the world held its breath, as if the whole of faerie had been waiting for him to say those words. I felt it in the pit of my stomach like the chime of a great bell. It was a beautiful sound, but so large, so heavy, that it could crush you with the music of its voice.

'What have you done?' Doyle asked, and I wasn't sure whom he had asked it of.

Sholto answered him. 'What I had to do.' He

stood there, stark and pale in the growing dark. The tattoo of his tentacles glowed as if outlined with phosphorus. The flowers of his crown looked ghostly pale, and I thought they would have attracted honeybees, if it had not been dark. Bees are not nighttime creatures.

The darkness began to lighten. 'What did you just think of?' Doyle asked.

'That if the sunlight had remained, there would have been bees to feed on the flowers.'

'No, it will be night here,' Sholto said, and the darkness began to thicken again.

I tried for a more neutral thought. What could come to his flowers in the dark? Moths appeared among the flowers, small ones, ones to match the moth on my stomach. Small flashes of light showed above the island, as if jewels had been thrown into the air. Fireflies, dozens of them, so that they actually glowed enough to drive back some of the dark.

'Did you call them?' Sholto said.

'Yes,' I said.

'You raised the wild magic together,' Ivar said.

'She is not sluagh,' Fyfe said.

'But she is queen to his king for tonight; the magic is hers, as well,' Ivar said.

'Will you fight me for the heart of my people, Meredith?' Sholto said.

'I will try not to,' I said softly.

'I rule here, Meredith, not you.'

'I do not want to take your throne, Sholto. But I can't help being what I am.'

'What are you?'

'I am sidhe.'

'Then if you are sidhe and not sluagh, run.'

'What?' I asked, trying to move a little away from Doyle and closer to Sholto. Doyle held me tight and wouldn't let me do it.

'Run,' Sholto said again.

'Why?' I asked.

'I am going to call the wild hunt, Meredith. If you are not sluagh, then you will be prey.'

'No, Sholto! Let us take the princess to safety first, I beg this of you,' Doyle said urgently.

'The Darkness does not usually beg. I am flattered, but if she can call back the sun to drive away the night, I must call the hunt now. She must be the prey. You know that.'

I was startled. Was this the same man who had refused to sacrifice me just moments ago? Who had looked on me with such tenderness? The magic was indeed working powerfully in him, to make this change.

Rhys's voice came, cautious: 'You wear a crown of flowers, King Sholto. Are you so certain that the wild hunt will recognize you as sluagh?'

'I am their king.'

'You look sidhe enough to be welcome in the queen's bed right now,' Rhys said.

Sholto touched his flat stomach with its healed

flesh and tattoo. He hesitated, then shook his head. 'I will call the wild magic. I will call the hunt. If they see me as prey and not as sluagh, then so be it.' He smiled, and even in the uncertain light it didn't look particularly happy. He laughed, and the night echoed with it. There was the call of some sweet-voiced bird, sleepy from the distant shore.

Sholto spoke again. 'It is a long tradition among us, Lord Rhys, to slay our kings to bring back life to the land. If by my life, or my death, I can bring my people back to their power, I will do it.'

'Sholto,' I said, 'don't. Don't say that.'

'It is done,' he said.

Doyle started moving us toward the other side of the island. 'Short of killing him, we cannot stop him,' he told me. 'You both reek of the oldest of magicks. I am not certain that he can be killed right now.'

'We need to leave then,' Rhys said.

Abeloec was finally pulling himself up on the shore. He still had his cup in his hand, and it seemed as if the weight of it had kept him from coming sooner. 'Don't tell me I have to get back in the lake,' he said. 'If she's touched with the magic of creation, let her create a bridge.'

I didn't wait. I said, 'I want a bridge to the shore.' A graceful white bridge appeared, just like that.

'Cool,' Rhys said. 'Let's go.'

Sholto spoke in a ringing voice. 'I call the wild hunt, by Herne and huntsman, by horn and hound, by wind and storm, and wreck of winter, I call us home.'

The dark near the roof of the cavern split open as if someone had cut it with a knife. It split open and things boiled out of it.

Doyle turned my face away and said, 'Do not look back.' He began to run, dragging me with him. We all began to run. Only Sholto and his uncles stayed on the island as the night itself ripped open and poured nightmares behind us.

Chapter 17

WE MADE THE FAR SHORE, BUT I TRIPPED ON A skeleton buried in the ground. Doyle picked me up and kept running. Gunshots echoed, and I saw Frost firing at Agnes as she threw herself on top of him. I had a glimpse of her face; something was wrong with it, as if her bones were sliding around under her skin. I screamed, 'Frost,' as a glint of metal showed in her hand. More shots sounded. Mistral was beside Frost, blades flashing.

'Doyle, stop!' I shouted.

He ignored me, and kept running with me in his arms. Abe and Rhys were with him.

'We can't leave Frost behind!' I said.

Doyle said, 'We cannot risk you, not for anyone.'

'Call a door,' Abe said.

Doyle glanced behind us, but not at Mistral and

Frost's fight with the night-hag. He glanced higher than that. It made me look up, too.

At first my eyes perceived clouds, black and grey rolling clouds, or smoke – but that was only my mind trying to make sense of it. I thought I had seen all the sluagh had to offer, but I was wrong. What was pouring down toward the island where Sholto stood was nothing my mind could accept. When I worked for the investigative agency . . . sometimes at a crime scene – if it's bad enough – sometimes your mind refuses to make an image out of it. It's just a jumble. Your mind gives you a moment to not see this horrible thing. If you have the chance to close your eyes and not look a second time, you can save yourself. This horror will not go into your mind and stain your soul. At most crime scenes I didn't have the choice of not seeing. But this; I looked away. If we didn't get away, then I'd have to look.

We had to get away.

Doyle yelled, 'Don't look. Call the door.'

I did what he asked. 'I need a door to the Unseelie sithen.' The door appeared, hanging in the middle of nowhere, just like before.

'No doors,' Sholto screamed behind us.

The door vanished.

Rhys cursed.

Frost and Mistral were with us now. There was blood on their swords. I glanced back at the shore, and saw Agnes – a dark, still shape on the ground.

Doyle started running again, and the others joined us. 'Call something else,' Abe said, near breathless trying to keep up with Doyle's pace. 'And do it quietly, so Sholto can't hear what you're doing.'

'What?' I asked.

'You have the power of creation,' he panted. 'Use it.'

'How?' My brain wasn't working under the pressure.

'Conjure something,' he said, and stumbled, falling. He rejoined us, blood pouring down his chest from a new cut.

'Let the ground be grass and gentle to our feet.' Grass flowed at our feet like green water. It didn't spread over everything like the herbs on the island. The grass sprang up in a path where we ran, and nowhere else.

'Try something else,' Rhys said from the other side of us. He was shorter than the rest, and his voice showed the strain of keeping up with the longer legs of the others.

What could I call from the ground, from the grass, that could save us? I thought it and had my answer; one of the most magical of plants. 'Give me a field of four-leaf clover.' The grass spread out before us wide and smooth, then white clover began to grow through the grass, until we stood in the center of a field of it. White globes of sweet-smelling flowers burst like stars across all the green.

Doyle slowed, and the others slowed with him. Rhys said it out loud: 'Not bad, not bad at all. You think well in a crisis.'

'The wild hunt is of ill intent,' Frost said. 'They should be stopped at the field's edge.'

Doyle sat me down amid the ankle-high clover. The plants brushed against me as if they were little hands. 'Four-leaf clover is the most powerful plant protection from faerie,' I said.

'Aye,' Abe said, 'but some of what is coming does not have to walk, Princess.'

'Make us a roof, Meredith,' Doyle said.

'A roof of what?'

'Rowan, thorn, and ash,' Frost said.

'Of course,' I said. Anywhere that the three trees grew together was a magical place – a place both of protection and of a weakening in the reality between worlds. Such a place would save you from faerie, or call faerie to you – like so many things with us, there was never a yes, or no, but a yes, a no, and a sometimes.

The earth underneath us trembled as if an earthquake were coming; then the trees blasted out of the ground, showering rock and dirt and clover over us. The trees stretched to the sky with a sound like a storm or a train, barreling down, but with a scream of wood to it. It was like nothing I'd ever heard before. While the trees knit themselves together above our heads, I looked back. I could not help it.

Sholto was covered in the nightmares he had called. Tentacles writhed; bits and pieces that I had no word for flowed and struck. There were teeth everywhere, as if wind could be made solid and given fangs to tear and destroy. Sholto's uncles attacked the creatures with blade and muscle, but they were losing. Losing, but fighting hard enough that they had given us time to make our sanctuary.

Frost moved to stand so that his broad chest blocked my view. 'It is not good to gaze too long upon them.' There was a bloody furrow down one side of his face, as if Agnes had tried to claw his eyes out. I made as if to touch the wound, and he pulled away, catching my hand in his. 'I will heal.'

He didn't want me to fuss over him in front of Mistral. If it had just been Doyle and Rhys, he might have allowed it. But he would not have Mistral see him weak. I wasn't sure how he felt about Abe, but I knew he viewed Mistral as a threat. Men don't like to look weak in front of their rivals. Whatever I thought of Mistral, that was how Frost and Doyle saw him.

I took Frost's hand and tried not to act concerned about his wounds. 'He called the hunt. Why are they attacking him?' I asked.

'I warned him that he looked too sidhe,' Rhys

said. 'I wasn't saying that just to stop him from doing something dangerous to us.'

Something warm dripped over my hand. I looked down to find Frost's blood painting my skin. I fought the spurt of panic and asked calmly, 'How badly are you hurt?' The blood was coming steadily – not good.

'I will heal,' Frost said, voice tight.

The trees closed overhead with a sound like the ocean waves rushing along a shore. Leaves tore and rained down on us as the branches wove a shield of leaves, thorns, and bright red berries above. The shadow it cast made Frost's skin look grey for a moment, and it frightened me.

'You heal gunshot wounds if the bullet goes through and through. You heal nonmagical blades. But Black Agnes was a night-hag and once a goddess. Is your wound of blade, or claw?'

Frost tried to take his hand back, but I wouldn't let him. Unless he wanted to be appear undignified, he couldn't break free. Our hands were covered in his blood, sticky and warm.

Doyle was at Frost's side. 'How badly are you hurt?'

'We do not have time to tend my wounds,' Frost said. He wouldn't look at Doyle, or any of us. He arranged his face in that arrogant mask, the one that made him impossibly handsome, and as cold as his namesake. But the terrible wounds on the right side of that face ruined the mask. It was like a chink in armor; he could not hide behind it.

'Nor do we have time to lose my strong right arm,' Doyle said, 'not if there is time to save it.'

Frost looked at him, surprise showing through the mask. I wondered if Doyle had never, in all these long years, called Frost the strong right arm of the Darkness. The look on his face suggested so. And maybe it was as close as Doyle would come to apologizing for abandoning him to the fight with Agnes in order to save me. Had Frost thought Doyle left him behind on purpose?

A world of emotion seemed to pass between the two men. If they'd been human men, they might have exchanged some profanity or sports metaphor, which is what seems to pass for terms of deepest affection between friends. But they were who they were, and Doyle said, simply, 'Remove enough weapons so we can see the wound.' He smiled when he said it, because of all the guards Frost would be the one carrying the most weapons, with Mistral a distant second.

'Whatever you're going to do, do it fast,' Rhys said.

We all looked at him, and then beyond him. The air boiled black, grey, white, and horrible. The hunt was coming toward us like a ribbon of nightmares. It took my eyes a moment to find Sholto on the island. He was a small, pale figure running – running full out – with that sidhe swiftness. But fast as he was, he wouldn't be fast enough – what chased him moved with the swiftness of birds, of wind, of water. It was like trying to outrun the wind; you just couldn't do it.

Doyle turned back to Frost. 'Take off your jacket. I'll make a compress. We're not going to have time for more.'

I glanced back toward the island. Sholto's guards, his uncles, tried to buy him time. They offered themselves as a sacrifice to slow the hunt. It worked, for a while. Some of that fearful boil of shapes slowed and covered them. I think I heard one of them scream over the high bird-like chittering of the creatures. But most of the wild hunt stayed on target. That target was Sholto.

He crossed the bridge and kept running. 'Goddess help us,' Rhys said, 'he's coming here.'

'He finally understands what he's called into being,' Mistral said. 'He runs in terror now. He runs to the only sanctuary he can see.'

'We stand in the middle of four-leaf clovers, rowan, ash, and thorn. The wild hunt cannot touch us here,' I said, but my voice was soft, and didn't hold the certainty I wished it had.

Doyle had ripped Frost's shirt away and torn Frost's own jacket into pieces small enough to be used as compresses.

'How bad is it?' I asked.

Doyle shook his head, pressing the cloth in an

area that seemed to run under Frost's arm and into his shoulder. 'Get us out of here, Meredith. I will tend Frost. But only you can get us out.'

'The wild hunt will pass us by,' I said. 'We stand in the middle of things that they cannot pass through.'

'If we were not its prey, then I would agree,' Doyle said. He was trying to get Frost to lie down on the clover, but the other man was arguing. Doyle pressed harder on the wound, which made Frost draw a sharp breath. He continued, 'But Sholto told us to run, if we were sidhe. He has conjured it to hunt us.'

I started to turn away, but couldn't quite tear my eyes from Frost. Once he had been the Killing Frost: cold, frightening, arrogant, untouched, and untouchable. Now he was Frost, and he wasn't frightening, or cold, and I knew the touch of his body in almost every possible way. I wanted to go to him, to hold his hand while Doyle tended his wound.

'Merry,' Doyle said, 'if you do not get us out of here, Frost will not be the only one hurt.'

I caught Frost's gaze. Pain, I saw there, but also something hopeful, or good. I think he liked that I was so worried about him. 'Get us out, Merry,' Frost said between gritted teeth. 'I am fine.'

I didn't call him a liar, but I did turn away so I couldn't watch. It would have distracted me too much, and I didn't have time to be weak.

'I need a door to the Unseelie Court.' I said it clearly, but nothing happened.

'Try again,' Rhys said.

I tried again, and again nothing happened.

'Sholto said *No doors*,' Mistral said. 'Apparently his word stands.'

Sholto's feet had touched the edge of the field I'd made. He was only yards away from the first of the clover. The air above him was thick with tentacles and mouths and claws. I looked away from it, because I couldn't think while I was staring into it.

'Call something else,' Abe said.

'What?' I asked.

It was Rhys who said, 'Where rowan, ash, and thorn grow close together, the veil between worlds is thinner.'

I looked up at the circle of trees that I'd called into being. Their branches had formed a lace of roof above us. They still hushed and moved above us the way the roses in the Unseelie Court moved, as if they had more life than an ordinary tree.

I began to walk the inside of the circle of trees, searching not with my hands, but with that part of me that sensed magic. Most human psychics have to do something to get themselves in the mood for magic, but I had to shield constantly not to be overwhelmed by it. Especially in faerie – there was so much of it that it became like the engine noise of some great ship, and you ceased to 'hear' it after a while, though it was always there thrumming along your skin, making your bones vibrate to its rhythm.

I reached out from behind those shields and searched for a place in the trees that felt . . . thin. I couldn't look simply for magic; there was too much of it around me. Too much power flowing toward us. I needed to cast out for something more specific.

'The clover has slowed them,' Mistral called.

This made me glance back, away from the trees. The cloud of nightmares rolled above the clover like a pack of hounds that had lost the scent.

Sholto just kept running, his hair flying behind him, the nude beauty of him beautiful in motion, like watching a horse run across a field. It was a beauty that transcended sex; simply beautiful for its own sake.

'Concentrate, Merry,' Rhys said. 'I'll help you look for a door.'

I nodded and went back to looking only at the trees. They thrummed with power, inherently magical and invested with further power because they had been called into being by one of the oldest magicks.

Rhys called from across the clearing. 'Here!'

I ran to him, the clover tapping at my legs and feet as if patting me with soft green hands. I passed Frost on the ground, where Doyle sat holding his wound. Frost was hurt, very hurt, but there was no time to help – Doyle would take care of him. I had to take care of us all.

Rhys was standing by a group of three of the trees that looked no different from the others, really. But when I put my hand out toward them, it was as if reality had been rubbed thin here, like a good-luck penny rubbed in your pocket.

'You feel it?' Rhys asked.

I nodded. 'How do we open it?'

'You just walk through,' Rhys said. He looked back at the others. 'Everybody gather around. We need to walk through together.'

'Why?' I asked.

He grinned at me. 'Because naturally occurring doorways like this don't lead to the same place every time. It'd be bad if we were separated.'

'Bad's one way of putting it,' I said.

Doyle had to help Frost to his feet. Even so, he stumbled. Abe came and offered his shoulder to lean on, still grasping the horn cup in one hand, as if it was the most important thing in the world. It occurred to me then that the Goddess's chalice had gone back to wherever it went when it wasn't mucking about with me. I had never held on to it the way Abe did with his, but then, I had been afraid of its power. Abe wasn't afraid of his cup's power; he was afraid of losing it again.

Mistral was backing toward us. 'Are we

waiting for the Lord of Shadows or leaving him to his fate?'

It took me a second to realize he meant Sholto. I looked toward the lake. Sholto was almost here, almost to the tree line. The sky behind him was totally black, as if the father of all storms was about to break, except that instead of lightning there were tentacles, and mouths that shrieked.

'He can escape the same way,' Rhys said. 'The door won't close behind us.'

I looked at him. 'Don't we want it to?'

'I don't know if we can close it, but if we can, Merry, he would be trapped.' There was a very serious look in his one eye – a measuring look. It was the look that I was beginning to dread from all the men. A look that said: *The decision is yours.*

Could I leave Sholto to die? He had called the wild hunt. He'd offered himself as prey. He'd trapped us here with his *no doors*. Did I owe him?

I looked at what chased him. 'I couldn't leave anyone to that.'

'So be it,' Doyle said from beside me.

'But we can go through ahead of him,' Mistral said. 'We don't have to wait.'

'You're sure he'll sense the door?' I asked.

Everyone answered at once. Mistral said, 'Yes.' Rhys said, 'Probably.' Doyle and Frost said, 'I do not know.' Abe just shrugged.

I shook my head and whispered, 'Goddess guide me, but I can't leave him. I can still taste his skin on my mouth.' I stepped in front of the men, closer to the farther edge of the trees. I yelled, 'Sholto, we're leaving, hurry, hurry!'

He stumbled, fell in the clover, and rolled to his feet again in a blur of motion. He dived through the trees, and I thought he'd made it, but something long and white whipped around his ankle just before it cleared the magical circle. It caught him in that instant when his body was airborne, not touching the clover, not inside the trees. The tentacle tried to lift him skyward, but his hands reached desperately for the trees. He caught a limb with his hands, and he was left suspended, feet above the ground.

I was running forward before I had time to think. I don't know what I planned to do when I got there, but I didn't have to worry, because a blur of movement rushed past me. Mistral and Doyle were there before me.

Doyle had Frost's sword in his hands. He leapt into the air in an impossibly graceful arc, and cut the tentacle in two. I smelled ozone a second before lightning crashed from Mistral's hand. The lightning hit the cloud and seemed to bounce from one creature to another, illuminating them. It was too much light. I screamed and covered my eyes, but it was as if the images were carved inside my lids.

Strong hands were on mine, pulling my hands away from my eyes. I kept my eyes tight shut, and Doyle's deep voice came. 'Clawing your eyes out won't help, Meredith. It's inside you now. You can't unsee it.'

I opened my mouth and screamed. I screamed and screamed and screamed. Doyle picked me up in his arms and started running toward the others. I knew Mistral and Sholto were behind us. Whimpers replaced my screams – I have no words for what I'd seen. They were things that should not have been. Things that could not have been alive, but they had moved. I had seen them.

If I had been alone, I would have fallen to the ground and shrieked until the wild hunt caught me. Instead I clung to Doyle and buried my nose and mouth against the curve of his neck, keeping my eyes fixed on the clover, and the trees, and my men. I wanted to replace the images that were burned inside me – it was as if I had to clean my eyes of the sight of the hunt. I breathed in the scent of Doyle's neck, his hair, and it helped calm me. He was real, and solid, and I was safe in his arms.

Rhys moved to help Abe with Frost. Doyle still had Frost's sword naked and bloody in his hand, held away from me. The blood smelled the way all blood smells: red, slightly metallic, sweet. If these creatures bled real blood, then they couldn't be what I had seen; they weren't nightmares. What I had seen in that lightning-kissed moment was nothing that would ever bleed real blood.

Doyle told Mistral to enter first, because we didn't know where the doorway led. The Storm Lord didn't argue, he just did what he was told. All of us, including Sholto, followed his broad back between the trees. One moment we were in the clover circle; the next we were in moonlight, at the edge of a snowbanked parking lot.

Chapter 18

THERE WAS A MARKED CAR AND SEVERAL UNMARKED cars sitting there. Inside, cops and FBI stared at us, eyes wide. We had simply appeared out of thin air; I guess it was worth a stare or two.

'How are we going to explain this?' Rhys asked softly.

The car doors started opening. Police of all flavors poured out into the cold. Then there was wind at our backs . . . warm wind, and a sound like birds, if birds could be too large, and too frightening for words.

'Oh, God,' Rhys said, 'they're coming through.'

'Mistral, Sholto, hold the door closed if you can. Give us time,' Doyle said.

Mistral and Sholto turned to face that warm, seeking wind. Doyle ran toward the cars; I was still in his arms. The others followed, though

Frost's wounds caused him to follow slowly behind us.

The police were calling to us. 'What's wrong?' 'Is the princess hurt?'

'Stay in your cars and you'll be safe,' Doyle yelled.

The closest car held two dark-suited men. One was young and dark, the other older and balding. 'Charles, FBI,' the younger one said. 'You don't give us orders.'

'If the princess is in danger, I can, by your own laws,' said Doyle.

The older one said, 'Special Agent Bancroft, what's happening? That's not geese I'm hearing.'

A uniform that was St. Louis city, one Illinois state trooper, and a local precinct cop joined us. Apparently, when the rest of the police went away after we'd last dealt with them here, they'd left a little bit of everybody behind. No one wanted to be left out, I guess.

'If you all stay in your cars, you will be safe,' Doyle repeated.

One of the younger uniforms said, 'We're cops. We're not paid to be safe.'

'Spoken like someone who is not even close to his pension,' another officer said, one with more weight around his middle.

'Jesus,' one of them said. I didn't have to glance back, for now Frost had caught up with us. He'd bled all over Rhys, so that it looked like Rhys was hurt worse. Abe was still bleeding from falling among the bones.

One of the uniforms touched his shoulder radio and started requesting an ambulance. Doyle yelled above the growing sound of wind and birds, 'There is no time. They will be upon us in moments.'

'Who?' Bancroft asked.

Doyle shook his head and moved around the agent. He laid me in the passenger seat of the car, then opened the backseat door, saying, 'Put Frost inside, Rhys.'

'I will not leave you,' Frost said. The men laid him in the seat even as he protested.

Doyle grabbed Frost's shoulder and said, 'If I die, if all of us die, if the others are gone into the ground for good, then you must survive. You must take her back to Los Angeles and not return.'

I started to get out of the car then. 'I won't leave you.'

Doyle pushed me back into the seat. He knelt down and gave me the full weight of his dark eyes. 'Meredith, Merry, we cannot win this fight. Unless help arrives, we will all die. You have never seen this wild hunt, but I have. We will give them sidhe to hunt, and they will ignore this car. You and Frost will be safe.'

I gripped his arms, so smooth, so muscled, so solid. 'I won't leave you.'

'Nor I,' Frost said, struggling to sit up in the backseat.

'Frost,' Doyle almost yelled it, 'I do not trust anyone but you and me to keep her safe. If it is not to be me, then it must be you.'

Bancroft said, 'Get in and drive, Charlie.'

The younger agent didn't argue this time; he got behind the wheel. I was still holding on to Doyle, shaking my head over and over. One of the other cops had gotten a first-aid kit out of the car. Bancroft took it and crawled into the back with Frost.

'No,' I said to Doyle. 'I am princess here, not you.'

'Your duty is to live,' Doyle said.

I shook my head. 'If you die, I'm not sure I want to.'

He kissed me then, hard and fierce. I tried to melt into that kiss, but he tore himself away and slammed the door in my face.

The doors locked. I glanced at the agent, who said, 'We have to get you to safety, Princess.'

'Unlock the door,' I demanded.

He ignored me and started the engine, hit the gas. Just then wind slammed into the car, so hard that it skidded the vehicle to the side. Charlie fought to keep the car in the parking lot and out of the trees.

'Drive,' Bancroft yelled, 'drive like a son of a bitch!'

I looked then, because I had to. The wild hunt had broken through, and it was like the moment in the cave – as if the darkness had split open and was spilling out nightmares. But the nightmares were even more solid now. Or maybe, now that I'd seen them, I couldn't unsee them.

A coat flew over my face, and I was left scrambling at it. 'Don't look, Merry,' Frost said, his voice choked, 'don't look.'

'Put on the coat, Princess,' Bancroft said. 'We'll get you to the hospital.'

I held the coat in my arms, but turned to look back.

The police were shooting at the hunt. Mistral lit the sky with lightning, and one of the police crumbled to the ground. Was he screaming? The horror spilled over Sholto, and he was lost to it. Doyle leapt toward the tentacles and teeth, the sword glittering in the moonlight. I screamed his name, but the last thing I saw before we drove into the dark was Doyle lost under a weight of nightmares.

Chapter 19

FROST'S HAND GRABBED MY SHOULDER, PRESSING ME against the seat. 'Merry, please, don't make Doyle's sacrifice in vain.'

I touched his hand, pressed it against me, and there was more blood on it. 'How can I let them drive us to safety and not fight it?'

'You must. I am too hurt to help, and you are too fragile. I would willingly die with them, but you must not die.'

Agent Charlie had us on the narrow road, driving a little too fast for the darkness and the snow. He hit ice and skidded.

'Slow down or you're going to put us in a ditch,' Bancroft said. 'And you, Frost, right, you need to lie back and let me finish putting pressure on this wound. You bleed to death and you can't keep the princess safe.'

'Did you see it?' Charlie said as he slowed

down. 'Did you see it?'

'I saw it,' Bancroft said in a strained voice. He pulled on Frost. 'Let me take care of the wound like your captain ordered.'

Frost let go of me, slowly, his hand pulling away. I started drawing the trench coat over me. I didn't know whose coat it was, but I was cold. Cold in a way that the coat wouldn't help, yet it was all I had.

Agent Charlie slowed at a sharp turn, and I caught a glimpse of something in the trees. It wasn't the wild hunt, and it wasn't our men.

'Stop,' I said.

He slowed further, almost stopped. 'What? What is it?'

I saw them in the trees: goblins. Goblins walking in single file, cloaked for the cold, bristling with weapons in the cold light of the moon. They were walking away from the fight, though some of them glanced back. That was enough to tell me they knew what was happening, and they were leaving my men to die.

'Drive,' Bancroft said.

'Stop,' I ordered.

Agent Charlie ignored me. The car picked up speed.

'Stop,' I repeated. 'There are goblins out there. They can tip the balance. They can save my men.'

'We're doing what your guard demanded,' Bancroft said. 'We're going to a hospital.'

I had to stop the car. I had to talk to the goblins – they were my allies. They had to help, if I asked it, or be forsworn.

I reached over, touched the agent's face, and thought about sex. I'd never done this to a human before, never used that part of my heritage for evil. And it was evil – I didn't know him, didn't want him, but I made him want me.

The agent slammed on the brakes, throwing me into the dash, and throwing the men in the back into the floorboards. Bancroft yelled, 'What the hell are you doing?'

Agent Charlie threw the car into park, skewing halfway across the road. He unbuckled his seat belt, pulled me toward him, and started trying to kiss me, his hands everywhere. I didn't care, as long as the car was stopped.

Bancroft came over the seat. 'Charlie, for God's sake, Charlie. Stop!'

I took advantage of the fight to reach across and unlock the door while the men fought almost on top of me. I opened the door and fell backward into the road. Charlie tried to crawl after me. Bancroft slid over the seat and on top of his partner.

I got to my feet on the icy road, huddling under the coat.

The goblins were there in the dark, just outside the headlight beams. Two faces looked at me, two nearly identical faces: Ash and Holly. The wind blew their yellow hair from their hoods. I couldn't tell which twin was which in the uncertain light – the only difference was eye color.

'Hail, goblins,' I called.

One of them touched the other and nodded toward the dark. They began to turn and leave. I yelled, 'I call on you as allies. To deny me is to be forsworn. The wild hunt is abroad, and oathbreakers are sweet meat to them.'

The twins turned back to us, and the goblins who were only dark shapes behind them shifted in the dimness. 'We did not make this oath,' one of them called.

'Kurag, Goblin King, did, and you are his people. Do you call your king a liar? Are you king now among the goblins, Holly?'

I had taken a chance on that. I wasn't certain which brother it was, but I'd guessed based on the fact that Holly had the worse attitude of the two. He bowed his head in acknowledgment. 'The princess sees well in the dark.'

'She merely has good ears,' his brother said. 'You complain more.'

Ash started down the side of the road, ignoring my plea, and some of the others followed. Most stayed in the shadows along the road's edge. There had to be nearly twenty of them. It was enough to make a difference, enough, maybe, to save . . . my men.

I heard a car door open behind me. Frost

crawled out and fell into the snow and ice of the road. I went to him but kept my gaze on the goblins.

'This is not our fight,' Holly said.

'I need your help as my allies; that makes it your fight,' I said. 'Or have the goblins lost their taste for battle?'

'You do not battle the wild hunt, Princess. You run from it, you join it, you hide from it. But you don't fight it,' Ash said. I could see his green eyes now. His hood framed a face as handsome as any at the Unseelie Court, golden-haired; only the pure, pupil-less green of his eyes and a bulkier body under the cloak betrayed his mixed heritage.

'Will you be forsworn?' I asked. I clung to Frost's hand in the snow.

'No,' Ash said. But he was not happy about it.

'We came out to see what the fuss was,' one of the other goblins said, 'not get ourselves killed for a bunch of sidhe.' The goblin was almost twice as broad as any sidhe. He turned into the light a face that was covered in hard, round bumps. 'Get a good look, Princess.' He threw back his cloak so I could see more of him. His arms were as covered as his face in bumps and growths, marks of beauty among the goblins. But these bumps were pastel colors – pink, lavender, mint green – not a skin tone that the goblins could boast.

'That's right, I'm half sidhe,' he said. 'Just like them, but I'm not so pretty, am I?'

'By goblin standards you are the more handsome,' I said.

He blinked eyes that bulged slightly from his face. 'But you don't judge by goblin standards, do you, Princess?'

'I ask as your ally for your aid. I ask as a blood-oathed ally to your king that the goblins aid me. Call Kurag and summon more goblins.'

'Why don't you call the sidhe?' the bumpy goblin asked.

Truth was, I wasn't certain there was anyone left who would risk themselves against the great hunt for me. Nor was I sure whether the queen would let them. She had been so unhappy with me when last we met.

'Are you saying that a goblin is a lesser warrior than a sidhe?' I asked, avoiding the question.

'No one is a greater warrior than the goblins,' he said.

Ash said, 'You don't know if the sidhe will come.'

I was out of time to prevaricate further. 'No, I don't,' I admitted. 'Aid me, Ash, help me, as my ally, help us.'

'Beg,' Holly said, 'beg for our aid.'

'The goblins seek to delay,' Frost said, voice hoarse, 'they seek to delay until the fight is over. Cowards!'

I gazed up at the three tall goblins, and the others waiting in the shadows. I did the only thing I could think of. I searched Frost until I found a gun. I pulled it free of the holster and got to my feet.

Bancroft had finally handcuffed his partner to the steering wheel, though Agent Charlie was still trying to get free and get to me. Bancroft joined us in the snow. 'What are you going to do, Princess?'

'I'm going to go back and fight.' I hoped that in the face of my determination, the goblins could do naught but join.

'No,' Bancroft said, and started to reach across Frost toward me.

I pointed the gun at him and clicked off the safety. 'I have no quarrel with you, Agent Bancroft.'

He had gone very still. 'Glad to hear it. Now give me the gun.'

I started to back away from him. 'I'm going back to help my men.'

'She's bluffing,' the warty goblin said.

'No,' Frost said, 'she's not.' He struggled to his feet, then fell back into the snow. 'Merry!'

'Bancroft, get him to the hospital.' I aimed the gun skyward and started running back the way we'd come. I tried to think of summer's heat. Tried to bring the idea of warmth to my shields, but all I could feel was the ice under my feet. If I was human enough to get frostbite, I'd lose feeling soon.

Ash and Holly came up beside me, one on either side. They loped along while I ran my fastest. They could have outdistanced me and gotten to the fight sooner, but they'd only obey the letter of our agreement. If I fought and asked for help, then they had to help me, but they didn't have to get to the fight one second before I did.

I prayed, 'Goddess, help me and my allies to arrive in time to save my people.' I felt someone pounding up behind us, but did not glance back – it was just one of the larger goblins.

Then hands, silver-grey in the moonlight. Before I knew it I was cradled against a chest almost as wide as I was tall. Jonty, the Red Cap, was ten feet of goblin muscle. He glanced down at me with eyes that in good light would be as red as if he looked at the world through a spill of fresh blood. His eyes were a match for Holly's. It had made me wonder if the goblin half of the twins was a Red Cap. The blood that dripped continuously from the cap on his head shone in the light. Little drops of it were flung behind him as he picked up speed and raced toward the fight. The Red Caps had earned their name by dipping their caps in the blood of enemies. Once, to be warlord among them you had to have enough magic to keep the blood dripping indefinitely. Jonty was the only Red Cap I'd ever met who could do the trick, though he wasn't a warlord, because the Red Caps were no longer a kingdom unto themselves.

Ash and Holly were forced to stretch to keep up with the much bigger man; Jonty was a small giant even among them. They had been in charge of this expedition, but goblins are a tough lot. If they let Jonty reach the fight first – if they showed themselves weaker, slower, than him – then they might not be in charge at the end of the night. Goblin society is survival of the fittest.

I cradled the gun carefully, pointing it away from Jonty. No one got ahead of us – no one else had the length of leg – and the others were fighting just to keep pace. Such a big creature, but he ran with the grace and speed of something lithe and beautiful.

I asked him, 'Why help me?'

In his deep voice, like gravel, he said, 'I swore a personal oath to protect you. I will not be forsworn.' He leaned over me, so that a drop of that magical blood fell upon my face. He whispered, 'The Goddess and God still speak to me.'

I whispered back, 'You heard my prayer.'

He gave a small nod. I touched his face, and my hand came away covered in blood, warm blood. I cuddled closer into the warmth of him. He raised his eyes again, and ran faster.

Chapter 20

THE SKY BOILED WITH STORM CLOUDS OVER THE SMALL woods that bordered the parking lot. The wild hunt wasn't a tentacled nightmare anymore. It looked like a storm, if storms could hover against the tops of trees and drape like black silk dripping between the trunks.

Lightning flashed from the ground into the clouds – Mistral was still alive and fighting back. Who else? Green flame flickered through the trees, and something hard and tight in my chest eased – that flame was Doyle's hand of power. He was alive as well. In that moment nothing else really mattered to me. Not crown, not kingdom, not faerie itself; nothing mattered except that Doyle was alive and not so hurt he could not fight.

Ash and Holly put on a burst of speed so that they were ahead of Jonty and me as we neared the open area closest the trees. There wasn't enough cover to hide anything in the open field, until from thin shadows, goblins appeared. They didn't materialize, but emerged like a sniper hidden in his gillie suit in the field – except that the only camouflage the goblins had was their own skin and clothes.

Ash had called Kurag, Goblin King, as we ran to this place. To do so, he had bared his sword and put a hand on my shoulder to come away with blood to smear upon the blade. Blood and blade: old magic that worked long before cell phones were a dream in a human's mind. Personally I wouldn't have wanted to run on the icy road with a bared blade. But Ash wasn't human, and he made it all look easy.

Ash and his brother ran ahead of Jonty – whoever got to the rendezvous first would lead the goblins without argument. But I didn't care – as long as we saved my men, I didn't care who led. I would have followed anyone in that moment to save them.

One of the brothers fell to talking with the waiting force. It wasn't until the other brother got close enough for his eyes to flash crimson that I knew it was Holly come back to Jonty and me. Holly was struggling to breathe normally. Outrunning someone whose legs were almost as tall as he was took more effort than was pretty, even for a warrior as formidable as he. His voice held only a hint of the breathlessness that made his shoulders and chest rise and fall so rapidly. 'The archers will be ready in moments. We need the princess.'

'I am not much of an archer,' I said, still cradled in the heat of Jonty's body, and the blood. The blood that flowed from his cap down to my body was warm. Warm as if it spilled from a freshly opened wound.

Holly gave me a look that appeared irritated even in the forgiving glow of moonlight. 'You carry the hand of blood,' he said. He let that anger that was always just below the surface for him fall into his voice.

I nearly asked what that had to do with archers. But the moment before I said it, I did know. 'Oh,' I said.

'Unless Kitto exaggerated what you did in Los Angeles to the Nameless,' Holly added.

I shook my head, the warm blood creeping down my neck between my skin and the borrowed trench coat. The blood should have been disturbing, but it wasn't – it felt like a warm blanket on a cold night: comforting. 'No, Kitto didn't exaggerate,' I said. I didn't like that Kitto had borne tales to the goblins, but forced myself to accept that he was half theirs and still had to answer to their king. He'd probably had little choice in what he told them.

'The full hand of blood,' Holly said, and his

voice wasn't so much angry as skeptical. 'Hard to believe it lies in such a fragile creature.'

'Look at my cap, if you doubt her power,' Jonty rumbled.

Holly gazed upward, but his eyes didn't stay on the cap long. His gaze slid down to me, and something in that look was both sexual and predatory. I could feel the blood plastering the back of my hair, my shoulders, arms; I must have looked like an accident victim. Most men would have found it frightening, but Holly looked at me as if I'd covered myself with perfume and lingerie. One man's nightmare, another's fantasy.

He reached a hand up, tentatively, as if he thought either Jonty or I would protest. When we didn't, he touched my shoulder. I think he meant to merely get a touch of blood on his fingers, but the moment his fingers brushed me, a look of wonder came over his face. He leaned in toward me, the wonder being eaten by something that was part desire, and part violence. 'What have you been doing, Princess, to feel like this?'

'I don't know what you're feeling, so I don't know how to answer.' My voice was small. Of all the men I'd agreed to have sex with, Holly and his brother were the ones who gave me the most pause.

Jonty's arms tightened around me, almost possessively. That was both good and bad. If all of Jonty was in proportion, then I could not satisfy him and live to tell the tale. But it was hard to tell with the Red Cap; his possessiveness might have had nothing to do with sex, and everything to do with the blood magic.

Holly drew his hand from my shoulder. He began to lick the blood from his hand like a cat that has dipped its paw in your glass of milk. His eyes fluttered closed as he licked. 'She calls your blood,' he said, in a low voice better suited for a bedroom than a battlefield.

'Yes,' Jonty said, and that one word from him had the same overly intimate tone.

I was missing something, but did not want to admit that I didn't know what was happening, or why they were so fascinated with the fact that touching me made the Red Cap bleed more. At a loss, I changed the subject. 'If you want me to call blood from our enemies, we need to get closer to the archers.' I fought to keep my voice matter-of-fact, as if I knew exactly what was happening and either didn't care or took it completely in stride.

'And who will hold you while you call blood, so those dainty feet do not touch the cold ground?' Holly said.

'I will stand on my own.'

'I will hold you,' Jonty said.

'You are a goblin, Jonty. Goblins fight among themselves as sport, which means it is likely there is at least a nick somewhere on your body. If you have a wound, even a small one, when I call blood, I will bleed you, too.'

'I am no Red Cap to brawl for the sake of brawling. I save my flesh for other things,' Holly said. He licked the last of the blood from his hand in a long smooth movement that should have been sensual, but managed to be mostly just unnerving.

'I will stand on my own,' I repeated.

'Your brother waves to get our attention,' Jonty said then to Holly, and moved forward.

Holly hesitated, as if he would block our way, but then moved aside, speaking as Jonty passed him. 'I will see you survive this night, Princess, for I mean to have you.'

'I remember our bargain, Holly,' I called back.

The smaller goblin hurried to keep up with Jonty's longer strides. It was like a child running after an adult, though Holly wouldn't have thanked me for the comparison. 'I hear reluctance in your voice, Princess, and the sex will be all the sweeter for it.'

'Do not torment her on the edge of battle, Holly,' Jonty said.

Holly didn't argue; he just abandoned the topic for the time being. 'The archers will cut them for you, but you have to weaken them enough to bring them down,' he said to me.

'I know what you want me to do.'

'You don't sound certain.'

I didn't voice my doubts, but this was a wild hunt. A true wild hunt, which meant it was the essence of faerie. The creatures could bleed, but how do you kill something that is formed of pure magic? This was ancient magic, chaos magic, primeval and horrible. How do you kill such things? Even if I bled them enough to bring them to earth, could they be truly slain by blade and ax? I had never heard of anyone fighting and winning against such a hunt.

Of course, I had never heard that the spectral hunts could bleed if cut. Sholto had called this one into being, using magic that he and I had raised as a couple. Was it my mortal blood that had made the hunt vulnerable to bleeding? Was my mortality truly contagious, as some of my enemies claimed?

Following this idea to its logical extension meant that if I sat on the throne of our court, it would condemn all of the sidhe to age and die. But at this moment if my mortal flesh had made this hunt mortal in turn, I was grateful for it. It meant they could bleed and die, and I needed them to die. We needed to win this battle. I would not spread my mortality through all of faerie, but to have shared it with these creatures – well, that would be a blessing.

Chapter 21

THE ARROWS CUT THE NIGHT SKY LIKE BLACK WOUNDS across the stars, vanishing into the boiling black silk of the clouds. We waited in the winter night for screams to let us know the bolts had found their mark, but there was nothing but silence.

I stood on the ground, pulling the borrowed trench coat around me. I stood on Holly's cloak, which he had thrown on the ground to keep my bare feet from the rough ground and the cold. 'The cloak gets in the way of my ax,' he'd said, as if he were afraid that I might think he was being gentlemanly. Then he moved forward to be with his brother and the other warriors.

Only Jonty and one other Red Cap stayed back with me, though every Red Cap who had come out tonight – a dozen of them – had touched me before they went to take their place in the ranks. They had laid their mouths, in a strange sort of kiss, against my shoulder where the coat hung heavy with blood from Jonty's cap. One had caught the coat in his pointed teeth and torn it before Jonty had slapped him away. The ones who came after had widened the hole until the lips of the last few touched my bare shoulder where the blood had begun to dry to my skin. I had neither offered the Red Caps the familiarity, nor been asked; Jonty had called them, and spoken in a Gaelic so old that I could not follow it.

Whatever Jonty had said to them had turned their faces to me, and the look in their eyes was that odd mix of sex, hunger, and eagerness that I'd seen in Holly. I hadn't understood the look – and hadn't had time to question it – but because it cost me nothing to have their lips pressed to my shoulder, I allowed it. Then I noticed that each of the Red Caps who touched me began bleeding afresh after touching Jonty's blood on my body.

I was fighting an urge to scream my impatience at them, but the Red Caps weren't the ones delaying; the other goblins squabbled about who would go where. If Kurag, Goblin King, had come, there would have been no arguments, but Ash and Holly, though feared warriors, were not kings, and all other leadership among the goblins is a constant state of struggle. The goblin society represented the ultimate in Darwinian evolution: only the strongest survive, and only the very strongest lead.

If I had been truly queen enough to lead them, they would have done what I ordered, but I didn't have their respect yet, so I knew better than to try to lead here. It would have undermined Ash and Holly, and gained me nothing. Besides, battlefield tactics wasn't my strongest suit, and I knew that. My father had drilled into me from an early age to know my strengths and weaknesses. Find allies who complement you, he'd said. True friendship is a type of love, and all love has power.

Jonty leaned over me and said, 'Call your hand of power, Princess.'

'How do you know they are hurt?'

'We are goblins,' he said, as if that settled it.

Another line of green flame flickered through the trees, and I was close enough now to see the black tendrils back away from it. I didn't argue again, but called the hand of blood.

I concentrated on my left hand. It didn't emit a beam of power, or anything like you see in the movies; it was simply that the mark, or key, to the hand of blood lay in the palm of my left hand. Or maybe *doorway* was a better term. I opened the mark in the palm of that hand, and though there was nothing to see with the naked eye, there was plenty to feel.

It was as if the blood in my veins had suddenly turned to molten metal. My blood tried to boil with the power of it. I screamed, and thrust my hand toward the cloud. I projected that burning, tearing power outward. I realized in that moment that it wasn't just the archers who were shooting blind – I had never before tried to use the hand of blood on a target I could not see.

For a heartbeat the power turned back on me, and every small scrape I'd accumulated in the past twenty-four hours bled. Each tiny wound bled like a fountain, and I fought my body, fought my own magic to keep it from destroying me.

Lightning struck the cloud, and illuminated it, as it had inside the sluagh's mound. But I wasn't horrified this time, I was joyous; a fierce triumphant joy. If I could see it, I could make it bleed.

I had the blink of an eye to spot my targets. A breath to see that the tentacled mass was white and silver and gold, not the black and grey and white it had been. I had an instant to note that the hunt had a terrible beauty before I thrust my power toward that shining mass and screamed, 'Bleed!'

Green flame climbed up the trees and lightning flared behind it so that both powers met mine in the cloud at the same instant. The cloud flashed green in reflected color. I called for blood and black fountains of it exploded into the green-yellow flare.

The light died, leaving the night blacker than before. My night vision had been ruined from staring into the light. Something spattered against the left side of my face, something that felt wet, but carried no shock of temperature difference. Only two things feel like that: water at body temperature, and very fresh blood. If I had been a warrior, I would have whirled, gun up, but I turned slowly, like a character in a horror movie who doesn't really want to see the blow before it falls.

All that met my eyes was the shortest of my Red Cap guards, Bithek. Someone had sliced open his scalp to spill blood in a gory mask down his face, so that even his eyes were lost to the dark flow of it. Then he shook his head like a wet dog, spattering me with warm drops. I closed my eyes, put up a protecting hand.

Jonty's chided Bithek. 'You're wasting the blood.'

'But so much, can't keep it out of my eyes. I'd forgotten that it was ever like this,' Bithek growled.

I looked behind me at Jonty and found him as bloody as the other guard. It made me look around at all of them. They were all covered in blood, but even by moonlight and starlight, I could see now that the blood welled from the caps on their heads.

'Your magic brings our blood, Princess,' Jonty said.

'I don't understand . . .'

'Make them bleed for us,' the last Red Cap said.

I looked at him. 'I can't remember your name,' I said.

'For this magic, I would follow you nameless, Princess Meredith. Bleed our enemies, and cover us in their blood.'

I turned away from the Red Caps. I didn't understand completely, but trusted. One mystery at a time – later, later I would unravel it all.

Even facing away from the Red Caps, I could still feel them. It was as if their power complemented mine, fed it. No; our powers fed each other; they were like a warm battery at my back, comforting, energizing.

I threw that warmth, that weight of power against our enemies. I called their blood by the flash of lightning and the flicker of green-gold flame. I called their blood and knew that the Red Caps at my back bled with them. I could feel it. The ones who waited ahead of us bled, too.

A goblin came running toward us in a blurring speed that would have done any sidhe proud. He was no taller than me, but had four arms to my two, and a face that was noseless and strangely unfinished. He dropped to his knees, and would not meet my eyes. He actually put two of his arms on the ground and abased himself – striking, because in goblin society the lower you go, the more respect you feel for the person you're addressing. I didn't usually get that kind of greeting from anybody. He said, 'A message from Ash and Holly: ' "Aim your magic better, Princess, before you bleed us all to death." '

Now I understood why he was abasing himself – he had been afraid I'd take the message badly.

'Tell them I'll aim better,' I said wryly.

He ducked his head, bumping his forehead to the earth, then sprang to his feet and raced back the way he had come. I drew my magic back, swallowed the hand of blood. The pain was instantaneous, grinding, and sharp, like broken glass flowing through my veins. I screamed my pain, wordlessly, but kept the magic inside me.

I fought to visualize the creatures inside the cloud. Tentacles, veined with silver and gold, white and pure, muscled magic. I fell to my knees with the pain. Jonty reached for me, and I hissed, 'No, don't touch me.' The magic wanted to bleed someone, anyone, and his touch would make him the target.

I closed my eyes so I could mentally draw the picture of what I sought. When I could see it, shining and writhing across the inside of my eyes, I reached my left hand out again, and threw that broken-glass pain into the image. My pain intensified for a shining, breathless moment – all there was in that second was the pain, so much pain. Then it eased, and I could breathe again . . . and I knew the hand of blood was busy else-where.

I kept my eyes closed so nothing else could catch my eye. I was afraid that if I saw the goblin warriors again, I'd bleed them by accident. I knew what I wanted to bleed, and that was above their heads in the sky. I thought about all the beautiful things that could have flown above their heads. Did it have to be frightening? There was such beauty in faerie, why did it have to be nightmarish?

I heard the sound of wings whistling overhead, and opened my eyes. I'd fallen to the ground on top of Ash's cloak, though I didn't remember falling. Above us, so close that the great white wings brushed Jonty's head, were swans. Swans gleaming white in the moonlight: There had to be more than twenty of them, and had I seen what I thought I saw on their necks and shoulders? Chains and collars of gold? It couldn't be – this was the stuff of legends.

It was the nameless Red Cap who voiced my thought: 'They had chains on their necks.'

I heard the wild call of geese next. They flew just overhead, following the line the swans had taken. I got to my feet, stumbling on the edge of the borrowed trench coat. Jonty caught me, but it didn't seem to hurt him or me. I felt light and airy, as if the hand of blood had become something else. What had I been thinking just before the swans flew overhead? That the beauty in faerie was too often nightmarish?

There was a flight of cranes then: my father's bird, one of his symbols. The cranes flew low and seemed to dip their wings at us, almost in a salute.

'They fall!' shouted Bithek.

I looked where he pointed. The storm cloud had vanished, and with it most of the creatures. There had been so many, a writhing mass of them, but now there were only a few – less than ten, maybe – and one of them had already crashed through the trees. A second fell earthward, and I heard the sharp crack of the trees breaking under the weight like a cannon shot, and men scattered, too far away for me to know who was who. Was Doyle safe? Was Mistral? Had the magic worked in time?

Inside my head, I could finally admit, it was Doyle I most needed to survive. I loved Rhys, but not like I loved Doyle. I let myself own that. I let myself admit, at least inside my own head, that if Doyle died, part of me would die as well. It had been the moment at the car, when he'd shoved Frost and me inside and given me to Frost. 'If not me, it must be you,' he'd said to Frost. I loved Frost, too, but I'd had my revelation. If I could have chosen my king this moment, I knew who it would be.

Pity that I wasn't the one doing the choosing.

Figures started toward us, and the goblins parted to form a corridor for my guards. When I finally recognized that tall, dark figure, something in my chest eased, and I was suddenly crying. I started walking toward him, then. I didn't feel the frozen grass under my bare feet. I didn't feel when broken stubble cut me. Then I was running, with the Red Caps jogging beside me. I picked up the edges of the borrowed coat like a dress, and held it out of my way so I could run to him.

Doyle wasn't alone; dogs, huge black dogs milled around his legs. Suddenly I remembered a vision I'd had of him with dogs like this, and the ground tilted under my feet, vision and reality melding before my eyes. The dogs reached me first, pressing warm muscled fur against me where I knelt, their great panting breath hot on my face as I held my hands out to touch them. Their black fur ran with a tingling rush of magic.

The bodies writhed under my hand, the fur growing less coarse, smoothing, the bodies less dense. I looked up into the face of a racing hound, white and sleek, with ears a shining red. The other hound's face was half red and half white, as if some hand had drawn a line down the center of it. I'd never seen anything so beautiful as that face.

Then Doyle was standing in front of me, and I threw myself into his arms. He lifted me off the ground and hugged me so hard it almost hurt. But I wanted him to hold me hard. I wanted to feel the reality of his body against me. I wanted to know he was alive. I needed to touch him to know it was true. I needed him to touch me, and let me know that he was still my Darkness, still my Doyle.

He whispered into my hair, 'Merry, Merry, Merry.'

I clung to him, wordless, and wept.

Chapter 22

EVERYONE LIVED, EVEN THE HUMAN POLICEMEN, though some were driven mad by what they had seen. Abeloec fed them from his cup of horn and they fell into a magical sleep, destined to wake with no memory of the horrors they had seen. Magic isn't always bad.

The black dogs were a miracle: They changed depending on who touched them. Abe's touch turned the great black dogs into lapdogs to lie before a cozy fire, white with red markings – faerie dogs. Mistral's touch turned them to huge Irish wolfhounds, not the pale, slender ones of today, but the giants that the Romans had feared so much – these were the hounds that could snap the spine of a horse with their bite. Someone else's touch turned a dog into a green-furred Cu Sith that loped off toward the Seelie mound. What would their king, Taranis, think of its return? He'd probably try to take credit for it, claim it as proof of his power.

In the midst of the return of so much that was lost, other things much more precious were returned to me. Galen's voice shouting my name turned me in Doyle's arms. He was running across the snowy field with flowers following in his wake, as if wherever he stepped, spring returned. All the rest who had vanished into the dead gardens were with him. Nicca appeared with a following of the winged demi-fey. Amatheon was there with the tattoo of a plow gleaming like neon blood on his chest. I saw Hawthorne, his dark hair starred with living blossoms. Adair's hair burned around him like a halo of fire, so bright it obscured his face as he moved. Aisling walked in a cloud of singing birds. He was nude, except for a piece of black gauze that he'd wrapped around his face.

Onilwyn was the only one who did not come. I thought the garden had kept him, until I heard another voice shrieking my name in the distance. Then I heard Onilwyn's frantic cry: 'No, my lord, no!'

'It cannot be,' I whispered, looking up at Doyle, watching fear cross his face, too.

'It is he,' Nicca said.

Galen wrapped himself around me as if I were the last solid thing in the world. Doyle moved so he could embrace me as well. 'It's my fault,' Galen whispered, 'I didn't mean to do it.'

Aisling spoke, and the flock of birds sang as if they were moved to joy by the sound of his voice. 'We reemerged in the Hallway of Mortality.'

'Major magic doesn't work there; that's why we're all so helpless to stop the torture,' Rhys said.

'We came out of the walls and floors – and trees and flowers, and shining marble came with us,' Aisling said. 'The hallway is forever changed.'

Galen started to shake, and I held him as hard as I could. 'I was buried alive,' he said. 'I couldn't breathe, I didn't need to breathe, but my body kept trying to do it. I came up through the floor screaming.' He collapsed to his knees while I fought to hold him.

'The queen was walling up Nerys's clan alive,' Amatheon said. 'Galen did not take well to that after his time in the earth.'

Galen shook as if he were having a fit, as if every muscle were fighting itself, as if he were cold, though fevered. It was too much power and too much fear.

Adair's glow had dimmed enough so that I could see his eyes. 'Galen said "No prisoners, no walls." The walls melted away, and flowers sprang up in the cells. He hadn't understood how much power he had gained.'

Another shriek approached in the distance. 'Cousin!'

Doyle said, 'Galen's exhortation, "No prisoners," freed Cel.'

Galen started to cry. 'I'm sorry,' he said.

'Onilwyn and the queen herself – and some of her guard – are wrestling Cel even now,' Hawthorne said, 'or he would be here already, trying to harm the princess.'

'He is quite mad,' Aisling said, 'and he is intent on hurting all of us. But most especially you, Princess.'

'The queen told us to run back to the Western Lands. She's hoping he'll grow more calm with time,' Hawthorne said. Even by starlight, he looked doubtful.

'She has admitted before her nobles that she cannot guarantee your safety,' Aisling said.

'We should flee, if we are going to,' Hawthorne said.

I realized what he meant. If Cel attacked me now, here, like this, we would be within our rights to kill him, if we could. My guards were sworn to protect, and Cel was no match for the strength and magic that stood with me now. Not alone, he wasn't.

'If I thought the queen would allow his death to go unpunished, I would say, *Stay, fight*,' Doyle said.

One of the great black mastiffs nudged Galen.

He reached for it, almost automatically, and it changed before my eyes. It became a sleek white hound with one red ear. It licked the tears from Galen's face and he stared at it in wonder, as if he hadn't seen the dogs until that moment.

Then came Cel's voice, broken, almost unrecognizable. 'Merry!' His screams broke off abruptly. The silence was almost more frightening than the shouting, and my heart was suddenly pounding hard in my chest.

'What happened?' I called out.

Andais walked over the rise of the last gentle hill, following Galen's trail of flowers. She was alone, save for her consort, Eamon. They were almost the same height, their long black hair streaming out behind them in a wind that came from nowhere. Andais was dressed as if she were going to a Halloween ball – and you were meant to fear her beauty. Eamon's clothes were more sedate, and also all black. The fact that Andais arrived with only him at her side meant she didn't want extra witnesses. Eamon was the only one who knew all her secrets.

'Cel will sleep for a time,' she called, as if in answer to a question we hadn't asked.

Galen fought to stand while I steadied him. Doyle moved a little in front of me. Some of the others did, too. The rest looked behind us into the night, as if they suspected their queen of treachery. Eamon might be on my side some of the time – he might even hate Cel – but he would never go against his queen.

Andais and Eamon stopped far enough away that they were out of easy weapon range. The goblins watched them, and us, from a tight huddled knot, as if they weren't sure whose side they were on. I didn't blame them, for I'd be going back to L.A. and they would be staying here. I could force Kurag, their king, to lend me warriors, but I couldn't expect his men to follow me into exile.

'Meredith, niece of mine, child of my brother Essus, greetings.' She'd chosen a greeting that acknowledged I was her bloodline. She was trying to be reassuring; she was just so bad at it.

I stepped forward until she could see me, but not beyond the protective circle of the men. 'Queen Andais, aunt of mine, sister of my father, Essus, greetings.'

'You must go back to the Western Lands tonight, Meredith,' said Andais.

'Yes,' I answered.

Andais looked at the hounds that still milled among the men. Rhys finally let himself touch them, and they became terriers of breeds long forgotten, some white and red, others a good solid black and tan.

The queen tried to call one of the dogs to her. The big mastiffs were what the humans called Hell Hounds, though they had nothing to do with the Christian devil. The big black dogs would have matched the queen's costume, but they ignored her. These wish hounds, the hounds of faerie, would not go to the hand of the Queen of Air and Darkness.

Had I been her, I would have knelt in the snow and coaxed them, but Andais did not kneel to anyone, or anything. She stood straight and beautiful, and colder than the snow around her feet.

Two other hounds had come to my hands, and they now bumped against me on either side, leaning in to be petted. I did it, because in faerie, we touch someone when they ask. The moment I stroked that silken fur, I felt better: braver, more confident, a little less afraid of what was about to happen.

'Dogs, Meredith? Couldn't you return our horses to us, or our cattle, instead?'

'There were pigs in my vision,' I said.

'Not dogs,' she said, her voice matter-of-fact, as if nothing special had happened.

'I saw dogs in a different vision, when I was still in the Western Lands.'

'True vision then,' she said, her voice still bland and faintly condescending.

'Apparently so,' I said, ruffling the ear of the taller of the hounds.

'You must leave now, Meredith, and take this wild magic with you.'

'Wild magic is not so easily tamed, Aunt Andais,' I said. 'I will take back with me what will go, but some of it is flying free, even as we speak.'

'I saw the swans,' Andais said, 'but no crows. You are so terribly Seelie.'

'The Seelie would say otherwise,' I said.

'Go, go back to where you came from. Take your guards and your magic, and leave me the wreck of my son.' It was tantamount to admitting that if Cel fought me tonight, he would die.

'I will go only if I can take all the guards who would come with me.' I said it as firmly and bravely as I could.

'You cannot have Mistral,' she said.

I fought not to look for him at my back, fought not to see his big hands touching the huge hounds that his caress had brought into being. 'Yes, I said. I remember what you told me in the dead gardens: that I could not keep him.'

'You will not argue with me?' she asked.

'Would it do any good?' The tiniest hint of anger seeped into my voice. The hounds tucked themselves tighter against my legs, leaning in for all they were worth, as if they would remind me not to lose control.

'The only thing that will call Mistral from my side to yours in the Western Lands is if you come up pregnant. If you become with child, I will have to let go of any who could be the father.'

'If I become with child, I will send word,' I said, and fought to keep my voice even. Mistral was going to suffer for being with me, I could see it in her face, feel it in her voice.

'I do not know what to wish for anymore, Meredith. Your magic runs through my sithen, changing it into something bright and cheerful. There is a field of flowers in my torture chamber.'

'What do you want me to say, Aunt Andais?'

'I wanted the magic of faerie to be reborn, but you are not enough my brother's daughter. You will make of us only another Seelie Court to dance and parade before the human press. You will make us beautiful, but destroy that which makes us different.'

'I would humbly disagree with that,' said a voice from the crowd of my men. Sholto stepped forward. His tattoo had become a nest of real tentacles again, glowing and pale, and strangely beautiful, like some underwater sea creature, some anemone or jellyfish. It was the first time I'd ever seen him display his extra bits with pride. He stood tall with the spear and knife of bone in his hands; at his side was a huge white hound with different red markings on each of its three heads. Sholto used the side of the hand that held the knife to rub the top of one of the huge heads.

Sholto spoke again. 'Merry makes us beautiful, yes, my queen. But the beauty is stranger than anything the Seelie Court would allow within their doors.'

Andais gazed at Sholto, and for a moment I thought I saw regret. Sholto's magic rode him, and power breathed off him into the night.

'You had him,' she said to me, simply.

'Yes,' I said.

'How was it?'

'It was our coming together that raised the wild hunt.'

She shivered, and there was a hunger on her face that frightened me. 'Amazing. Perhaps I will try him some night.'

Sholto spoke again. 'There was a time, my queen, when the thought of a chance at your bed would have filled me with joy. But I truly know now that I am King Sholto of the Sluagh, the Lord of That Which Passes Between, Lord of Shadows. I will no longer take crumbs from the table of any sidhe.'

She made a sharp sound, almost a hiss. 'You must be an amazing bit of ass, Meredith. One fuck with you and they all turn against me.'

To that, there was no safe answer, so I said nothing. I stood in the midst of my men, with the weight and press of the hounds milling around us. Would she have been more aggressive if the dogs – war dogs, most of them – had not been there? Was she afraid of the magic – or the more solid form the magic had taken?

One of the small terriers growled, and it was like a signal to the others. The night was suddenly thick with growls, a low chorus that shivered down my spine. I petted the heads of those I could touch, hushing them. The Goddess had sent me guardians, I understood that now. I thanked her for it.

'Cel's guards who did not take oath to him – you promised they could go with me,' I said.

'I will not strip him of all signs of my favor,' she answered, and her anger seemed to crackle on the cold air.

'You gave your word,' I insisted.

The dogs gave another low chorus of growls. The terriers began to bark, as terriers will. I realized in that moment that the wild hunt was not gone, only changed. These were the hounds of the wild hunt. These were the hounds of legend that hunted oathbreakers through the winter wood.

'Do not dare to threaten!' said Andais. Eamon touched her arm. She jerked away from him, but seemed chastened. The wild hunt had been a great leveler of the mighty. Once you became their prey, the hunt did not end until the quarry was dead.

'I do not believe I am the huntsman,' I said.

'It would be a bad night, Queen Andais, to be an oathbreaker.' Doyle's deep molasses voice seemed to hang on the night, as if his words had more weight on the still, winter air than they should have.

'Are you the huntsman, Darkness? Would you punish me for breaking faith?'

'It is wild magic, Your Majesty; there is sometimes little choice when it fills you. You become an instrument of the magic, and it uses you for its own ends.'

'Magic is a tool to be wielded, not some force one allows oneself to be overcome by.'

'As you will, Queen Andais, but I ask that you do not test these hounds tonight.' Somehow it seemed Doyle wasn't talking about just the dogs.

'I will honor my word,' she said in a voice that made it clear that she did so only because she had no choice. She had never been a gracious loser, not in anything, large or small. 'But you must leave now, Meredith, this moment.'

'We need time to send for the other guards,' I said.

'I will bring all those who wish to come to you, Meredith,' Sholto said.

I turned, and there was an assurance in him, a strength that had not been there before. He stood there with his 'deformity' plain to see. He now made it seem just another part of him, though, a part that would have been as surely missed as an arm, or a leg if it were gone. Had being stripped of his extra bits made him realize he valued them? Maybe. It was his revelation, not mine.

'You would side with her,' Andais said.

'I am King of the Sluagh; I will see that an oath given and accepted is honored. Remember, Queen Andais, that the sluagh was the only wild hunt left in faerie until tonight. And I am the huntsman of the sluagh.'

She took a step toward him, as if in threat, but Eamon pulled her back. He whispered urgently against her cheek. I could not hear what he said, but the tension left her body, until she allowed herself to lean back against him. She let him hold her; in the face of those who were not her friends, she let Eamon's arms hold her.

'Go, Meredith, take all that is yours, and go.' Her voice was almost neutral, almost free of that rage that always seemed to bubble just underneath her skin.

'Your Majesty,' Rhys said, 'we cannot go to the human airport like this.' His gesture seemed to note how many of the guards were naked, and bloody. The terriers at his feet gave happy barks, as if it looked all right to them.

Sholto spoke again. 'I will take you to the edge of the Western Sea, just as I took the sluagh when we hunted Meredith in Los Angeles.'

I looked at him and shook my head. 'I thought you came by plane.'

He laughed, and it was a joyous sound. 'Did you picture the dark host of the sluagh on some human airplane sipping wine and ogling the flight attendants?'

I laughed with him. 'I hadn't thought about it that clearly. You are the sluagh – I didn't question how you got to me.'

'I will walk the edge of the field where it touches the woods. It is an in-between place, neither field nor forest. I will walk, you will all follow, and we will be at the edge of the Western Sea, where it touches the shore. I am the lord of the between places, Meredith.'

'I didn't think any royals could still travel so far,' Rhys said.

'I am the King of the Sluagh, Cromm Cruach, master of the last wild hunt of faerie. I have certain gifts.'

'Indeed,' the queen said, drily, 'use those gifts, Shadowspawn, and take these rabble from my sight.' She'd used the nickname that the sidhe called him behind his back, but that even she had never used to his face before.

'Your disdain cannot touch me tonight, for I have seen wonders.' He held up the weapons of bone, as if she had missed them before. 'I hold the bones of my people. I know my worth.'

If I'd been closer to him I would have embraced him. Probably just as well that I wasn't, as it might have ruined the power of the moment, but I promised myself to give him a hug the moment we had some privacy. I loved seeing that he valued himself at last.

I heard a sound like the breaking of ice. 'Frost,' I said. 'We can't leave him behind.'

'Didn't the FBI take him to the hospital?' Doyle asked.

I shook my head. 'I don't think so.' I looked out across the snow. I couldn't see anything, but . . . I started moving, and the hounds followed at my side. I started to run across the snow, and felt the first sharp pain in my cut feet. I ignored it, and ran faster. Time and distance shortened – as they never before had outside the sithen. One minute I was with the others, the next I was miles away, in the fields beside the road. My twin hounds had stayed with me, and half a dozen of the black mastiffs were there, too.

Frost lay in the snow, unmoving, as if he couldn't feel the dogs snuffling at him or my hands turning him over. The drifts underneath him were soaked with blood, and his eyes were closed. His face was so cold. I lowered my lips to his and whispered his name: 'Frost, please, please, don't leave me.'

His body convulsed, and his breath rattled back into his chest. Death seemed to be reversed. His eyes fluttered open, and he tried to reach for me, but his hand fell back into the snow, too weak. I lifted his hand to my face and held it there. I held his hand there while it grew warm against my skin.

I cried, and he found his voice, hoarse. He whispered, 'The cold cannot kill me.'

'Oh, Frost.'

He raised his other hand and touched the tears on my face. 'Do not weep for me, Merry. You love me, I heard it. I was leaving, but I heard your voice, and I couldn't leave, not if you loved me.'

I cradled his head in my lap and wept. His other hand, the one that I wasn't clutching, brushed the fur of one of the huge black dogs. The dog stretched and grew tall and white. A shining white stag stood over us. It had a collar of holly, and looked like some Yule card brought to life. It pranced in the snow, then ran in a white blur across the snow until it was lost to sight.

'What magic is abroad this night?' Frost whispered.

'The magic that will take you home.' Doyle spoke from behind us. He fell to his knees in the snow beside Frost, and took his hand. 'The next time I send you to a hospital, you are to go.'

Frost managed a wan smile. 'I could not leave her.'

Doyle nodded as if that made perfect sense.

'I don't think the magic will last until morning,' Rhys said. They were all there, trailing behind, except Mistral. He was with the queen, I supposed. I hadn't even gotten to say good-bye.

'But for tonight,' Rhys said, 'I am Cromm Cruach, and I can help.' He knelt on the other side of Frost and laid hands on him, above where his clothing was black with blood.

Rhys was suddenly formed of white light, not just his hands, but all of him glowing. His hair moved in the wind of his own magic. Frost's body jerked upward, leaving my lap and our hands. He fell back against Doyle and me, and said in a voice that was almost his own, 'That hurt.'

'Sorry about that,' said Rhys, 'but I'm not a healer, not really. There is too much of death in my power to make it painless.'

Frost touched his own shoulder and chest, taking his hands from out of Doyle's and mine. 'If you are not a healer, then why do I feel healed?'

'Old magic,' Rhys said. 'The morning light will find this magic gone.'

'How can you be certain?' Doyle asked.

'The voice of the God in my head tells me so.'

No one questioned after that. We just accepted it as true.

Sholto led us to the edge of the field and forest. The dogs moved around us, some choosing their masters, others making it plain that they did not belong to anyone here. The ones that chose among us followed as Sholto walked, but the other black dogs began to fall back and vanish into the night, as if we had imagined them. The hound at my side bumped my hand for a pat, as if to remind me that it was real.

I wasn't certain the hounds would stay, but they seemed magically to give each of us what we needed tonight. Galen walked surrounded by dogs, circled by sleek-looking greyhounds and a trio of small dogs dancing at his feet. They made him smile, and helped chase the shadows from his face. Doyle moved in a circle of black dogs; they fawned and capered about him like puppies. The terriers followed Rhys like a small army of fur. Frost held my hand over the back of the smallest of the greyhounds. He had no dog at his side – only the white stag that had run into the night. But he seemed perfectly content with my hand in his.

The air was warm, and I looked from Frost's face to Sholto, and found that Sholto was walking on sand. One moment we were walking in snow-covered fields at the edge of the trees, and the next moment sand sucked at my feet. Water swirled over my bare toes, and the bite of salt let me know that I was bleeding.

I must have made some small sound, because Frost picked me up. I protested, but it did me no good. The greyhounds stayed at his side, dancing around us, half afraid of the curl of ocean, and seemingly worried that they couldn't stay in contact with me.

Sholto led us up on dry land. The three-headed dog and the bone weapons had vanished, but somehow I didn't think they were any more gone than the chalice was from me. True magic cannot be lost or stolen; it can only be given away.

We stood in the darkness, hours before dawn. I could hear the rushing of cars on the highway nearby. We were hidden by cliffs, but that would change as the dawn grew near. Surfers and fishermen would come down to the sea, and we needed to be gone before then.

'Use glamour to hide your appearance,' Sholto said. 'I have sent for taxis. They will arrive very soon.'

'What magic is it,' I asked, 'that lets you find taxis in L.A. at a moment's notice?'

'I am the Lord of That Which Passes Between, Merry, and taxis are always going between one place and another.'

It made perfect sense, but it made me smile all the same. I reached for Sholto, and Frost let him take me, though not just with his arms. The thick muscular tentacles wrapped around my body, the smaller ones playing along my thighs, somehow finding their way under the borrowed trench coat.

'Next time you are in my bed, I will not be half a man.'

I kissed him, and whispered against his lips, 'If that was you as only half a man, King Sholto, then I can hardly wait to have you in all your glory.'

He laughed, that joyous sound that had

brought the singing of birds in the sluagh's dead garden. I thought there would be no answer here, but suddenly over the sighing of surf came singing, one birdsong after another, sliding in joyous celebration in the dark. It was a mockingbird, singing for Sholto's laughter.

We stood for a moment on the edge of the Western Sea with the mockingbird's song pouring over us, as if happiness could have a sound.

Sholto kissed me back, hard and thorough, leaving me breathless. Then he handed me back, not to Frost, but to Doyle. 'I will return so I can bring the rest of the guards who wish to come into exile with you.'

Doyle cuddled me in against his body and said, 'Beware the queen.'

Sholto nodded. 'I will be wary.' He began to walk back the way we had come. Somewhere before he vanished from sight I saw the white shine of a dog at his side.

'Everybody remember that the glamour is supposed to hide the fact that we're naked, and bloody,' Rhys said. 'Anyone who doesn't have enough glamour to pull it off, stand next to someone who does.'

'Yes, Teacher,' I said.

He grinned at me. 'I can cause death with a touch and a word; I can heal with my hands for tonight. But damn, conjuring this many taxis out of thin air – now, that's impressive.'

We walked up to the line of waiting taxis, laughing. The drivers all seemed a little puzzled to find themselves in the middle of nowhere, waiting beside an empty beach, but they let us get in.

We gave the taxis the address of Maeve Reed's Holmby Hills house, and they drove. They didn't even complain about the dogs. Now, that was magic.

THE END

The new Merry Gentry novel

A Lick of Frost

is now available from Bantam Press

Here's the first chapter to
tickle your fancy . . .

CHAPTER 1

I WAS SITTING IN AN ELEGANT CONFERENCE ROOM IN the top of one of the gleaming towers that make up part of downtown Los Angeles. The room's far wall was almost entirely of glass, so that the view was nearly agoraphobic. They're predicting that if the big one—the big earthquake that is—hits, this section of L.A. will be eight to fifteen feet deep in glass. Anything on the streets below will be cut to pieces, crushed, or trapped underneath an avalanche of glass. Not a pretty thought, but it was a day for ugly thoughts.

My uncle Taranis, King of Light and Illusion, had pressed charges against three of my royal bodyguards. He had gone to the human authorities with charges that Rhys, Galen, and Abe had raped one of his court's women.

In all the long history of his reign in the Seelie Court he had never gone outside to the humans for justice. Faerie rule; faerie law. Or truthfully, sidhe rule; sidhe law. The sidhe had ruled faerie for longer than anyone could remember. Since some of those memories stretched back thousands of years, maybe the sidhe had always been in charge, but it tasted like a lie. The sidhe do not lie, for to truly lie is to be cast out of faerie, exiled. Since I knew that the three bodyguards in question were innocent, that raised interesting problems with Lady Caitrin's testimony.

But today we were just giving statements, and, depending on how that went, King Taranis was standing by for a group call. Which was why Simon Biggs and Thomas Farmer, both of Biggs, Biggs, Farmer, and Farmer, were sitting beside me.

"Thank you for agreeing to this meeting today, Princess Meredith," one of the suits across the table said. There were seven suits across the wide, gleaming table, with their backs to the lovely view.

Ambassador Stevens, official ambassador to the courts of faerie, was sitting on our side of the table, but he was on the far side of Biggs and Farmer. Stevens said, "A word on faerie etiquette: You don't say thank you to the people of faerie, Mr. Shelby. Princess Meredith, as one of the younger royals, will probably not be offended, but you will be dealing with some nobility who are much older. Not all of them will allow a thank you to pass without grave insult." Stevens smiled when he said it, his blandly handsome face sincere from his brown eyes to his perfectly cut brown hair. He was supposed to be our voice to the world, but, truthfully, he spent all his time at the Seelie Court sucking up to my uncle. The Unseelie Court where my aunt Andais, Queen of Air and Darkness, ruled, and where I might rule someday, was too scary for Stevens. No, I didn't like him.

Michael Shelby, a U.S. Attorney for L.A. said, "I am sorry, Princess Meredith. I didn't realize."

I smiled, and said, "It's fine. The ambassador is correct, a thank-you won't bother me."

"But it will bother your men?" Shelby asked.

"Some of them, yes," I said. I looked behind me to Doyle and Frost. They stood behind me like darkness and snow made real, and that wasn't far from the truth. Doyle had black hair, black skin, a black designer suit; even his tie was black. Only the shirt was a rich royal blue, and that had been a sop to our lawyer. He thought black gave the wrong impression, made him seem threatening. Doyle, whose nickname was Darkness, had said, "I am the captain of the princess' guard. I am supposed to be threatening." The lawyers hadn't known what to say to that, but Doyle had worn the blue shirt. The color almost glowed against the rich, perfect black of his skin, which was so black there were purple and blue highlights to his body in the right light. His black eyes were hidden behind wraparound black-on-black sunglasses.

Frost's skin was as white as Doyle's was black. As white as my own. But his hair was uniquely his own, silver, like metal beaten into hair. It gleamed in the tasteful lighting of the conference room. Gleamed like something you could have melted down and made into jewelry. He had tied the top layer of it back with a barrette that was silver, and older than the city of Los Angeles itself. The dove-gray suit was Ferragamo, and the white of his shirt was less white than his own skin. The tie was darker than the suit, but not by much. The soft gray of his eyes was bare to the room as he scanned the far windows. Doyle was doing it, too, behind his glasses. I had bodyguards for a reason, and some who wanted me dead could fly. We didn't think Taranis was one of the people who wanted me dead, but why had he gone to the police? Why had he persisted in these false charges? He would never have done all this without an agenda. We just didn't know what that agenda was, so just in case, they watched the windows for things that the human lawyers couldn't even begin to imagine.

Shelby's gaze flicked behind me to the guards. He wasn't the only one who kept fighting not to glance nervously at my men, but it was Assistant District Attorney Pamela Nelson who was having the most trouble keeping her eyes, and her mind, on business. The men across the table gave the guards the glances men give when they see another man whom they are almost certain could take them physically without breaking a sweat.

U.S. Attorney Michael Shelby was tall, athletic, and handsome, with a gleam of white teeth, and the look of someone who had plans to rise above being the U.S. attorney for the Los Angeles area. He was over six feet, and his suit couldn't hide the fact that he worked out pretty seriously. He probably didn't meet many men who made him feel physically weak. His assistant Ernesto Bertram was a slender man who looked too young for his job, and far too serious with his short dark hair and glasses. It wasn't the glasses that made him look too serious; it was the look on his face, as if he'd tasted something sour. The U.S. attorney for the St. Louis area, Albert Veducci, was here, too. He didn't have Shelby's tan.

In fact, he was a little overweight, and he looked tired. His assistant was Grover. He'd actually introduced himself only as Grover, so I didn't know if it was his first, last, or only name. He smiled more than the rest of them and was attractive in that friendly, walk-you-home-on-campus way. He reminded me of guys in college who were either as nice as they seemed or absolute bastards who only wanted sex, for you to help them pass a class, or, for me, to be close to a real live faerie princess. I wouldn't know which kind of "nice guy" Grover was for a while. If things went well, I'd never figure it out, because I'd probably never see him again. If they went badly, we might see a lot of Grover.

Nelson was the assistant district attorney to *the* district attorney for Los Angeles County. Her boss, Miguel Cortez, was short, dark, and handsome. He looked great on camera. I'd seen him on the news often enough here. The trouble was that he, like Shelby, was ambitious. He liked being on the news, and wanted to be on the news more. This accusation of rape against my men had all the earmarks of a case that could make your career or break it. Cortez and Shelby were ambitious; it meant that they would either be very cautious, or very incautious. I wasn't sure which mood would help us the most, yet.

Nelson was taller than her boss, close to six feet in her not-too-high heels. Her hair was a vibrant red that fell in waves around her shoulders. It was that rare shade that is deep, rich, and as close to true red as human hair can get. Her suit was well cut, but conservative and black, her button-up shirt white, her makeup tasteful. Only that flame of hair to ruin the almost mannish exterior she portrayed. It was as if she were hiding her beauty and drawing attention to it at the same time. Because she was beautiful. A sprinkling of freckles underneath the pale makeup didn't detract from the flawless skin, it added. Her eyes were green and blue at once, depending on how the light caught them. Those undecided eyes couldn't stop looking at Frost and Doyle. She tried to concentrate on the legal pad she was supposed to be making notes on, but her gaze kept rising, and finding them, as if she couldn't help herself.

That made me wonder if there was more going on than just handsome men and a distracted woman.

Shelby cleared his throat sharply.

I jumped and looked at him. "I'm terribly sorry, Mr. Shelby, were you speaking to me?"

"No, I was not, and I should have been." He looked down the table on his side. "I was brought into this as a more neutral voice, but let me ask my fellow members of the bar if they are having trouble forming questions for the princess."

Several of the lawyers spoke at the same time. Veducci just raised his pencil in the air. Veducci got the nod. "My office has dealt more closely with the princess and her people than the rest of you, which is why I'm carrying certain remedies against glamour."

"What sort of remedies?" Shelby asked.

"I won't tell you what I'm carrying, but cold steel, iron, four-leaf clover, Saint-John's-wort, rowan and ash—either the wood or the berries—have been known to work. Some say bells will break glamour, but I think high-court sidhe won't be bothered much by bells."

"Are you saying that the princess is using glamour against us?" Shelby asked, his handsome face no longer pleasant.

"I am saying that sometimes when dealing with King Taranis or Queen Andais, their presence over-whelms humans," Veducci responded. "Princess Meredith, being part human, though beautiful—" He nodded in my direction.

I nodded at the compliment.

"—has never affected anyone so strongly, but a lot has been happening in the Unseelie Court in the last few days. Ambassador Stevens has filled me in, as have other sources. Princess Meredith and some of her guard have moved up the power grid, so to speak." Veducci still looked tired, but now his eyes showed the mind inside that overweight, over-worked camouflage. I realized with a start that there were other dangers besides ambition. Veducci was smart, and hinted that he knew something about what had happened inside the Unseelie Court. Did he know, or was he fishing? Did he think we'd give something away?

"It is illegal to use glamour on us," Shelby said, angry. He looked at me now, and his look was no longer in the least friendly. I looked back. I gave him the full force of my tricolored eyes: molten gold at the outer edge, then a circle of jade green, and last emerald to chase around my pupil. He looked away first, dropping his gaze to his own legal pad. His voice was tight with controlled rage. "We could have you arrested, or deported back to faerie for trying to use magic to sway these proceedings, Princess."

"I'm not doing anything to you, Mr. Shelby, not on purpose." I looked at Veducci. "Mr. Veducci, you say that simply seeing my aunt and uncle was difficult; am I difficult now?"

"From my colleagues' reactions, I believe you are."

"So this is the reaction that King Taranis and Queen Andais have on humans?"

"Similar," Veducci said.

I had to smile.

"This is not funny, Princess," Cortez said, his words full of anger, but when I met his brown eyes, they dropped from me.

I looked at Nelson, but it wasn't me distracting her; her problem was behind me.

"Which one are you staring at the most?" I asked. "Frost or Doyle; light or dark?"

She blushed in that pretty way human redheads have. "I'm not . . ."

"Come, Ms. Nelson, confess, which one?"

She swallowed hard enough that I heard it. "Both," she whispered.

"We will charge you and these two guards with undue magical influence in a legal proceeding, Princess Meredith," Cortez said.

"I agree," Shelby said.

"Neither I, nor Frost and Doyle, are doing this on purpose."

"We are not stupid," Shelby said. "Glamour is an active magic, not a passive one."

"Most glamour, yes, but not all," I said. I looked down the table at Veducci. They'd put him farthest from the center of the table, as if being from St. Louis made him less. Or maybe I was just overly sensitive for my hometown.

"Did you know," Veducci said, "that when you see the Queen of England, they call it being in the presence? I've never met Queen Elizabeth, and I'm not likely to, so I don't know how it works for her. I've never spoken to a human queen. But the phrase 'in the presence,' to be in the presence of the queen, means more when it's the queen of the Unseelie Court. To be in the presence of the king of the Seelie Court is also a treat."

"What does that mean?" Cortez asked. "A treat?"

"It means, gentleman, and ladies, that being king or queen in faerie gives you an unconscious aura of power, of attractiveness. You live in L.A. You see that it works in lesser ways for major stars or politicians. Power seems to breed power. Dealing with the faerie courts has made me believe that even us poor humans do it. To be around the powerful, rich, beautiful, talented, whatever, it isn't just human nature to suck up. I think it's glamour. I think that success of a certain level has a glamour to it, and you attract people to you. They want to be around you. They listen to you more. They do what you say more. Humans have a shadow of real glamour; now think about someone who is the most powerful figure in faerie. Think about the level of power surrounding them."

"Ambassador Stevens," Shelby said, "shouldn't you have been the one who warned us about this effect?"

Stevens smoothed his tie, played with the Rolex watch Taranis had given him as a present. "King Taranis is a powerful figure with centuries of rulership. He does have a certain nobility that is impressive. I have not found Queen Andais as impressive."

"Because you only talk to her from a distance, over the mirrors, with King Taranis by your side," Veducci said.

I was impressed that Veducci knew that, because it was absolutely true.

"You're the ambassador to faerie," Shelby said, "not just to the Seelie Court."

"I am the United States Ambassador to the courts of faerie, yes."

"But you never step foot into the Unseelie Court?" Shelby asked.

"Uh," Stevens said, running his fingers over and

over the watchband, "I find Queen Andais a little less than cooperative."

"What does that mean?" Shelby said.

I watched him play with the watch, and a tiny bit of concentration showed that there was magic on it, or in it. I answered for him, "It means he thinks the Unseelie Court is full of perversion and monsters."

They were all looking at him now. If it had been purposeful glamour on our part, they wouldn't have. "Is that true, Ambassador?" Shelby asked.

"I would never say such a thing."

"But he believes it," I said, softly.

"We'll all make a note of this, and make sure the proper authorities know of your gross dereliction of your duties," Shelby said.

"I am loyal to King Taranis and his court. It is not my fault that Queen Andais is a sexual sadist, and quite mad. She and her people are dangerous. I have said so, for years, and no one has listened to me. Now we have these charges, proving what I have been saying."

"So you told your superiors that you feared the queen's guard would rape someone?" Veducci asked.

"Well, I, no, not exactly."

"What did you tell them?" Shelby asked.

"I told them the truth, that I feared for my safety

at the Unseelie Court, and that I would not be comfortable there without an armed escort." Stevens stood up, very tall, very certain of himself. He pointed at Frost and Doyle. "Look at them, they are frightening. The potential in them to do carnage, why, it just radiates off of them."

"You keep touching your watch," I said.

"What?" He blinked at me.

"Your watch. King Taranis gave it to you, didn't he?" I asked.

"You accepted a Rolex watch from the king?" Cortez made it a question. He sounded outraged, but not at us.

Stevens swallowed, and shook his head. "Of course not. That would be totally inappropriate."

"I saw him give it to you, Ambassador," I said.

He ran his fingers over the metal. "That's simply not true. She's lying."

"The sidhe don't lie, Ambassador, you know that. That's a human habit."

Stevens's fingers were practically rubbing a hole through the watchband. "The Unseelie are capable of every evil. Their very faces show them for what they are."

It was Nelson who said, "Their faces are beautiful."

"You are fooled by their magic," Stevens said. "The king gave me the power to see through their deceptions." His voice was rising with each word.

"The watch," I said.

"So this," Shelby gestured at me, "beauty is illusion?"

"Yes," Stevens said.

"No," I said.

"Liar," he screamed, shoving his chair back so that it rolled on its wheels. He started walking past Biggs and Farmer, toward me.

Doyle and Frost moved like two halves of a whole. They simply stood in front of him, blocking his way. There was no magic to it, except the force of their physicality. Stevens stumbled back from them as if he'd been struck. His face contorted in terror, and he cried out, "No, no!"

Some of the lawyers were standing now. Cortez said, "What are they doing to him?"

Veducci managed to yell above Stevens's screams. "I can't see anything."

"We are doing nothing to him," Doyle said, his deep voice cutting under the higher-pitched voices like water undercutting a cliff face.

"The hell you aren't," Shelby yelled, adding to the noise of Stevens's screams and those of the others.

I tried yelling above the noise, "Turn your jackets inside out!" No one seemed to hear me.

Veducci bellowed, "Shut up!" in a voice that smashed through the noise like a bull through a fence. The room was stunned into silence. Even Stevens stopped screaming and stared at Veducci. Veducci continued in a calmer voice, "Turn your jackets inside out. It's a way to break glamour." He moved his head toward me, almost a bow. "I forgot that one."

The others hesitated for a second. Veducci took off his own jacket and turned it inside out, then put it back on. It seemed to galvanize the rest. Most of them began taking off their jackets.

Nelson said, as she folded her jacket so the seams showed, "I'm wearing a cross. I thought that protected me from glamour."

I answered her. "Crosses and bible verses would only work if we were of the devil. We have no connection to the Christian religion, either for good or ill."

She looked down, as if embarrassed to meet my eyes. "I didn't mean to imply anything."

"Of course not," I said. My voice was empty as I said it. I'd heard the insult too often to take it to heart. "One of the things the early church did was to paint anything they could not control as evil.

Faerie was something they could not control. As the Seelie Court became more and more human-friendly, the parts of faerie that could not, or would not, play human, became part of the Unseelie Court. Since the things that humans perceive as frightening are mostly at the Unseelie Court, we got painted as evil over the centuries."

"You *are* evil!" Stevens screamed. His eyes bulged, his pulse was racing, and his face was pale and beaded with sweat.

"Is he sick?" Nelson asked.

"In a way," I said, softly enough that I wasn't sure any of the other humans in the room heard me. Whoever had done the spell on the watch had done too good a job, or a bad one. The spell was forcing Stevens to see nightmares when he looked at us. His mind wasn't coping well with what he was seeing and feeling.

I turned to Veducci. "The ambassador seems ill. Perhaps he should be taken to see a doctor?"

"No," Stevens yelled. "No. Without me here they will take over your minds!" He grabbed Biggs, who was closer. "Without the king's gift you will all believe their lies."

"I think the princess is right, Ambassador Stevens," Biggs said. "I think you *are* ill."

Stevens's hands dug into the inside-out designer jacket that Biggs was now wearing. "Surely you see them for what they are now?"

"They look like all the sidhe to me. Except for the color of Captain Doyle's skin, and the princess being petite, they look like nobles of the sidhe court."

Stevens shook the bigger man. "The Darkness has fangs. The Killing Frost has skulls hanging from his neck. And she, she is withered, dying. Her mortal blood contaminates her."

"Ambassador . . ." Biggs began.

"No, you must see it, as I do!"

"They didn't change at all when we turned our jackets inside out," Nelson said. She sounded a little disappointed.

"I told you, we are not doing active glamour on any of you," I said.

"Lies! I see the horror of you." Stevens hid his face against Biggs's broad shoulders, as if he could not bear the sight of us, and perhaps he could not.

"It is easier not to look at them, though," Shelby said.

Cortez nodded. "I can focus better now, but they look the same."

"Beautiful," Bertram said.

Shelby gave him a sharp look, and the assistant apologized, as if that one word was totally out of line.

Stevens had begun to sob into Biggs's designer suit. "You must get him away from us," Doyle said.

"Why?" one of the others asked.

"The spell on the watch makes him see monsters when he looks at us. I fear his mind will break under the strain of it without King Taranis nearby to ease the effects."

"Can't you just undo the spell?" Veducci asked.

"It is not our spell," Doyle said simply.

"Can't you help him?" Nelson asked.

"I think the less contact with us, the better for the ambassador."

Stevens had seemed to be trying to bury his face into Biggs's shoulder. The ambassador's hands twisted in the seams and lining of the coat.

"Being near us is hurting him," Frost said, speaking for the first time since the introductions. His voice did not have the depth of Doyle's, but the width of his chest gave it weight.

"Get some security up here," Biggs said to Farmer. And though Farmer was a very powerful man in his own right, and a full partner, he moved for the door. I guess when your daddy is one of the founders of a firm and you are the leading active partner, you still have clout, even over other partners.

We stood in silence, the humans' awkward body language and facial expressions saying that they were terribly uncomfortable with the display of mad emotion. It was a type of madness, but the three of us sidhe had seen worse. We'd seen madness that had magic to it. The kind of magic that could steal the breath from your body on a laughing whim.

Uniformed security came. I recognized one of the guards from the entrance desk. They had a doctor with them. I remembered reading several doctors' names on the board beside the elevator. Apparently, Farmer had exceeded his orders, but Biggs seemed very pleased to hand the sobbing man over to the doctor. No wonder Farmer had made partner. He followed orders to the letter, but built on them, made them better.

No one said anything else until they led the ambassador from the room and the door closed quietly behind him. Biggs straightened his tie and tugged at the wrinkled suit jacket. Inside out, or right side out, the suit was ruined until a dry cleaner got hold of it. He started to take the jacket off, then glanced at us and stopped.

I caught his eye, and he looked away, embarrassed. "It's all right, Mr. Biggs, if you're afraid to take your jacket off."

"Ambassador Stevens's mind seems quite broken."

"I would advise the doctor to have a licensed practitioner of the arts look at the watch before you simply remove it."

"Why?"

"He's worn that watch for years. It may have become a part of his psyche, his mind. To simply remove it could do more harm."

Biggs reached for a phone.

"Why didn't you say something before he was led away?" Shelby asked.

"I only now thought of it," I said.

"I thought of it before they left," Doyle said.

"Why didn't you speak up?" Cortez asked.

"It is not my job to protect the ambassador."

"It's everyone's job to help another human in such a state," Shelby said, then he looked surprised, as if he'd just heard what he'd said.

Doyle gave the smallest curl of lips. "But I am not human, and I think the ambassador is weak and without honor. Queen Andais has lodged several complaints with your government about the ambassador. She has been ignored. But even she could not have foreseen such treachery as this."

"Treachery of our government against yours?" Veducci asked.

"No, King Taranis's treachery against someone who trusted him. The ambassador saw that watch as a mark of high favor, when in fact it was a trap and a lie."

"You disapprove," Nelson said.

"Do you not also disapprove?" Doyle asked.

She started to nod and then looked away, blushing. Apparently, even with her jacket turned, she couldn't help reacting to him. He was worth reacting to, but I didn't like that she was having this much trouble. The charges would be hard enough without us making the prosecutors blush.

"What would the king have gained from poisoning the ambassador against your court?" Cortez asked.

"What have the Seelie always gained from blackening the name of the Unseelie?" I asked.

"I'll bite," Shelby said. "What *have* they gained?"

"Fear," I said. "They have made their people fear us."

"What did that gain them?" Shelby asked.

Frost spoke. "The greatest punishment of all is to

be cast out of the Seelie Court, the golden court. But it is punishment because Taranis and his nobles have convinced themselves that once you join the Unseelie Court you become a monster. Not just in actions, but in body. They tell their people that they will become deformed if they join with the Unseelie."

"You talk like you know," Nelson said.

"I was once part of the golden throng, long, long ago," Frost said.

"What did you do to earn exile?" Shelby asked.

"Lieutenant Frost doesn't have to answer that," Biggs said. He had stopped fussing with his suit and was back to being one of the best lawyers on the West Coast.

"Is the answer prejudicial to the charges brought against the other guards?" Shelby asked.

"No," Biggs said, "but since the lieutenant is not included in the charges filed, the question is outside the scope of this investigation."

Biggs had lied, smoothly, effortlessly; lied as if it were the truth. He actually didn't know if Frost's answer would have been prejudicial, because he had no idea why anyone but the three guards in question had been exiled from the Seelie Court. (Though in Galen's case, he hadn't been exiled because he'd been born and raised in the Unseelie Court; you can't be exiled from what you've never been a part of.) Biggs had carefully not allowed any questions that might interfere with a linear defense of his clients.

"This is a very informal proceeding," Veducci said with a smile. He radiated harmless good-ol'-boy charm. It was a trick, bordering on a lie. He'd researched us. He'd dealt with the courts more than any of the other lawyers. He was either going to be our greatest ally or our most difficult opponent.

He continued, still smiling and letting us see those tired eyes. "We are all here today to see if the charges that King Taranis filed on behalf of the Lady Caitrin should be followed up with more formal proceedings. Cooperation would give strength to the princess' guards' denials."

"Since all of the guards have diplomatic immunity, we are here out of courtesy," Biggs said.

"We do appreciate that," Veducci said.

"Do bear in mind," Shelby said, "that King Taranis has stated that all of the queen's guard, and now the princess' guard, are a danger to everyone around them, most especially women. He stated that this rape did not surprise him. He seemed to think it was the inevitable outcome of allowing the queen's Raven Guard unlimited access even inside faerie. One of the reasons he brought these charges to the human authorities, an unprecedented action in all the history of the Seelie Court, is that he feared for us. If a sidhe noble of Lady Caitrin's magical powers could be so easily taken, then what hope did mere humans have against their . . . lusts?"

"Unnatural lusts," I said.

Shelby shifted his gray eyes to me. "I did not say that."

"No, you didn't, but I'm betting my uncle Taranis did."

Shelby gave a little shrug. "He doesn't seem to like your men much, that is true."

"Or me," I said.

Shelby's face showed surprise, and I wished I could have told if it was genuine, or if he were lying with his face. "The king had only good things to say about you, Princess. He seems to feel that you have been"—he seemed to change what he was about to say at the last moment—"led astray by your aunt, the queen, and her guards."

"Led astray?" I made it a question.

He nodded.

"That's not what he said, is it?"

"Not in so many words, no."

"It must have been truly insulting for you to pretty it up like this," I said.

Shelby actually looked uncomfortable. "Before I saw Ambassador Stevens and his reaction to you, and the possible spell on his watch, I might have simply stated what the king said." Shelby gave me a very straightforward look. "Let's say that Stevens has made me wonder at the vehemence of King Taranis's dislike of all your guard."

"All my guard?" Again I made it a question with the upward lilt of my voice.

"Yes."

I looked at Veducci. "He charges all my men with crimes?"

"No, only the three mentioned, but Mr. Shelby is correct. King Taranis stated that your Raven Guard is a danger to all women. He thinks that having been made celibate for so long has driven them insane." Veducci's face never changed as he let out one of the biggest secrets of the faerie courts.

I opened my mouth to say, "Taranis wouldn't have told you that," but Doyle's hand on my shoulder stopped me. I looked up at his dark figure. Even through his black glasses, I knew the look. That look said "Careful." He was right. Veducci had stated earlier that he had sources at the

Unseelie Court. Taranis might not have said it at all.

"This is the first we've heard that the king is accusing the Raven Guard of being celibate," Biggs said. He had glanced at Doyle, but now put his attention back on Shelby and Veducci.

"The king felt that the long-enforced celibacy was the reason for the attack."

Biggs leaned in to me, and whispered, "Is this true? Were they forced to be celibate?"

I whispered against his white collar, "Yes."

"Why?" he asked.

"My queen willed it so." That was true, as far as it went, but it kept me from sharing secrets that Queen Andais wouldn't want shared. Taranis might survive her wrath; I wouldn't.

Biggs turned back to the opposing side. "We are not conceding that this alleged celibacy took place, but if it did, the men in question are no longer celibate. They are with the princess now, and not the queen. The princess has stated that the three of them are her lovers. There would be no alleged celibacy-induced"—Biggs seemed to search for the right word—"madness." He made light of it with his voice, his face, and a hand gesture. It was a glimpse of what he'd be like in court. He just might be worth all the money my aunt was paying.

Shelby said, "The king's statement, the charges filed, are enough to allow the United States government to confine all of the princess' guard to the lands of faerie."

"I know the law you're referring to," Biggs said. "Many in Jefferson's government didn't agree with him allowing the fey to settle here after they were exiled from Europe. They insisted on a law that would allow them to permanently confine to faerie any citizen of faerie deemed too dangerous to be allowed among the human citizenry. It is a very broad law, and has never been invoked."

"It's never been needed before," Cortez said.

Doyle had stayed at my back, his hand resting on my shoulder. Either he knew I needed comforting, or he needed it. I laid my hand on top of his, so we could touch bare skin to bare skin. He was so warm, so solid. Just the touch made me feel more certain that it would be all right. We would be all right.

"It's not needed now, and you all know it," Biggs said. He *tsked* at them. "Trying to scare the princess by threatening to send all her guards back to faerie. Shame on you."

"The princess doesn't look scared," Nelson said.

I gave her the full weight of my tricolored eyes, and she couldn't hold my gaze. "You are threatening to take the men I love away from me," I said. "Shouldn't that frighten me?"

"It should," she said, "but it doesn't seem to."

Farmer touched my arm, a clear let-me-talk gesture. I leaned back into the weight of Doyle at my back and let the lawyers talk. "Which brings us to the law in question," Farmer said. "The royals of any court are exempt from the law Mr. Shelby has mentioned."

"We are not proposing to exile Princess Meredith to faerie," Shelby said.

"You know that the threat to put all her guards under some sort of legal confinement to faerie is outrageous," Farmer said.

Shelby nodded. "Fine, then just the three who are charged with rape. Mr. Cortez and I are both duly appointed officers of the United States attorneys' office. We are within our duty and rights to simply put the three guards back into the land of faerie until these charges are settled."

"I repeat, the law, as written, cannot be applied to the royals of any court of faerie," Farmer said.

"And I repeat that we aren't threatening to do anything to Princess Meredith," Shelby said.

"But we aren't referring to that royal," Farmer said.

Shelby looked down the line of lawyers on his side. "I'm not sure we're following your argument."

"Princess Meredith's guard are royal, for now."

"What does that mean, for now?" Cortez asked.

"It means that when inside the Unseelie Court, they have a throne on the royal dais in which they take turns sitting beside the princess," Farmer said. "They are her royal consorts."

"Being her lover doesn't make them royal," Cortez said.

"Prince Phillip is technically still Queen Elizabeth's royal consort," Farmer said.

"But they're married," Cortez said.

"But in faerie, at any court, you aren't allowed to marry until you are with child," Farmer said.

"Mr. Farmer," I said, touching his arm, "since this is informal, perhaps it would go more quickly if I explained."

Farmer and Biggs whispered back and forth, but finally I got the nod. I was going to be allowed to talk. Oh, goody. I smiled at the other side of the table, leaning a little forward, hands nicely folded on the table. "My guards are my lovers. Which makes them royal consorts until one of them makes me pregnant. Then that one will be king to my queen. Until the choice is made, they are all royalty in the Unseelie Court."

"The three guards who have been charged by the king should be sent back to faerie," Shelby said.

"King Taranis was so afraid that Ambassador Stevens would see that the Unseelie Court was beautiful that he put a spell on the man. A spell that forced him to see us as monstrous. A man who would do such a desperate thing would do many other desperate things."

"What do you mean, Princess?"

"To lie is to be cast out of faerie, but to be king is sometimes to be above the law."

"Are you saying these charges are falsified?" Cortez asked.

"Of course they are false."

"You would say anything to save your lovers," Shelby said.

"I am sidhe, and I am not above the law. I cannot lie."

"Is that true?" Shelby leaned down and asked Veducci.

He nodded. "It's supposed to be true, but either the princess is lying, or Lady Caitrin is lying."

Shelby looked back at me. "You cannot lie."

"I have the ability, but to do so is to run the risk

of being cast out from faerie." I squeezed Doyle's hand tightly. "I just got back. I don't want to lose it all again."

"Why did you leave faerie the first time, Princess?" Shelby asked.

Biggs answered that. "That question is off limits, and outside the charges in question." The queen had probably given him a list of questions I couldn't answer.

Shelby smiled. "Very well. Is it true that the Raven Guard were forced into centuries of celibacy?"

"May I ask a question before I answer that?"

"You can ask anything you like, Princess, but I may not answer."

I smiled at him, and he smiled back. Doyle's hand tightened on my shoulder. He was right— mustn't flirt, until we knew exactly how it would be perceived. I toned the smile down, and asked my question. "Did King Taranis himself say that the Ravens were forced into centuries of celibacy?"

"I've so stated," Shelby said.

"No, I mean as truth, Mr. Shelby. Please bear in mind that even a princess may be tortured for going against her queen's orders."

"You admit that they torture people at the Unseelie Court," Cortez said.

"They torture people at both courts, Mr. Cortez. Queen Andais just doesn't hide what she does, because she's not ashamed of it."

"Are you stating for the record . . . ?" Cortez said.

"This will be a sealed record," Biggs said, "unless it goes to court."

"Yes, yes," Cortez said, "but are you stating for the record that King Taranis allows torture to be used as a punishment in the Seelie Court?"

"Answer my question truthfully, and I will answer yours."

Cortez looked at Shelby. They exchanged a longer-than-normal look, then both of them turned back to me. "Yes," they said at the same time. The two men looked at each other, and finally Cortez nodded at Shelby, who said, "Yes, King Taranis stated that the fact that the Raven Guard had been forced into centuries of celibacy was the reason they were a danger to women. He further stated that to then have the forced celibacy lifted for only one little girl, referring to you, Princess, was monstrous. For no one woman could satisfy the lusts of centuries."

"So the celibacy was the motive for the rape," I said.

"That seems to be the king's reasoning," Shelby said. "We haven't looked for a motive beyond the usual for rape."

The usual, I thought.

"I've answered your question, Princess. Now, are you stating for the record that the Seelie Court tortures its prisoners?"

Frost came to stand beside Doyle. "Meredith, think upon this before you answer."

I looked behind me, met his worried eyes, the soft gray of winter skies. I held my other hand out to him, and he took it. "Taranis let our cat out of the bag, Frost. It's only fair we let one of his out."

Frost frowned at me. "I do not understand this talk of cats, but I fear his anger."

I had to smile at him even as I agreed with him. "He began this, Frost. I will only finish it."

He squeezed my hand, and Doyle squeezed the other, so that my hands were crisscrossed over my chest, holding them. I held their hands while I said, "Mr. Shelby, Mr. Cortez, you asked me, am I stating for the record that King Taranis's golden court tortures as a punishment? I am so stating."

The record was supposed to be sealed, but if either of these secrets got into the press. . . This little family feud was going to get very ugly, very fast.

Let temptation get the better of you – A *Lick of Frost* is available from all good bookshops now.